An Alaska Wilderness Mystery Novel

# MURDER OVER KODIAK

# ROBIN BAREFIELD
Alaska Wilderness Mystery Author

PO Box 221974 Anchorage, Alaska 99522-1974
books@publicationconsultants.com—www.publicationconsultants.com

ISBN 978-1-59433-617-1
eBook ISBN 978-1-59433-616-4
Library of Congress Catalog Card Number: 2016931186

Manufactured in the United States of America.

# Chapter One

S eagulls cried overhead, and the diesel engines of fishing boats thrummed in the distance. I paced the dock and wondered why the plane was so late. A sharp explosion cracked like a shotgun blast, and I whirled around in search of the source of the noise. My gaze met the watery, black eyes of a twelve-hundred-pound Steller sea lion bobbing ten feet from the end of the dock. The blast had been his exhalation when he'd surfaced, and now, he seemed to be sizing me up as a food source.

I backed toward the center of the dock, holding his gaze. "Go away, big guy. There's nothing for you here." My nerves were already taut, and I was in no mood to be chased by a grouchy sea mammal.

He swam closer. "I don't have fish in my pocket, and I don't taste good." I did not need this aggravation. "Go away. Go away!"

He stretched his neck, watched me a moment longer, and must have decided I wasn't worth the effort. He arched his back and dove.

I laughed at myself and my pounding heart. No place was safe; danger lurked everywhere. Even waiting for an airplane was perilous business. I glanced at my watch. I'd been sitting on this dock waiting for the floatplane for an hour, and while the warm afternoon sun felt good, I had work to do.

Only one plane had left the dock in the last hour, and none had arrived. The plane for which I was waiting was, according to my rough estimate, about an hour late. I knew the pilot had several stops to make, any or all of which could have taken longer than planned, but I hadn't expected to wait more than an hour.

I was meeting my young assistant, who was bringing clam and mussel samples that we needed to rush to the lab at the marine center and prepare for protein-separation analysis. We had to deal with the samples immediately, and if the plane didn't arrive soon, we would have to work the entire night to achieve our task. I glanced at my watch again; thirty seconds had passed. It was now 4:32 and thirty seconds. *Where was that confounded plane?*

I knew the gurgling in the pit of my stomach wasn't caused by irritation or impatience. Overdue planes make me nervous. I'd been in a small plane accident two-and-a-half years earlier, and now I stuck to ground transportation whenever possible. The weather on this late June day provided perfect flying conditions, though. There wasn't a cloud in the sky, and only a slight breeze ruffled the surface of the channel.

The dispatcher had told me there were sightseers on the plane, so maybe the pilot was showing them bears or goats or whales. Perhaps he'd misjudged the falling tide at one of his stops, and the plane now was stuck on the beach, where it would remain until the next flood tide. I hoped this last imagined scenario wasn't the case. I wanted to get the samples to the lab as soon as possible. Any delay in handling the organisms could affect the results of the electrophoresis.

I took a deep breath, closed my eyes, and enjoyed the smell of processed fish from the nearby canneries. I licked my lips and tasted salt mingled with seaweed, clams, and mussels. I never grew tired of the sea air. I managed to let my mind drift for a few minutes, but my thoughts soon returned to reality, and I kicked at the dock; something was wrong. From the tingling in my fingers to the dull beginnings of a tension headache, I had a bad feeling.

My unease, in part, was due to guilt. My assistant, Craig, was twenty years old and a college junior. This was the second summer he'd worked for me, and we'd become good friends. He was more mature and better organized than other college helpers I'd had, and I trusted him with important tasks. I should have supervised the collection of these bivalve samples directly, though, because it was important that the quality of the field work be above question.

A lady on the west side of Kodiak Island had died after eating steamed clams, and her reported symptoms were similar to those for paralytic shellfish poisoning (PSP). If our protein-separation analysis indicated a high level of PSP in the clams Craig collected, it would offer further proof that my analysis was accurate in determining the presence of PSP. This lady was the third person on the island to die this spring after eating bivalves, and we successfully had detected PSP in the source populations of mussels and clams that provided the final meals for the other two victims.

Craig and I had collected those bivalve samples together, and I was confident he knew the correct procedure, but I should have gone with him this time, too. I didn't mind field work, and I enjoyed camping, but I dreaded the small plane flights that were a necessary part of any field work on this island. Besides, I was busy at the marine center, and Craig was willing, so I'd sent him alone on this mission. Now, as the muscles tightened in my stomach, I wished I had gone and left Craig safely recording data at the lab.

I waited another half-hour and then climbed the steep ramp to the parking lot above the floatplane dock. I took two steps across the gravel toward my Explorer, when the charter plane company's grey van sped into the lot and skidded to a stop next to the ramp. I turned and jogged toward the van, fear mounting in my chest.

The driver of the van jumped to the ground, slammed the door, and galloped down the ramp. I sprinted as fast as I could to catch him. He heard my footsteps on the metal ramp and turned to see who was following him. I stopped, bent over, and put my hands on my knees, panting to catch my breath.

"What's wrong?" I asked.

The man, a pilot named Steve Duncan, recognized me, and I saw his face change. The tight wrinkles around his hazel eyes relaxed. He ran his fingers through his short, dark hair. "Oh, nothing. Bill is just a couple minutes late, and I'm going to see if he got stuck. The tides are miserable on that side of the island, and there's a particularly low one this evening."

Bill, whose last name I didn't know, was the pilot of Craig's flight. I knew this, because when I'd called the dispatcher to inquire about the ETA of Craig's flight, she had informed me that she only could make a rough guess at the arrival time, because Bill had several pickups to make.

"Couldn't they just be looking at animals? Your dispatcher told me two of the passengers were flight-seers."

Steve paused, and I watched the gold flecks in his eyes reflect the sun. "Yeah, that's probably it, but we can't get him on the radio, so I think I'll make sure he didn't get stuck when he stopped to pick up your guy."

Although Steve tried to hide it, I heard an urgency in his voice, and I knew he wasn't telling me everything.

"How far overdue is the flight?"

"Not too long."

"Come on, tell me the truth. I have a right to know."

Steve stared at me, debating with himself about how much he should tell me. Finally, he sighed and slapped the steel handrail. "He's nearly two hours late. We didn't expect him to be right on schedule, but he doesn't have enough fuel to fly around this long. Of course, he had to make several stops, but we talked to someone at Uyak Cannery, so we know he picked up Darren

Myers there three hours ago. He already had Dick Simms and the two wildlife viewers on board then, so he only had to pick up your guy and fly to town." Steve shrugged. "That shouldn't have taken him this long."

"I'm going with you."

"What?"

"I'm going with you to look for the plane."

"No." Steve shook his head and held up his hands. "That isn't necessary."

"Please, I'll be a nervous wreck waiting here."

Steve turned. "Fine then, come along."

I hurried after him, and when I saw he wasn't going to offer me a helping hand, I jumped onto the float of the white and blue plane, opened the passenger door, and climbed into the small seat. Steve untied the plane and taxied away from the dock. The Cessna 206 could seat three passengers comfortably, or four small passengers with no gear. I looked behind me. Except for an orange emergency bag and a sleeping bag, the rear of the plane was empty.

Steve was too preoccupied to give me the standard emergency speech. I glanced at him and saw him speaking into the microphone on his headset. I looked up and saw my headset dangling on a hook overhead. I put it on and listened to Steve talk to the tower. He then radioed his office to tell the dispatcher he was departing and to ask if she had heard from Bill.

"No luck. No radio contact," she replied. Her voice sounded heavy with fear. I glanced at Steve, but he stared straight ahead as he increased the throttle.

The plane glided smoothly across the surface of the calm ocean, and soon we were airborne. I looked below us at the town of Kodiak nestled at the ocean's edge. Most of the downtown had been wiped out during the tsunami generated by the 1964 earthquake, and the hastily-rebuilt metal structures looked out of place in one of the most beautiful harbors in the world.

Kodiak had been my home for a year and three months, and the more I got to know the island and the people, the more I liked the place. A secretary at the marine center recently told me that she and the other office workers had made a bet that I wouldn't last six months on what the locals lovingly called "The Rock."

It was true; this environment was at the opposite end of the spectrum from my last home in Tucson. The climate here was cool and wet, and the nightlife consisted of half a dozen bars and one small movie theater. Kodiak, though, had spirit and spunk. It was an isolated community with soul, and after only a year, I knew I wanted to stay here. The grey, rainy days, the North Pacific storms, and the early summer fog all got me down from time to time, but one sunny day on this emerald island made up for weeks of bad weather.

Here, weather talk was more than idle chitchat. For the inhabitants of a city that boasted one of the world's most profitable fishing ports, weather was all-important. Winter storms killed, and too many boats disappeared each year in thirty-foot seas. A good weather forecast heralded good fishing, and a bad forecast meant the skipper should seek the safety of a harbor or bay. People who had lived here their entire lives cursed the weather, but I never failed to notice the gleam in an old-timer's eyes as he spoke about the forecasted one-hundred-knot winds of an approaching storm. I'd known I wasn't brave before I moved here, but on Kodiak, I was reminded daily of my inferior nerves as I watched courageous fishermen and women leave port in their small vessels to make a living on the high seas.

An eagle flew in front of the plane, and seeing something edible in the ocean beneath him, he angled into a sharp dive.

My self-esteem was at rock bottom now. I never would forgive myself if something bad had happened to Craig. *I should have been the one on that plane.* I tried to calm my mind. There was no reason to think the worst. Even if the plane had suffered engine failure, it was a floatplane, and would be over or near water the entire trip. The pilot could glide to a safe landing and then row the plane to shore. Only a slight breeze ruffled the ocean beneath us; a landing would be possible on any one of the many bays around the island today.

Small plane accidents, like boats lost at sea, were not uncommon in this area of the world. Kodiak is a mountainous island with steep peaks rising from sea level, punctuated by deep fjord-like bays that carved the shoreline. No place on the thirty-five-hundred square mile island is further than fifteen miles from the ocean. In addition to this unique geography, the Alaska Current, an offshoot of the warm Japanese Kuroshio Current, flows northward near Kodiak, bringing warm water to the frigid Gulf of Alaska and spawning weather conditions that are often violent, change rapidly, and may vary considerably from one area of the island to another. Blue skies can predominate in the city of Kodiak while low-hanging fog fills a bay fifteen miles away, and high winds blow across the south end of the island.

One of the few pieces of advice that my boss at the marine center had given me when I'd accepted the position here was to fly with pilots who had flown around the island for a while and had gained experience with the unique conditions here. I had no idea whether Craig's pilot, Bill, had been flying here long. Since I hadn't been flying with him, I hadn't bothered to check. Of course, the weather was perfect today, so I hadn't worried about the pilot or the flight. In this weather, there was no way the pilot could lose sight of a mountaintop in the fog or get blown into the side of a mountain because he misjudged a wind current. This was one of those rare bluebird days when weather wasn't a factor.

I positioned the microphone of the headset near my mouth and spoke into it. "How long has Bill been flying here?"

Steve looked at me. "Seven or eight years. He's a local boy; he grew up here. He got his pilot's license as soon as he graduated from high school. He's young, but he's a good pilot, and he knows the island." Steve paused for a moment. "I really think he's stuck on the beach somewhere. Bill's one weakness is that he's too nice and lets people push him around. I've flown with Simms a lot, and he's a pain in the butt. I can imagine him insisting that Bill detour and land somewhere, so he could impress his important bear viewers. Bill would probably do it, even if it was against his better judgment, and now they're all stuck on the beach, and Simms is giving Bill the what for."

I could imagine the same situation. I didn't know Bill, but I knew Dick Simms, the Kodiak Fish and Wildlife Refuge manager. The man considered the Kodiak National Wildlife Refuge that covered two-thirds of the island his own personal playground. The strict refuge rules applied to everyone except him, and I would bet he had been somewhere he shouldn't have been today. I swore to myself that I would murder the man if he was the cause for our concern.

"Didn't Bill have a satellite phone? Wouldn't he call your office if he was stuck?"

"He has a phone with him, but he forgot to bring it into the office to charge it last night, so it's probably dead."

"How will you know where to look? If Bill made an unscheduled landing, the plane could be anywhere."

"True," Steve said. "First, I'll fly over the area where your guy was camped. If the plane isn't there, I'll fly around until we see something, or until we're low on fuel."

"Have you notified the Coast Guard yet?" I asked.

"No. It's a little premature for that. I'm sure Bill is stuck on the beach, and I don't want to waste the Coast Guard's time and resources just to embarrass him. Besides," Steve looked at me, "if the plane crashed, the ELT would have activated, and the Coast Guard would know there was an emergency. They would have immediately called our office and then would have initiated a search and rescue."

I was quiet for a few moments, and then I asked the question I couldn't get out of my mind: "If the plane went into the ocean, would the ELT activate?"

"Maybe not," Steve said, "and if we don't hear from Bill and can't find any trace of the plane in a couple of hours, we'll notify the Coast Guard then. There's really no reason to think the worst, Jane. Planes are overdue all the time, and ninety-nine-point-nine percent of the time the plane, pilot, and passengers are fine. I'm sure that's the case here. If the weather was bad, I'd be a little more concerned, but these are perfect flying conditions."

*Why does he look so grim then, and why is my stomach boiling with dread?* I stared out the passenger window. Lush green vegetation swept down a pointed mountain, stopping abruptly at the grey shale beach. A wide path of orange rockweed littered the low edge of the beach, indicating an extreme low tide. Beyond the rockweed, the bay reflected a murky, dark grey. The ocean water was alive with phytoplankton, the food base for one of the richest fisheries in the world. I saw two salmon seiners deploying their nets at the mouth of the bay. The salmon season had been open for two weeks, and the fishermen worked every minute of the long, June days to catch the valuable red salmon on their way to their spawning grounds on the south end of the island. I reminded myself that there were fishermen all around the island. *If the plane had gone down, someone would have seen it.* That thought made me feel better, and I sat back and tried to relax.

Steve and I remained silent for the next several minutes. I glanced out my window occasionally, but I didn't allow myself to scan the mountainsides for mangled metal or burning debris.

"Your guy was camped south of Larsen Bay, right?"

The sound of Steve's voice in my headphones startled me, and I sat forward to study the scenery below us. "Yes, he was camped about a mile south of Cycek's cabin."

Steve brought the plane in low and buzzed the small wooden cabin belonging to the man who'd lost his wife to PSP. We flew along the coastline, and I studied the shore for any sign of life. If Craig was still here waiting to be picked up, he most likely would be sitting by a pile of gear stacked on the beach. We flew along the beach for five miles until we came to Uyak Cannery, but there was no sign of Craig or his gear.

"Do you plan to stop at the cannery?"

"No," Steve said. "They won't know any more than they told us over the phone, and I don't want to worry anyone."

"They're probably already worried. They can guess we aren't sightseeing."

"It would be a waste of time, anyway." We circled and climbed.

"Now where?" I asked.

"Your guess is as good as mine. I think I'll try to follow the route Steve would fly from his last pickup point to town."

"I thought you said he planned to fly around for a while before heading to town."

"I said that I believed Simms wanted him to take his guests flight-seeing, but Bill had a hot date tonight, and I know he wanted to get back to town as soon as possible. If no one complained, I'm sure he'd fly straight to town."

I stared at Steve. He hadn't bothered to tell me this earlier. "That's why you're so concerned, isn't it? You knew Bill planned to immediately return to town."

"Well, yes." Steve said the words slowly. "I think Bill has had a problem, and that's why I'm looking for him. I just don't think the problem is serious. He may have to spend the night on the beach with his airplane, but I can shuttle his passengers to town, and if he has a mechanical problem, I can bring him the tools and parts to fix it."

I didn't reply. I just hoped the problem was as simple as that. I focused my attention on the ocean and beach below us. I looked for a stranded plane, I looked for parts of a plane, and I looked for debris. Steve flew low across Uyak Bay. An afternoon breeze rippled the ocean, and reflected sunlight sparkled off the small waves. I saw two aluminum skiffs and three fishing boats. We were only a few miles from the village of Larsen Bay. *If the plane had experienced trouble here, someone would have spotted it.*

We crested the north end of Amook Island, then Carlsen Point, followed by Zachar Bay. I saw several cabins that belonged to gill-net fishermen, and two fishermen picking salmon from their net looked up at us as we flew low overhead. We crossed the mouth of Spiridon Bay, and I began to relax. People were everywhere. Any serious plane accident would have been reported by now.

We flew inland between two mountains, and I noticed that Steve was leaning forward, scrutinizing the ground below us. There was no sign of human habitation here, and an accident could go unseen. I knew that the lush green vegetation that looked like a mat covering the mountain was actually four or five feet high. A shiny metal plane could lay hidden in the jungle-like growth. I'd heard a story about a plane that had crashed on the island in the forties, and despite the fact that it lay nearly intact below a major flight path, the wreckage only had been discovered a few years ago.

"They might have landed at Spiridon Lake," Steve said. "I'll fly around it a couple of times."

I stared down at the small lake, studying the shoreline for a stranded plane, but all I saw were three Sitka black-tailed deer, two does, and a fawn. The deer ran into the brush when they heard the airplane's engine. I looked at Steve and he shrugged, angling the plane toward the next mountain pass.

As soon as I looked down again, I saw what I thought was litter, a piece of something white and teal blue sticking out of the fireweed. Then, I saw a glint of silver, and my mouth felt dry.

"Oh …!" Steve said. "What happened here?"

Sweat rolled down my forehead as I fought back nausea. I saw larger pieces of white metal, one with a black "N" and a "9" painted on it. I didn't have to ask; I knew what I was looking at. I also knew there were no survivors. The plane had splintered into small pieces, and the pieces were scattered over a hundred-square-foot area. I saw a large section that looked like part of the fuselage and tail. I also could make out a piece of one wing and a chunk of metal that appeared to be the front of a float. The rest of it, though, looked like scraps of white and teal foil, and if I hadn't known, I would not have guessed I was looking at the remains of an airplane.

Steve circled the wreckage. "What in happened? The plane blew apart."

"Bill must have hit the mountain." My voice cracked.

"No way," Steve said. "That plane is in a million pieces."

"Couldn't it have exploded on impact?"

"Maybe, but I've seen my share of plane wrecks, and I've never seen anything like that. I want to land and take a closer look."

"Shouldn't we get back to town and notify the Coast Guard?"

"Dr. Marcus," Steve's eyes locked on mine, "there's no hurry. No one lived through that."

"Yeah, I know." A vision of good-looking, curly-haired Craig flashed in my head. I doubted there was enough left of him to identify. His parents lived in Olympia, Washington. *How will I tell them this news? How can I explain that I'd sent their son on an assignment, and now there was not even enough left of him to ship home to them?* I sat back hard in the airplane seat. A hole opened in my stomach. *I sent Craig to his death.*

# Chapter Two

I don't remember Steve circling and landing on Spiridon Lake. I must have jumped from the plane into the shallow water lapping at the lake shore, mindless that I wasn't wearing rubber boots. The first thing I recall is pushing my way through the dense vegetation, my feet numb in my wet sneakers and socks. I trotted to keep pace with Steve and tripped over a fallen alder, ripping the leg of my jeans. My knee burned, and blood oozed down my leg. The pain felt good. I wanted to be punished for what had happened to Craig. *How would I ever forgive myself for this?*

I was watching my feet, trying not to trip again, when Steve stopped abruptly, and I bumped into him. We had arrived at the crash site, and Steve was staring at the piece of metal with "9N" painted on it.

"The bodies?" I said.

Steve shook his head. "Disintegrated, I guess."

My tongue stuck in my mouth. The saliva was gone. "There's got to be something left."

I began poking through the weeds and found several scraps of heavy, red nylon. *Wasn't Craig's backpack red?* I couldn't remember. I saw a small, jagged piece of corrugated metal that looked like the skin of a camera case. Maybe it had belonged to the tourists.

I saw a leather object a few feet away, and as I walked closer, I realized it was a leather shoe or part of a boot. I thought it strange that the shoelace was still woven through the eyelets. How had that small piece of string survived, when nearly everything else had evaporated? I bent down to look at the shoe. I didn't think I should touch anything, so I held back my long hair with one hand and twisted my face close to the singed, brown leather. There was something in the shoe. I squinted, fighting back the urge to touch the object.

I screamed and jumped up. I ran into the woods and stumbled into a thick mass of alders. Black waves broke in front of my eyes. I fell onto my hands and knees and retched, emptying my stomach.

"What did you find?" I heard Steve's footsteps behind me.

I tried to stand, but my legs were liquid. Steve reached out his hand to me, and I clutched it, pulling myself upright. I put my hand over my mouth and thought I was going to be sick again.

"A foot." I could barely hear my voice above the roar in my head, and Steve frowned at me.

"What?"

"There's part of a foot in a shoe."

"Oh crap!" Steve turned around and threw his head back. He stared at the sky for a few moments and then said, "Let's get out of here. We'd better contact the Coast Guard and the FAA. Human remains will attract wild animals."

He didn't expand on his explanation, but I got the picture. Before long, bears, foxes, eagles, ravens, and a host of other scavengers would begin picking through the wreckage, searching for the remains of the pilot and five passengers.

I clung to Steve's arm while we retraced our steps to the lake shore. Thunder crashed in my head, driving away coherent thoughts. Once I'd climbed into the airplane seat, I leaned back, closed my eyes, and tried to quiet the noise.

"What do you think happened?" I asked Steve, after we had been flying for fifteen minutes.

He remained quiet, and I was just about to repeat my question when his voice cracked in my headphones. "If I ask you something, will you promise not to mention it to the FAA?"

"Okay."

"What kind of Haz Mats did your guy have?"

Haz Mats was airline jargon for hazardous materials, and the heading covered everything from paint to batteries to fuel. I had signed an FAA form for Kodiak Flight Services stating I understood that my representatives and I would be flying on charters with hazardous materials. Since it is impossible to set up a camp without some sort of hazardous material, I had considered my signature a formality.

"He had a battery, a small tank of propane, and some white gas. Why?" I thought I knew the answer.

"It's possible that Bill did something we're all guilty of doing."

I stared out the windshield, seeing Bill's actions like a movie in my mind. "He threw the propane tank, the battery, and the gas in the same compartment in the float."

"We don't know that," Steve said. "It's just a possibility."

I thought it sounded like a good possibility. "Could those fuels have done that much damage?"

"I don't know." Steve paused. "But something blew that plane to pieces. I'm no expert, but twisted metal and embedded particles are evidence of a powerful explosion."

"Couldn't the plane have crashed and then exploded?"

"No. It blew up in the air."

I didn't understand how Steve could know the plane had exploded in the air, and as he'd said, he was not an explosives expert. I hoped the FAA would be able to determine the source of the explosion, because I didn't think I could live the rest of my life not knowing what had caused Craig's death. I felt responsible for him being on that plane, and I wanted to know what had happened to it. I wouldn't volunteer any information to the FAA that would make Bill look negligent, but if I was asked, I would tell the investigator about the fuels and the battery in Craig's gear.

Steve didn't say anything else to me on the way to town. He didn't radio the Coast Guard or his office, and I guessed that he wanted to wait until he got to town and the privacy of a telephone before he made those calls. The Coast Guard and other authorities would have several hours before dark to secure the crash site.

I wondered who would investigate the crash. Once the Coast Guard determined there were no survivors, the Alaska State Troopers and the FAA probably would take over the investigation. *Would a trooper call me tonight?* I didn't want some anonymous policeman contacting Craig's parents. I had never met Craig's parents, but I was sure Craig had talked about me, so they would know my name. I'd place the call as soon as I got back to the lab. Since I hadn't seen Craig's body, I had trouble believing he was dead. Still, his campsite was gone, so he must have been on the plane, and no one had lived through that crash.

I glanced at Steve as we taxied up to the floatplane ramp. His teeth were clenched, and he stared forward. He had called his dispatcher to report he was landing, but when she asked if he'd found Bill, he told her he would call her in a few moments. As soon as he cut the engine, he jumped onto the float and leapt to the dock. He bent and tied the plane to the dock in one fluid movement. Then, he turned and ran.

I was still unbuckling my seat belt as Steve sprinted up the ramp to the parking lot. I had none of his energy. My wet feet felt glued to the metal floor of the plane. My body trembled as I climbed to the dock. The air smelled sour. I inhaled rotting seaweed and processed fish. I bent over the side of the dock and vomited into the ocean.

I sat in my Explorer and looked at my watch. It was 6:37. With any luck, the lab would be deserted, because I couldn't face my coworkers now. I considered driving to my apartment, but I had to go to the lab to look up Craig's parents' number, and I knew I should call them as soon as possible.

I drove down Rezanof, where I saw kids skating and riding bicycles, their parents standing in their yards, enjoying the perfect June evening. Baskets brimming with blue lobelia, yellow begonias, and red fuchsias framed porches, while the last round of brightly-colored tulips made way for budding lilies. The beautiful evening only deepened my despair. Craig never would smell another flower, watch another movie, or date another girl. His life had been blown apart in its prime.

*How had it happened?* I asked myself that question for the hundredth time since I'd first seen the scattered bits of metal. *Had the pilot put the propane bottle and the battery in the same float compartment?* If the metal propane bottle fell across both battery terminals, causing a spark, and if the propane bottle leaked, it could have exploded. Still, that was a lot of ifs, and there had been no turbulence to cause the propane tank to shift in flight. I could think of no better explanation for the explosion, though.

I drove slowly as I bumped along the winding road to the marine center and was relieved to see the empty parking lot. I parked, slid from my Explorer, and dragged myself through the large glass doors. The Kodiak Braxton Marine Biology and Fisheries Research Center was one of the most beautiful laboratories I ever had seen. Huge glass windows fronted the two-story building, offering a panorama of the Pacific Ocean and a bird's-eye view of the arrival and departure of the Kodiak commercial fishing fleet. The lushly carpeted lobby and breathtaking scenery were meant to impress visitors and inspire donations. I'm not sure impressed visitors would feel the marine center needed a donation, but that was not my department. As long as I had a job, I would not worry about the economical side of operating this showpiece facility.

My office was located down a long corridor on the parking lot level of the building. Laboratories and a small fish-processing plant occupied the lower level. I unlocked my office door, flipped on the fluorescent light, and sunk down into the swivel chair in front of my desk. I pulled Craig's personnel file from my desk drawer, stared at the desk telephone a moment, and then pushed my chair forward.

I placed the heart-wrenching call to Craig's parents. Craig's father answered the phone, and when I told him who I was, and why I was calling, he said nothing and handed the phone to his wife. She remained calm, but didn't seem to believe me. When I hung up the receiver a few minutes later, I wasn't sure I had convinced them that their son was dead. I was afraid they thought I was a prank caller, but I didn't know what else I could do. *How could I expect them to believe Craig was dead?* I couldn't believe it myself, and I had seen the wreckage. They would not even be able to look at his body and tell him goodbye. I remembered the pale flesh in the brown leather shoe, and bile rose in my mouth.

My fingers still were gripping the receiver when the phone buzzed. I jerked my hand away and then eased it back to the smooth plastic. I expected to hear the voice of one of Craig's parents, calling to confirm my identity.

"Marcus," I answered.

"Dr. Marcus," a deep voice said. "I am Alaska State Trooper James Hostler. I understand that you have an assistant by the name of Craig Pederson."

"Yes."

"I regret to inform you that we believe Mr. Pederson was killed this afternoon in an airplane-related accident."

"Yes, I know. I was in the plane with Steve Duncan when we found the wreckage."

Trooper Hostler was quiet for a moment, undoubtedly rereading the information he had been given. "I see." He recovered nicely. "Have you contacted his nearest kin?"

"Yes, but I'm not sure they believed me. Perhaps you should also call them." I recited the Pedersons' telephone number to the trooper, and he was just about to hang up, when I asked, "Are the troopers at the crash site yet?"

"I'm sorry, I can't comment on the investigation."

"Please."

Hostler paused. "Yes ma'am. Several troopers and an FAA representative have flown out to look at the wreckage."

I sighed. I felt a measure of relief knowing that professionals were handling the details of the disaster. I needed to call Peter Wayan, the director of the marine center, and tell him about Craig. Then, I planned go home and take a long, hot bath.

Doctor Wayan answered his phone on the third ring. My relationship with Wayan was formal. He treated me with respect but kept his distance, as he did with everyone who worked at the marine center. We were his colleagues, not his friends.

Wayan responded with alarm when I told him the news, but once he decided the marine center was not liable, he clicked his tongue and uttered condolences. I didn't inform him that the marine center's fuel may have caused the explosion; we would cross that bridge when we came to it.

I grabbed my purse and briefcase, turned out my office light, and locked the door. I drove out Spruce Cape Road and pulled into the parking lot of my condominium complex. Six young girls were skating in the lot, giggling and all talking at once. Their gaiety made me sadder.

My two-bedroom condominium with a partially-obstructed view of the ocean never had seemed so bleak. I stumbled into the bathroom and ran hot water into the tub. I peeled off my clothes and sank into the steaming water. I don't know how long I sat there, but when I climbed out of the tub, the water was cold. I climbed into my bed and wished I'd never have to get out. Staying home alone would be even worse, though. Somehow, I had to find the strength to carry on. I would never shake the belief that I had sent Craig to his death, but I had to get past it and find a way to deal with my guilt.

Grief hung in the air as I walked down the hall of the marine center the following morning. Craig had been popular with the staff, joking with everyone from the janitor to the director. I walked into the main office to check my messages and fought back a sob when I saw the tear-stained faces of the two middle-aged secretaries. Glenda, a plump, short, dark-haired woman stood, walked around her desk, and held out her arms to me. I wanted to bolt out the door, but I forced myself to stand still and be consoled.

"So sad, dear," Glenda said and patted my back.

I dared not speak, and I blinked as two tears snaked their way down my cheeks.

Glenda released me and looked at my face. "And I hear you found the wreckage."

"News travels fast." My voice sounded breathy and high. I glanced at Betty, a petite, grey-haired woman who sat in her chair with her palms flat on the desk top. I wasn't certain if I imagined her look of disapproval. She was usually more restrained and less affectionate than Glenda, but now she looked as if she were judging me. I wanted to blurt that yes, I should have been on that plane instead of Craig. I should have been the one who evaporated, my life wiped away as if I never had existed.

The room began to look dark and far away. I struggled to breathe, and I heard Glenda's voice call to me from a distance. "Are you okay, dear? You look pale. Maybe you should sit down."

I held onto the wall for support as I pulled myself toward the door frame. Once in the hallway, I kept my hand on the wall and shuffled toward my office. I passed someone who said something to me, but I couldn't respond. Sweat dripped from my face and black swirls danced in front of my eyes. I had fainted only once before, during my miscarriage, but I remembered the sensation that had preceded that event, and I feared I was about to end up in a heap on the hall floor.

I reached my office door and tried to find the key ring in my purse. As soon as I looked down, everything went black. I pushed my back to the wall and slid to the floor. I don't think I lost consciousness. I bent my knees to my chest and rested my head on them. I hoped no one would walk by and see me.

Slowly, the heat subsided, and my face began to cool. My head pounded, but when I lifted it from my knees, I was relieved to see my foggy vision had cleared. My body felt spent, and I didn't think my legs would support me. The corridor was empty, so I decided to sit a few minutes longer.

*What was wrong with me? Was I sick?* I'd had my share of trauma, and I never before had responded to it by fainting. Maybe this was a symptom of guilt. How could I move beyond this terrible feeling? What could I do to ease my burden of responsibility for Craig's death? Maybe if I knew what had caused the explosion, I would find some consolation. I could call Steve Duncan at Kodiak Air Services and see if he had any new information.

My plan of action gave me strength. My knees vibrated as I stood, but I managed to find my keys and let myself into my office. I opened a warm bottle of water and washed down two aspirin. Then, I scooted the chair to my desk, pulled the phone in front of me, and dialed the number for Kodiak Flight Services.

The dispatcher answered the phone, and I asked for Steve. There was a long pause, and then a deep voice said, "Hello, Dr. Marcus."

"Hi Steve. Have you heard anything about the crash?"

"Two FAA inspectors and the troopers are out there now. I was planning to call and warn you that they'll want to interview you sometime today."

"Why?"

"We were the first two on the scene of the crash. I think they want to know what you saw and make sure you didn't touch or move anything. They may also want to ask you about Craig's gear."

I paused for a moment. "I can't lie about it, Steve."

"I don't want you to lie, but please don't tell them what I said or volunteer any information."

"I won't say anything to get Kodiak Flight Services in trouble, but I want the FAA to get to the bottom of this. I need to know why that plane exploded."

"We may never know," Steve said.

"I hope you're wrong."

I hung up the phone and slumped in the padded chair. I stared at the walls of my office, and my eyes settled on the large tide calendar to the left of my desk. I had to get my mind off Craig and the plane crash and focus on work. That was the only way I would get through this mess. I needed to collect samples to replace those lost in the plane crash. I stood and peered closer at the calendar.

The calendar was printed with the tidal fluctuations for the Kodiak District. Uyak Bay, where the lady had died from PSP, had tides that correlated with the Seldovia district. I'd written in the Seldovia fluctuations for the months of June and July.

The times and intensities of the tides changed daily. To collect the clam samples, I needed at least two days of extreme low tides. Today was June twenty-sixth; the next series of minus tides began on July fourth. The marine center had planned a Fourth of July picnic, but I wasn't in a partying mood. I could fly to Uyak on the third and camp for three days.

Maybe I would stop by Mr. Cycek's cabin and explain why it was taking so long to get the test results on the population of clams that had killed his wife. I couldn't believe he wouldn't know about the plane crash, but I'd heard he lived the life of a hermit. I had only met the man once, at the hospital after his wife, Doris, had been pronounced dead. He had been devastated by the loss of his wife, and when I explained that we would test the clams from the beach where he and Doris had dug the poisonous bivalves, he offered his assistance and even reluctantly suggested that we stay with him.

I knew from talking to Craig on the radio that Mr. Cycek had been helpful and interested in our work. Craig had said that Mr. Cycek was lonely and talked about little other than his wife's death. It was unfair to keep the man waiting and wondering about the results of our test. I was certain Doris had died from PSP, but only the presence of saxitoxin in clams from the beach where she had been digging would confirm the diagnosis

Saxitoxin, the compound that causes PSP, is one of the most lethal poisons known to man. A nerve agent one-thousand times more potent than cyanide, it paralyzes its victims, much like curare. Saxitoxin is produced by a marine dinoflagellate, a type of algae. Bivalves, such as mussels and clams, ingest the poisonous algae along with their usual fare of nonpoisonous plankton. The poisonous dinoflagellates do not harm the bivalves, but the shellfish concentrate the poison, and when humans dine on these bivalves, they suffer the effects of the accumulated toxin.

A human may begin to feel the effects of PSP as soon as five minutes after eating toxic shellfish. The first symptom is usually a tingling or numbness around the lips, gums, and tongue. In a mild case of poisoning, the tingling may spread to the face and neck. The victim also may feel a prickly sensation in the fingertips and toes and suffer from a headache, dizziness, and nausea. These are the only symptoms most people feel.

In moderate cases of poisoning, the victim's speech becomes incoherent, and the prickly sensation spreads to the arms and legs, causing stiffness and a loss of coordination in the limbs. The victim feels light headed, has a rapid pulse, and may have trouble breathing.

If the poisoning is serious, the victim will suffer muscular paralysis, a choking sensation, and severe respiratory difficulty. Unless ventilatory support is available, the victim probably will die.

A mouse bioassay is the only currently-approved method to test bivalves for the presence of saxitoxin. This test involves feeding extracts of the suspected shellfish to mice and then watching the mice to see if they die. This procedure leaves much to be desired. Not only is it labor-intensive, but it is non-specific for saxitoxin and only can be performed in a certified biological laboratory. Only one lab performs this test in the state of Alaska, and no monitored PSP-tested beaches exist in the state.

Unfortunately, even though everyone realizes the risk, many people continue to eat shellfish. Most residents of Kodiak follow certain legends or taboos that have been passed down from their ancestors or from the native Alutiiq people Don't eat bivalves in months without Rs or during a red tide. These taboos help, because the dinoflagellate responsible for PSP does bloom in the early summer, and a large bloom often produces a blood-red color in the water.

However, other algae also produce a dark-red color when they bloom, and the deadly dinoflagellate can be present when there is no change in the color of the water. Also, some bivalves, such as the butter clam, can hold the toxin in its tissues for as long as a year. Additionally, deadly cysts produced by sexual reproduction of the dinoflagellates are even present in the winter and may be ingested by bivalves during the coldest months of the year, all of which have Rs in their names.

At no time is one safe from PSP, and for some reason, Kodiak Island is one of the most dangerous places in the state for the toxin. These facts prompted Dr. Wayan to apply for a grant to develop an accurate, fast, inexpensive chemical assay to detect the presence of saxitoxin. While experimental chemical assays have been developed, none has been tested thoroughly or approved for monitoring purposes.

I am a biologist, not a chemist, but the position at the marine center interested me, mainly because it was in Kodiak, a town that had enchanted me when I'd visited it a year earlier. The position also happened to become available just as my job at the genetics lab at the University of Arizona was ending. I had hoped to find another genetics position, but was dismayed by the surplus of brilliant geneticists and the scarcity of jobs. I knew that I didn't stand a chance in that marketplace. Since I have a Ph.D. in fishery biology, I thought this job might lead to something in my field. I find the problem of PSP interesting, but chemistry is not my forte.

Why Dr. Wayan hired someone with my credentials for this study is a mystery I never may unravel. I know that Dr. Cenau, the director of the genetics lab in Tucson, gave me a great reference. She felt guilty about cutting my position, and she wanted to do everything she could to help me land a new job. I also believe the marine center has trouble attracting chemists to Kodiak. This isn't an intellectual mecca, and while the location provides many opportunities for scientists interested in the ocean, most chemists can find jobs at better chemical laboratories.

I am lucky to work with a group of brilliant graduate students, and I am certain that I have learned more from them than they have from me. In addition to the research project, I teach classes in physiology and marine biology, and the fact that I am one of the few people on the staff with a strong background in biology may be another reason I was chosen for this position.

The primary mission of the marine center is to provide research and developmental support to Alaska's seafood industry. Experimental projects range from producing good-tasting foods packed with high-protein fish meal to finding a way to neutralize the enzyme that causes arrow tooth flounder to fall apart when the fish is cooked. In addition to the laboratories and the small fish processing plant on the lower level, the center has a test kitchen to evaluate new seafood items before they are sold commercially. As with any good scientific laboratory, the projects are endless, but the funding isn't.

I think of my work as a short-term project, and I don't expect my funding to last long. In addition to developing a chemical assay, I am assisting a Nova Scotia microbiology company to evaluate and refine their cell-based test for PSP, and in many ways, I like their test better than ours. It is cheap and easy, and even though it doesn't provide as much data as a chemical assay, if their test proves to be accurate, I think it and not ours will become the test of the future. The main problem their test has at this point is that it often produces false positives. I get positive results nearly every time I use it, even when a comparative mouse bioassay turns out negative.

If they can solve this problem, though, they will have an inexpensive, portable test kit that is simple enough to be used by a layman. A guy can dig a bucket of clams, use his cell-based pocket kit, and an hour later, know if the clams are safe to eat. Our test is expensive and complex and must be performed in a well-equipped laboratory by highly-paid technicians and scientists. So far, though, our test produces much more accurate results.

By helping the Canadian company refine their test kit, I am cutting my own throat. I don't think state legislators will find it in their hearts to give me more money to work on PSP if an accurate detection test is already on the market. After all, this is the same state that didn't splurge for oil-containment equipment until after the Exxon Valdez disaster. On the other hand, it is also a state rich with oil money, and from what I've seen, there is no rhyme or reason as to how that is spent. If the right politician in Juneau decides this is a worthy project, we might be able to fund this venture for years. I'm along for the ride, always watching and listening for new job openings.

My desk clock buzzed its 10:00 warning, and I shook my head to clear it. *What day is it?* I stared at the calendar, until I recalled it was Thursday. I taught a 10:00 class on Monday, Wednesday, and Friday, but I didn't have anything today. I should clean up the lab. I'd prepared it to run Craig's samples, and I would have to put away the chemicals and equipment. I couldn't face the graduate students this morning, though. Perhaps I would sneak down there during the lunch hour.

I turned my attention to the stack of paperwork on my desk but accomplished little. At 11:30, my telephone buzzed and Betty announced that an FAA inspector was waiting in the main office to talk to me.

"Send him to my office," I said. I unlocked and opened the door and set a chair in front of my desk. I was just returning to my chair when a sharp knock rattled the door frame.

"Hello. Come in."

The tall man bent his head and walked through the doorway. He would have cleared the seven-foot frame by several inches even without this maneuver, but I suspected he did it out of habit.

He walked across my office, shifted the paper sack he was carrying from his right to his left hand, and shoved his long, thin right hand toward me. "Dr. Marcus, I'm Frank Hayman with the FAA."

I shook the dry palm, wishing my own hand didn't feel so sweaty. "Please, sit down." I gestured toward the chair in front of my desk.

He folded his long body onto the seat and sat quietly for a moment, staring at my face. His thin black hair was combed straight back from his forehead, enhancing his prominent nose. The nose provided a solid base for his wire-rimmed glasses, and from behind these glasses, his brown eyes studied me, shifting their focus from my left to my right eye and then back to my left again. I imagined he could read the guilt in my eyes and was trying to decide how he should question me. What did I know about the plane crash, and how could he extract that information?

I waited with my hands folded in my lap. I willed myself to breathe evenly and to hold Hayman's gaze. I hoped he could not see the beads of perspiration that were forming on my forehead.

Finally, he spoke. "Dr. Marcus, as I'm sure you have guessed, I am investigating the loss of Kodiak Air Services' Beaver. I spoke with Steve Duncan, and he told me that you were with him when he discovered the wreckage."

Hayman paused, so I answered. "That's right."

"Can you tell me what you saw?"

"Not much, just twisted pieces of metal."

"Did you find any human remains?"

I paused, and as the image of the singed flesh in the shoe filled my mind, the world started to go black again. "Yes," my voice was weak, "a shoe with part of a foot in it."

"Did you touch the shoe or anything else?"

"No."

Hayman sighed and said nothing. He watched me, and I knew I must look terrible.

"Could you identify anyone?" The question came out as a whisper, but Hayman heard me.

"There was more left from the crash than you might think. The underbrush was heavy, and once we cleared it away, we found enough remains to identify the pilot and three of the passengers." Hayman paused. "That's one of the reasons I want to talk to you.

He lifted the paper sack from the floor and withdrew a piece of purple and green nylon material from it. "Does this material look familiar to you?"

The saliva drained from my mouth. "Yes. It's part of Craig's jacket."

"I think we can confirm his identity then."

"That's all you need?"

"That's all we're going to get." His eyes held mine until I looked away.

"Do you know yet what caused the crash?" I phrased my question carefully, making sure to say crash instead of explosion.

Hayman didn't answer. Instead, he asked, "Was Mr. Pederson carrying any explosive materials?"

I felt my cheeks grow hot. "Do you mean fuels or batteries?"

"Why don't you tell me what gear he had?"

I stared at my desk. "Personal gear: A tent, shovels, cooler, dry ice, a three-burner stove, a Coleman lantern." I closed my eyes as if thinking about the gear, even though I knew exactly what camping supplies Craig had packed. "Radio, antenna, Blazo, propane, and a twelve-volt battery." I continued to stare at my desk as I said the last three items.

When Hayman didn't respond, I looked into his dark eyes. "Do you think the fuels caused an explosion?" I had to ask. Hayman was no fool. If he believed the plane had exploded, hazardous materials would be the first thing he would check.

"That's certainly a possibility." He spoke slowly. "However, Mr. Duncan felt certain that the pilot would have loaded the fuels in the floats, not in the cabin with the passengers. What do you think?"

I felt like a bug under a magnifying glass as Hayman studied me. "I've never flown with that pilot before," I said, "but the other pilots have always loaded the fuels in the floats." What could I do? I didn't want to say anything to damage Kodiak Air Services' reputation, but Hayman had asked me a direct question, and I wasn't going to lie.

"If that's the case, then the fuels did not cause the explosion."

"Really?" I sat straight and didn't try to conceal the surprise I felt.

"The explosion originated in the rear section of the cabin. We're certain of that, because that is the most damaged portion of the plane." Hayman shrugged. "To be more precise, we can't find any pieces of the rear section of the cabin. It seems to have evaporated."

"How could you tell? I didn't see much of any portion of the plane."

"We found the wings and large pieces of both floats. If an explosion of the caliber that destroyed this plane originated in the floats, at least one of the floats would be gone, blown to bits."

My mind struggled to sort through this new information. I had been so certain that the gas and battery had caused the explosion that I had not thought of an alternative explanation. "Do you think someone planted a bomb?" The idea was ludicrous. This was not a flight from JFK to Cairo. Terrorism was not a major threat on Kodiak Island.

"I don't know, ma'am," Hayman said, "but the FBI thinks it's a possibility. Their bomb specialists arrive tomorrow."

# Chapter Three

"Why would someone blow up a floatplane?"

"I agree, Dr. Marcus, this is unusual, but there were some special passengers on that plane."

"Who?"

"You haven't heard?"

I shook my head.

"Well, it's not a secret. The news is all over the local radio station. I assume you know who Dick Simms was."

I nodded. "The Kodiak National Wildlife Refuge manager."

"He was acting as tour guide yesterday for Senator Margaret Justin and her husband, George."

"George Justin, the corporate raider?" I knew his name, because his picture had been in *USA Today* a few days earlier.

"That's right. His wife is, or was, a U.S. senator from New York, and she was on the Senate Appropriations Subcommittee for the Interior and the Environment. Apparently Simms was trying to convince her to allocate more funds to the Department of the Interior."

"And she had enemies who disliked her enough to blow up her sightseeing plane?"

Hayman shrugged. "It's not my job to figure out motive. I'm trying to assign a less sinister cause to the explosion. The fuels and battery are a possibility. If you think of any other explosives Mr. Pederson may have had, please contact me."

Hayman stood, handed me his business card, and walked out of my office. I sat, staring at the open door. My headache seemed to be letting up, but I still felt responsible for Craig's death. *I should have been on the plane, and he should have been safe at the marine center.* I now realized, though, that I had been so convinced that our fuels caused the explosion, I'd believed myself partially responsible for the deaths of everyone on the plane. If something else caused the explosion, my burden of guilt was reduced to one.

Geoff Baker, one of the graduate students at the marine center, always had the radio blaring in his lab. I picked up my phone and dialed his extension.

"Yo," a deep voice answered.

"Geoff, this is Jane."

"Hey Doc, sorry to hear about Craig."

"Thanks, Geoff. Have you been listening to the radio this morning?"

"Always. I never miss the hotline."

"What have you heard about the crash, about the passengers on the plane?"

Geoff's voice softened. "Speculation about whether or not someone planted a bomb and talk about the senator and problems with her reelection campaign."

"What problems?"

"Keep in mind, Doc, this is KDKI, not CNN, but apparently the senator was in a tight race for the primary this August. Her campaign ads claim that her opponent has ties with a Mexican drug cartel. Sounds as if she may have made some powerful enemies."

"Anything else?"

"Did you know her husband was George Justin?"

"I heard that."

"Her Senate ties probably didn't hurt his career."

"You're cynical, Geoff."

"Apparently he had plenty of enemies, too, and KDKI is now exploring the possibility that he may have been the target."

"While they're at it, why don't they consider Simms?"

"Yeah, no loss there."

"Geoff!"

"Don't tell me you don't feel the same way. Everyone at the refuge office hated Simms. He had more enemies running around Kodiak than some senator from New York."

"Simms wasn't my favorite guy, but I didn't wish him blown to bits, especially not while he was flying on the same plane as Craig." I paused. "Thanks for the update, Geoff. I'll talk to you later."

"Hey Doc, who was the fifth passenger? They haven't said his or Craig's name on the radio."

"Darren Myers. He owned Uyak Cannery."

"Don't know him. Talk to you later, Doc."

The line went dead. I replaced the receiver in its cradle and stood. *Time to get to work.*

The lab-cleaning job that I had been avoiding all morning took less than ten minutes to complete. I put away the blender, ethanol, centrifuge, petri dishes, and lab tools. I looked at the tidy corner where Craig kept his books and personal gear. Tears raced down my cheeks, and I dropped onto a stool. This is what I had been dreading. Usually when I came into the lab, Craig was huddled at his corner desk, pouring over data sheets or researching something. His beloved laptop stared blankly at me, waiting for Craig to wake it up with the touch of his finger. I would have to pack and send his gear to his parents, but I didn't have the strength for that today.

"Hey, Doc, you okay?"

I realized I still was crying, and I turned away from the open door to wipe my cheeks with my shirt sleeve.

"Here, take this." A handkerchief appeared in front of my eyes.

"Thanks, Geoff. Sorry."

"Nothing to be sorry about, Doc. We all miss Craig. He was a smart kid with a bright future." He paused. "What a waste."

"You're doing a lousy job of cheering me up."

Geoff laughed. "Think it's a good thing I didn't become a priest like my mom wanted?"

I smiled at Geoff's unshaven face, taking in his shoulder-length red hair that was bundled in a ponytail. "You would have struggled with that gig for more than one reason."

"I didn't mean to barge in on you," Geoff said, plunging his hands into the front pockets of his jeans, "but I heard something on the radio that will tick you off."

"What?"

"The Kodiak Flight Services pilot picked up Simms, the senator, and her husband from Bradford Creek."

"He took them bear viewing in an area closed to the public?"

"Exactly. Apparently special people can get special permits to go into those areas that are closed to the rest of us."

"Simms makes," I caught myself, "made the rules as he went along. That's why it was impossible to respect him. He threw a tantrum until Bradford was closed to public use, and then he turns around and goes in there any time he wants. I heard he went in there a dozen times last year, once with ten people."

"Unfortunately, no one calling into the radio station seems to think there is anything wrong with the refuge manager taking bear viewers into a closed area."

I sighed. "Well, he won't do it again." I turned my face away from Geoff, aware that my eyes must be bright red. "Do you honestly think Simms could have been the target?"

Geoff's long, thin frame rested against the wall of the lab. He was one of the oldest students at the center, nearly my age. He nodded his head, blue eyes blazing. "I think it's possible."

Geoff and I locked eyes for several moments and then he pushed himself away from the wall, walked to me, patted my shoulder, turned, and left the lab.

I stared at the door for fifteen minutes, lacking the energy or desire to move. When I did stand, it was only to take five steps and sit again, this time in the chair in front of Craig's computer.

I turned on the laptop and laughed when the image of a shrieking raven filled the screen.

On the first field trip Craig took with me, he had been humbled by one of these shrewd birds. After we pitched our tents, I assigned him the task of storing the gear, while I walked the beach to inspect a mussel bed. He put everything in the tents except the two food boxes, and when I returned, I found him stretched out on his sleeping bag, reading a novel, while a raven systematically carried away our food. He'd been so embarrassed that I couldn't possibly get mad at him, but the story was too good not to share with my colleagues and graduate students at the marine center, and Craig caught a lot of flak. "Beware the raven," was a chant that haunted him for his first summer at the center, and only a few days ago, I'd heard a graduate student yell the words down the hall to him.

Craig loved practical jokes, and he was good-natured about the ribbing. After his initial embarrassment wore off, he announced he was adopting the raven as his personal totem. I'd given him a Ravens Brew coffee sweatshirt as a going-away present when he returned to school after his first summer as my assistant, and he still wore it often. I didn't know he had a raven as his computer wallpaper, but I wasn't surprised.

As I watched his program icons materialize on top of the sleek black image, I felt tears snake down my cheeks. Craig had mentioned a raven only two nights earlier when I'd spoken with him on the sideband radio. I'd been in a hurry and cut the conversation short. I now regretted that.

Craig had been in his usual high spirits, and in the midst of promising me I would be proud of his work, he told me the only problem he'd had was with a strange, old raven. I told him to save the story until he got back to town. Now, I never would hear it.

I shook my head and wiped my eyes. I exited and turned off the computer. I needed to look through the computer files and copy anything that pertained to our project, but I couldn't bear to do that today.

I returned to my office and thumbed through the file folders stacked in a neat pile on the right side of the desk. I slid the one marked "Cycek" out of the stack and opened it.

The first thing I saw was the photo of Doris Cycek and an unexpected giggle escaped my lips. I'd asked Mr. Cycek to send us a photo of his wife to put in her file. It's too easy in a project like ours to forget the victims were human beings with hopes, dreams, memories, and families. Our focus is the molecular structure of saxitoxin, our task to develop a chemical test that could reveal the presence of the lurking poison. Our procedure only would be successful if it worked every time and detected even low levels of the toxin. The photos of those who had died from PSP were to remind us why these high standards were necessary, and Craig had posted the photos on the bulletin board in the lab.

The families of the other victims had sent us posed photos of their loved ones, but the picture of Mrs. Cycek was horrible. "Do I have to look at this every day?" Craig had asked when the photo arrived, and after two days, he took it down from the bulletin board and stuffed it in her file. As I looked at it now, I couldn't blame him.

The photo was slightly out of focus, and the photographer obviously had surprised Mrs. Cycek. Her eyes were open wide; her mouth turned downward into a frown. She stood on the beach with the ocean behind her and was dressed in an outfit so ridiculous I thought it had to be a joke. A red paisley scarf secured her grey hair, which shot straight upward like a geyser. A baggy, red-and-white, polka-dot dress hung over her small frame like a tent, and orange, rubber, knee-high boots and yellow work gloves accessorized the ensemble.

I thought at first that perhaps this was the only snapshot of his wife Mr. Cycek could bear to part with, but then a more logical explanation occurred to me: *This was probably the most recent photo Mr. Cycek had of his wife, and he thought that's what we wanted.* I turned the photo over and shook my head. His wife would not have been happy with him. I doubted this was the way Doris Cycek would have wanted to be remembered.

The following ten pages in the folder were a typed transcript of the conversation I'd had with Mr. Cycek at the hospital soon after his wife had been pronounced dead. I'd told Craig to take notes, but I had no idea he'd taken down our conversation verbatim. For a moment, thinking I would tease him about being an overachiever, I forgot he was gone. A weight dropped in my stomach when I remembered.

I thumbed through the pages of dialogue between Mr. Cycek and myself. I vividly remembered the small man, dressed in brown coveralls, a red flannel shirt, and brown rubber boots. He clutched a dirty baseball cap in his right hand while we talked. His grey hair had been smashed flat by his hat, drooping on his forehead and curving around his big, brown ears. His back was hunched, and his eyes were glazed. His answers were concise but wooden, his pitch unvaried. He didn't look at my face as he spoke, but stared into the air over my right shoulder. I worried he was going into shock, and after I'd finished talking to him, I quietly asked the doctor to examine him.

I read Craig's notes. The symptoms Mr. Cycek reported were textbook:

Jane: Do you know how many clams your wife ate?
Cycek: No more than ten. She said she wasn't feeling well, so she laid down on the couch.
Jane: Did you save the shells or the clams she cooked but didn't eat?
Cycek: No. I cleaned up. I didn't know the clams made her sick.
Jane: What about raw clams? Did she cook everything she dug?
Cycek: Yes. There's nothing left.
Jane: I know this is difficult Mr. Cycek, but can you describe your wife's symptoms?
Cycek: She said she felt light headed and her stomach was upset, so she laid down on the couch. I washed the dishes, and maybe twenty minutes later I walked out of the kitchen to find her coughing and gasping for breath. I called right away for the Coast Guard, and by the time they got there—maybe an hour later—she'd stopped breathing. I didn't know what to do.

Poor Mrs. Cycek. The doctors believed her heart just gave out. If she'd been younger and stronger, she might have lived until the Coast Guard arrived. After a few hours on respiratory support, she could have recovered fully.

I closed the file and pushed it away from me. It would be up to me to take the notes from now on, and I did not have the time or energy to do as good a job as Craig had. I stood and stretched, and my thoughts returned to Dick Simms. Simms had made enemies, but I couldn't believe someone hated him enough to kill him.

I dialed the number for the Kodiak National Wildlife Refuge. The bear biologist at the refuge was a friend of mine, and she usually had few qualms about divulging department secrets. She had detested Simms, and more than once we had shared a bottle of wine while she unloaded her frustrations about working with him.

"Dana Baynes, please," I said to the receptionist.

"Baynes."

"Hi Dana. This is Jane Marcus."

"Jane. I was going to call you this evening. I was sorry to hear about your assistant. I know how much you liked him."

"Thanks, Dana. I can't seem to think about anything else; that's why I'm calling." I paused, remembering that Dana just had lost her boss. "How are things around there today?"

"Well, we're not exactly having a wake; none of us liked Dick. It's pretty quiet here, though. I guess we're all in shock."

"An FAA guy stopped by my office earlier, and he said someone may have planted a bomb on the plane."

"I heard that," Dana said. "I gather that Senator Justin had a few enemies."

"What was Simms doing with her and her husband?"

"Acting the big-shot host, his favorite role. I guess that's how he made it to refuge manager, because heaven knows it wasn't his intellect that got him there. He knew who to brown nose."

"Was it legal for him to take the senator to Bradford?"

Dana said nothing for a moment. Then, slowly, she said, "Yes, legally he could break the rules, and it wouldn't have been so bad if he had only done it occasionally, but he went into restricted areas on a regular basis and left it to the rest of us to justify his actions. I don't know how many times I talked to him about it, but he just laughed."

"Do you think anyone hated Simms enough to kill him?"

Dana's voice was so low I could barely hear it. "Yes."

"Can you think of anyone in particular?"

I expected a sarcastic reply, but she sounded strained as she said, "Yes, but I can't talk now. I'll stop by your place tonight. Is 7:00 okay?"

"I'll buy the wine."

I disconnected with Dana and dialed the number for Kodiak Flight Services. Steve Duncan answered the phone.

"Hi, Steve. The FAA inspector stopped by my office, and he told me that the explosion originated in the cabin."

"Yeah, he told me the same thing."

"Do you think someone planted a bomb?"

"I don't know, Dr. Marcus. I'd be happy for any explanation that removes the liability from Kodiak Flight Services, but a bomb sounds far-fetched to me. Think about it. When and how would someone have hidden it on the plane? We made three flights with that plane yesterday before the explosion. I don't think we left the plane unattended in Trident Basin all day, and you know what that place is like, with pilots and charter service employees buzzing around the docks all the time. We all know each other, and any one of them would have told me if he or she had seen a stranger poking around one of my planes."

I remembered how quiet the floatplane docks had been when I was waiting for Craig's plane, but I didn't mention this.

"I also think Bill would have noticed if a strange object had been put in the plane," Steve continued.

I didn't know much about explosives, but I thought a small bomb easily could have been hidden from Bill's view. "Did you meet the senator, Steve?"

"No."

"Did anyone at the office receive a call asking about the senator's flight?"

"Hayman asked us the same thing, and we've all thought about it, but we can't remember anything. That's just it. How would a stranger know what plane we would use for the senator's flight? We could have used either of the two Beavers, or for that matter, we could have flown the three of them in the two-oh-six."

"Why did Simms charter you guys in the first place? The refuge has its own plane."

"The refuge plane was unavailable for some reason. It was either being used for something else or was down for maintenance. Simms had his secretary call two days ago to set up a charter, and we really didn't have anything available. That's why we ended up combining their charter with the charter to pick up Craig from his campsite and Darren Myers from the cannery. Bradford is just over the mountain from Uyak Cannery and where Craig was camped, so it made sense to combine their flights. We didn't make that decision, though, until yesterday morning, so no one would know what plane we planned to use to shuttle Simms and his pals to Bradford."

I didn't have an argument for this point, and I had to admit the bomb theory was shaky at best. "I guess we'll have to wait to hear what the bomb experts say."

"Someone is going down for this," Steve said. "If there is no evidence of a bomb, then my little charter service will get ground to pieces. The government will see that someone pays for the senator's death."

I knew that Steve owned part of Kodiak Flight Services, but now I wondered how much of the company was his. He'd always kept a low profile, but now he kept referring to the airlines as his. Would he be able to hang on to his business through this crisis? "At this point, I hope it was a bomb," I said.

"Me too, Dr. Marcus."

"Steve," I said, "after all we've been through together, I think you can call me Jane."

He laughed. "Jane. Okay, I can do that."

Dana Baynes rang my doorbell at 7:00, and when I opened the door, the aroma of pepperoni and cheese greeted me.

"I know you, Jane. You haven't eaten a thing since this whole mess began, so I picked up a delicious, well-balanced meal for us." Dana's dark curls bounced as she hurried into my apartment. She sported a flannel shirt and blue jeans on her petite frame. As I followed her to the kitchen, I noticed that her shoulder-length hair looked as if a comb hadn't touched it in a week.

I had to admit the pizza smelled good, and I hadn't eaten in twenty-four hours. I poured the Merlot while Dana dished up pizza. We sat at the kitchen bar and ate in silence. After devouring two pieces, I pushed my plate away and sipped the wine. The Merlot had a calming effect on me. My shoulders sagged as the tension drained from them.

"You look tired," Dana said.

"This hasn't been a good day."

Dana squeezed my arm and squinted her green eyes. "I know. I didn't like Simms, but the thought of him being blown to pieces has haunted me all day. I didn't know Craig well, but what a terrible loss. I can only imagine how you must feel."

I fought back tears. "It's more than that, Dana." I grasped the edge of the bar. "I should have been on that plane. I sent Craig in my place to collect the bivalve samples, because I hate to fly."

"You can't do that, Jane." She crossed her arms over her small chest. "You're being too hard on yourself. You can't control everything. You are in charge of your lab. You shouldn't be the one to go on these piddly little collection trips. Those jobs are exactly why you hire assistants. Unless you planted the bomb, you're not responsible. Got it?"

I laughed. Dana always could make me feel better. I knew I wouldn't be able to shake off my guilt so easily, but at least my mood lightened. "You're bossy for such a little thing."

"Yeah, that's what Simms used to say."

"Let's go in the living room. I'll get the dishes later." I picked up the bottle of wine and my glass and walked ten steps to the recessed portion of the condo that I grandly called the living room. I sank into the soft cushions of the couch and set the wine bottle on the glass coffee table. Dana sat in the oversized chair on the other side of the table.

"Do you really believe Simms could have been the target?"

"I not only believe it, but I think it makes a lot more sense than imagining Mexican terrorists skulking through the back alleys of Kodiak."

"And you know a likely suspect?"

Dana sipped her wine and stared at the coffee table. "I could give you a list of likely suspects, including two people at the office who would dance on Simms' grave if his death meant they would be promoted to refuge manager. I don't honestly think either one of them has the balls to plant a bomb, though."

"Then who?"

Dana sighed, set her glass on the coffee table, and sat forward in her chair. She placed her elbows on her knees and looked at my face. "Simms used his position to do many things I didn't approve of. You know I fought with him constantly over programs he implemented that I felt were harmful to the bears or their habitat." Dana massaged her nose.

"Our biggest responsibility on this refuge is to protect the brown bear habitat, and I often believed Simms went out of his way to sabotage our mission. He managed to make enemies of most of the primary users of the refuge. No one liked him. He was terrible." Dana waved her hand in front of her face, as if swatting a mosquito.

"He didn't have a clue about scientific procedure, and he was a running joke among the fish and game biologists. He antagonized guides, the native corporations, commercial fishermen, and air transport carriers. I'm not exaggerating, Jane. I think you would be surprised to know how many people called our office with complaints. This man was not well-liked." She picked up her glass and drank. As she lowered it to the table, she said, "But if he was the target, I think he was killed for following through with a good decision, not for all the things he did that were wrong."

"What do you mean?"

"Have you heard of George Wall?"

"No, I don't think so."

"Wall is a renegade sport-fishing and photography guide. I don't know how he convinces people to book with him, but he takes a steady stream of people every summer."

"Where does he take them?"

"That's just it. He isn't licensed to guide anyone on the refuge. He has applied for a special use permit, but he has a list of fish and game violations, he runs an unsafe operation, and the Alaska Department of Fish and Game showed us a thick folder of complaints from his past clients. To top it off, he can't get insurance, and no one gets a special use permit without insurance." Dana shrugged. "There are a few shady guides operating on Kodiak, but we try to keep them off the refuge, and the legitimate guides that work on the refuge aren't shy about letting us know when an unlicensed guide appears where he shouldn't be. That's what happened to Wall."

"Someone reported him?"

"A guide saw Wall running float trips down Uganik River, and he called us. I was impressed with Simms. This is just the sort of thing he usually waffles on. He puts off doing anything about it until it's too late to catch the guy. This time, though, he called in the troopers and they set up a sting operation in a few days." Dana took another sip of wine and sat back in the chair. A smile played across her lips as she remembered the event.

"A male and female trooper posed as husband and wife and booked with Wall. He had an opening on his next float trip." She shook her head. "What an idiot. Not only were the troopers able to charge him with operating on the refuge without a permit, but he baited a brown bear with salmon so his clients could get photos of it. Then, he shot the bear in the butt with birdshot to chase him away. He strung a section of gill net across the river to catch his party's supper, and then instructed his clients on the proper procedure for snagging salmon." Dana laughed. "I can't remember what else he did, but the troopers snapped photos of everything, and Wall was arrested on eight counts as soon as he returned to town."

"Unbelievable," I said.

"The guy was furious about being caught, and of course, Simms didn't sit quietly in the background. He was present at Wall's arrest, and he couldn't resist telling Wall what a fool he was and laughing in his face. Wall threatened he would get even with Simms."

I shrugged. "People make threats like that, but they usually don't carry through," I said. "Isn't Wall in jail?"

"No. He's out on bail. His case won't come to trial for a few months." Dana sat forward again. "I know this sounds crazy, Jane, but Wall is bad news. I can't remember why, but I was in Simms' office when he was looking through Wall's file. This was before the sting operation. I wasn't involved in any of this, but for some reason I was in Simms' office, and I remember him saying that Wall had served time in Colorado. He worked with the state highway department there and was part of the excavation crew for digging tunnels. He worked with explosives." Dana paused, her eyes locked on my face. "A few sticks of dynamite disappeared from the worksite, and two days later, Wall's girlfriend's father's truck blew into a million pieces. It didn't take Sherlock Holmes to piece the facts together."

"Was the father killed?"

"No, something went wrong. No one was in the truck when it exploded, so Wall only had to serve a few years."

"Have you told the police this?"

"Not yet," Dana said. "I'll wait until someone official states that the crash was not an accident."

"It could be too late by then."

Dana shrugged. "I hope not."

"Does anyone else at the refuge know about Wall's record?"

"I don't know. It wasn't a secret. Simms told me, and it was none of my business. Marty Shires, the assistant refuge manager, must know, but he was so busy trying not to look happy today, that I doubt it occurred to him. We're not a close-knit group in that office."

I smiled. "It's a regular Peyton Place there. I don't know how any work gets done."

"Not much does." Dana handed her glass to me for a refill.

I was awake and staring at the ceiling the next morning at 6:00 when my alarm buzzed. I hadn't slept well, but I felt restless and bursting with energy. I brushed my teeth, combed my hair, and gathered it into a ponytail. I pulled on sweats and jogging shoes and headed out the front door.

Fog and drizzle enveloped the mountains. Visibility was less than half a mile, and the ceiling was no more than a hundred feet. I considered driving to Abercrombie Park for my jog, but I recalled that an overzealous bear had treed two joggers there recently, and I decided to stick to the city sidewalks. The town was slow to awaken on this misty morning, and I doubted I would run into much traffic on the sidewalk.

The morning air felt cool, and even though the air oozed moisture, I didn't notice the humidity until I had been running for a few minutes. Suddenly, my lungs clogged, and I stopped, head up, gasping for air. I sat on a low wall that bordered the sidewalk and stared at the wet pavement. My head ached, and I regretted the four glasses of wine I'd consumed with Dana.

Could George Wall have planted a bomb to settle the score with Simms? Dana was not taken to flights of fancy. She rarely accepted any notion without scientific proof. I hoped she would tell the police her suspicions before Wall left the island. If he planted the bomb, though, he probably already was gone.

I slid off the wall and began to walk home. The drizzle had saturated my sweats, and cold was beginning to soak through my skin.

I didn't hear the car pull up beside me until a familiar voice said, "Walking in the rain?"

I stopped and turned toward the red Audi. Peter Wayman's dark face smiled at me through the open window. He wore a suit and tie, and I glanced at my watch to see if I was late for work.

"It's not even 7:00 yet, Peter. Are you headed to work already?"

"I have to take off early today, so I thought I'd get a head start. Can I give you a ride home?"

I looked down at my wet clothes. "I don't want to get your car wet."

He waved his hand. "Don't worry about it. Come on."

His words sounded more like an order than an offer, and I meekly complied with the wishes of my boss. As I slid into the immaculate car, I tried to touch as few surfaces as possible. Dr. Wayman watched me, his brown eyes intense, and as soon as I shut the car door, he drove slowly toward the center of town.

"How are you doing, Jane?" He kept his eyes forward, but I glanced at the side of his face. Peter was in his mid-forties, and he was the most beautiful man I ever had seen. His black hair was cropped close to his head, and a tinge of grey at the temples offered the only clue to his age. His milk-chocolate skin was flawless. He didn't even have wrinkles around his eyes, and I wondered how he managed this. Maybe after I had consumed a few glasses of champagne at the next Christmas party, I'd get him to divulge his beauty secrets. Peter was also a sharp dresser, especially for a scientist. He ran the marine center with an iron fist, but he was a good boss, and I respected him. I also liked his wife, a high school math teacher, and I occasionally baby sat their three-year old daughter.

"Jane?"

"I'm sorry, Peter. I'm fine."

"Are you planning to hire a replacement for Craig?"

"No, I don't think so. I'll get someone next year, but I think I can handle the research this summer."

"Okay, but don't get behind. With the high levels of PSP this summer, you'll want to take as many samples as possible."

"I know," I said. "I'm planning to get more samples from Uyak in a few days on the next series of low tides."

"Good."

An uneasy silence followed. I sensed Peter trying to form his next question, and as he made a slow U-turn through a grocery store parking lot, I realized that our meeting had not been accidental. Peter had been looking for me. He wanted to talk to me about something outside the office.

"Have you heard any more from Craig's parents?"

"No. Why?"

"No reason. I'm just surprised they haven't asked more questions about the accident."

"Maybe they've been talking to the troopers."

"Betty told me that an FAA inspector visited you yesterday, and then he called the office later in the afternoon to check on the size of the propane tank Craig took with him."

*Good old Betty. Run to Dr. Wayman and tattle on Jane.* "It's just a formality, Peter. We didn't do anything wrong." If only I could believe those words.

Peter braked at a stop sign and turned to look at me, his intelligent eyes searching my face. "Did our fuels cause that explosion?"

"I don't know, Peter." I met his gaze. "It is possible, but the FAA inspector told me that the explosion originated in the cabin. The pilot probably put the battery and the propane tank in the float."

I saw the muscles in Peter's cheeks relax. *He'd better be careful; all that tension would produce lines on that perfect face.*

Peter accelerated slowly from the stop sign. "The FBI is sending an explosives expert to see if a bomb caused the crash."

Peter swung his face toward me. "I heard that rumor, but I didn't believe it. Are you sure?"

"That's what the FAA inspector told me."

"Does he think someone was trying to kill the senator?"

"He didn't speculate, but I think the only reason the FBI is getting involved in this is because the senator was on the plane."

Peter snorted. "Yes, if five unknown tourists had been killed, the event would have barely rated a blurb in the *Kodiak Mirror*."

"I don't know," I said. "I can't believe someone would follow the senator all the way to Kodiak to kill her."

"What about the other passengers?"

"What do you mean?"

"Maybe someone else was the target."

I expected Peter to tell me about Simms' many enemies. Peter still thought of me as a recent arrival on the island, and he liked to explain things to me. His next words surprised me.

"This isn't something I want you to repeat to anyone, Jane, but I've played poker a few times with Darren Myers. Darren was the owner of Uyak Cannery."

*Peter played poker?* I couldn't visualize that. "What about Darren Myers?" I asked.

"Like I said, this is just wild speculation, but he was going through an extremely ugly divorce. His wife, Maryann, threatened to kill him."

"No offense, Peter, but I doubt his wife would plant a bomb to get rid of him. If she really hated him that much, she could stir a little cyanide into his coffee. This doesn't strike me as a jealous-wife type of crime."

Peter shrugged. "I hear she has quite a temper." He pulled into the parking lot of my complex and stopped in front of the walkway.

I doubted that Peter and his poker buddies were a good source of unbiased information, and I was surprised that Peter didn't sense this.

I opened the car door. "I'm beginning to realize that everyone has enemies, but it takes either a ruthless or a warped individual to kill six people just to rid yourself of one person. I don't think most people are capable of that kind of random killing. Do you?"

Peter stared at me but said nothing. He seemed to be thinking about what I had said. Maybe he was thinking about Maryann Myers, and I wondered how much he knew about the woman.

# Chapter Four

I unlocked my office door at 8:30, and a woman from the Alaska Department of Environmental Conservation Lab in Palmer called five minutes later. "Doctor Marcus. We never received your bivalve samples. We were ready to perform the bioassay yesterday, but we don't have your samples."

I'd forgotten to call Palmer and cancel the mouse bioassay. My plan had been to prepare the bivalve tissues Craig was bringing me. I would use a small amount for the cell-based test we were running for the Canadian lab and then divide the remainder in half. I would keep one half for our chemical assay and send the other half to Palmer for a bioassay. Then, we could compare the results of the two assays and the cell-based kit. I had alerted the Palmer lab that I would be sending them a sample, but in the aftermath of the crash, I'd forgotten to call and cancel.

I explained the situation to the technician. She was less than sympathetic, and I couldn't blame her. Their lab was busy, and they were under pressure to determine the level of saxitoxin in the bivalves from Uyak. In cases of suspected PSP, the lab usually was sent a bivalve sample from the victim's last meal. In this case, however, the clams had been eaten and the dishes cleared away before the victim began experiencing her first symptoms of PSP. Only Mrs. Cycek had eaten the clams, and according to her husband, she had consumed ten or twelve butter clams.

I assured the technician that I would fly out in a few days and collect more samples.

"Please let us know when to expect them," she said, and then disconnected.

I taught my 10:00 class without much enthusiasm. Craig had assisted me with this class, and the students were glum and withdrawn. I let them leave twenty minutes early and then returned to my office and called Kodiak Flight Services to set up a charter to Uyak Bay for July third·

"Dr. Marcus," the dispatcher said. "I think Steve wants to talk to you."

A moment later, Steve said, "Hi Jane. I just want to let you know that we're having a memorial service for Bill and his passengers today at 3:00."

"Where?"

"Trident Basin. We're trying to keep it small and informal. Hopefully the press won't hear about it."

I thought Steve was being dramatic. Kodiak's press corps couldn't consist of more than two reporters, one from KDKI and one from the *Kodiak Mirror*. However, when I searched for a parking place at Trident Basin at 2:30, I understood what Steve had meant.

"For crying out loud," Geoff said.

I'd given him a ride to the service. Peter had previous plans and said he wouldn't be able to attend, but Glenda and Betty and two graduate students who had roomed with Craig were in a car behind us. I motioned to them to back up, and we parked along the side of the narrow dirt road. Several more cars pulled in behind us.

As we walked down the road, I became aware of television crews and video cameras. "What's going on?"

"We're famous, Doc. This is our fifteen minutes."

A guy with CNN embroidered on his coat nearly shoved me off the road as he ran past. "I guess this is the press Steve was worried about. They must have heard about the memorial service."

They weren't the only ones who had heard. A trooper's van rolled slowly past us down the steep road. "Maybe something else has happened," I said. "I can't believe all this excitement is for the memorial service. I've heard about slow news days, but why would folks in Cleveland care about a memorial service in Kodiak, Alaska?"

Geoff glanced sideways at me. "When a U.S. senator gets blown up in a plane, it's news, Doc."

I now regretted promising Steve I would say something at the service. I thought I would be speaking to a few acquaintances, and I wasn't prepared to address the nation.

The crowd was gathering in a semicircle above the ramps leading down to the floatplanes. Steve saw me approach and motioned to me. He wore a long-sleeved, tan shirt and tie his straight, blonde hair combed back from his forehead. He chewed on his upper lip.

"Looks like we have more of a crowd than I wanted."

I looked around. The camera crews were setting up their equipment, and a nervous rumble filled the air. "We'll get through it," I said. "I wish I'd planned what I was going to say a little better, though. Who else is speaking?"

"I'll go first, and then Father Ivanof will say a prayer. Next, I'll say a few words about Bill and then introduce you. When you get done, you need to introduce David Sturman. He will say something about Darren Myers."

"Is that it?" I asked.

"No. Father Ivanof will say a final prayer."

"What about Simms? Isn't anyone planning to eulogize him?"

"I called the refuge office, but no one wanted to stand up and say anything. I guess we should have planned this earlier."

"It's not your fault. I can't believe Marty Shires or someone at the refuge can't think of something nice to say about Simms. I bet if Shires knew all these camera were here, he would volunteer to say something."

"Speak of the devil."

I turned around and saw a short, thin, dark-haired man approaching. He ignored me and held out his right hand to Steve.

"Say," Shires said. "I've been thinking, and I'd like to say a few words about Dick."

"These cameras didn't scare you away?" I said.

Shires spun around to look at me. I don't think he recognized me, and my words confused him.

"Okay," Steve said. "You'll speak after David Sturman. I'll tell him to introduce you."

I wandered back to my group from the marine center and found them huddled together in conversation.

"Hey, Doc," Geoff said. "Does that guy look familiar to you?" He tilted his head toward an ABC crew standing beside him.

I looked at the crew. The cameraman was pointing the camera at a reporter who was dressed in the latest outdoor gear. He looked out of place in Kodiak, as if he had just stepped out of the pages of an Eddie Bauer catalog.

"He does look familiar, but I'm not much of a news junkie. I don't know his name."

"You'll be on the evening news, Doc."

"Unless I say something incredibly stupid, I'm sure my bit will be edited out. Ten seconds of Father Ivanof is what they're after." I knew what I said was true, but the words failed to ease the burning in my stomach.

The crowd began to hush, and I turned my attention toward Steve, who stood atop four stacked pallets in front of the semicircle of people.

"Thank you all for coming today. This is just a simple ceremony to remember Bill Watson and his passengers."

I looked around the crowd. The news teams were quiet, the cameras fixed on Steve. Steve seemed calm, his voice strong. I hoped I would do as well. At the mention of Bill's name, a young woman sobbed loudly. Three other women huddled around her, shielding her from the invasive eyes of the cameras. I wondered if this was the young woman Bill had planned to take to dinner on the day of the crash.

Near the young women, a tired, middle-aged couple leaned against each other for support. I knew they must be Bill's parents, and as I watched their bent frames, my anxiety disappeared. Craig had been even younger than their son, and his parents grieved alone. I would do my best to tell this crowd about the short life of that very special person. Perhaps some of what I said would be carried on the evening news, and maybe Craig's parents would see it and know their son had been valued and loved by his coworkers.

Steve introduced Father Ivanof and then helped the elderly priest up onto the makeshift platform. A deep voice boomed from the small man, and as he lifted his arms, his long black robe billowed.

I lowered my head and thought about Craig during the long prayer. I still couldn't believe he was dead. My mother had died a slow, tortuous death from cancer. Watching her suffer had scarred me and my view of life in ways I still was discovering, but I never had trouble believing she was dead. In the end, her death was a relief, because I no longer had to watch her cry from pain and fear. Craig had been here one minute and gone the next, his body evaporated. I kept expecting a radio call from him asking when the plane would arrive to pick him up.

"Thank you, Father Ivanof," Steve said.

His words brought me back to reality, and I lifted my head, aware that I was the last person in the crowd to do so.

Steve paused for a minute and seemed to be gathering his thoughts. He looked at the ground and then allowed his gaze to drift around the crowd. "We still don't know what caused the crash of Nine Nine November, and we may never know what caused the Beaver to explode in midair on a calm, clear day. All we know is that the lives of six people were snuffed out." As he paused, I heard scattered sniffles among the spectators.

"Bill Watson was a good pilot, and I'm certain the investigation will reveal no error on his part." Steve seemed to be staring at one of the cameras when he said this, and I thought it was a bold statement to make so early in the investigation.

"Bill grew up in Kodiak, and according to his parents, as soon as he could talk, he told anyone who would listen that he wanted to be a pilot." I glanced at Bill's parents, and saw them grip each other tighter. "He began working for Kodiak Flight Services as a freight handler when he was sixteen years old, and when he was seventeen, he started working on his pilot's license. I thought of him as a younger brother." Steve's voice cracked, and he stared at the ground.

"Bill was proud to be a pilot, and even though he was young, he took the responsibility of his job seriously. Today, I want to remember his competence and afford him the respect he deserves."

Steve then told a story about a daring medevac Bill had performed when he landed on stormy seas to transport a young girl from a boat to the hospital. The girl had fallen and badly cut herself, and Bill heard the distress call and diverted from his original flight plan to rescue her. The doctor at the hospital said that if Bill hadn't gotten her there so quickly, she would have bled to death.

Next, Steve told a humorous story about Bill stopping to pick up deer hunters. They loaded their gear on the plane, and Bill saw that their campsite was still a mess, littered with trash and five-gallon fuel cans. He tossed their duffel bags and boxes of deer meat on the beach and told the hunters that first he would haul their garbage to town and then he would take their gear. The men were irate, but they were forced to comply with Bill's wishes. When they balked about paying for the extra flying time, Bill threatened to report them to the troopers. Steve said that the hunters were twice as big as Bill, but by the time they arrived in town, they were meek and polite and made reservations with Kodiak Flight Services for the following fall hunting season, even requesting Bill as their pilot.

Steve told two more stories about Bill, but I didn't listen. I was too busy rehearsing my own talk in my mind. I noticed the television camera crews continued to film throughout Steve's talk, but I knew they would not show all of this on the news.

"Now I would like to introduce Dr. Jane Marcus from the Kodiak Braxton Marine Biology and Fisheries Research Center to say a few words about Craig Pederson."

The crowd shuffled, turning to see who I was. I swallowed and walked forward. I was glad I'd worn slacks as Steve pulled me up on the pallets.

"Hello," I said in what I thought was a loud voice. The greeting seemed to be sucked into the air, though, and I saw the crowd inch forward. I counted five cameras pointed at me, and for a moment, I wasn't sure I could do it. I inhaled and yelled my next sentence. "Most of you probably don't know who

I am, or who Craig was. I'm on the staff at the Marine Research Center, and I have only lived in Kodiak a little more than a year. In that short time, though, I've come to call Kodiak home, and I hope to stay here for a long while." The crowd seemed to relax and move back. Everyone could hear me now, but I wasn't sure how long my voice could endure yelling.

"Craig was from Oregon, and this was his second summer as a student assistant at the center. He was bright, personable, funny, and efficient." I tried not to picture Craig as I said these words, because I knew if I thought about him, I would lose control, and that's the last thing I wanted to happen.

"He was so capable, that I sent him alone on a sample-collecting trip, and he was on his way back from this trip when the plane exploded. This was the first collection trip he had gone on alone. I went with him on all the others." My voice didn't falter, but I felt tears roll down my cheeks, and I knew I wouldn't be able to talk much longer.

"Craig had a loving family, many friends, and a bright future. The world will be a little darker without his shining spirit." I looked at the group from the marine center and saw Betty sobbing into her handkerchief. I felt my lips quiver, and I knew I'd better wrap it up.

"Thank you," I said, and I was stepping down from the platform when I saw Steve waving frantically to me. "Oh!" I stood straight. "I would like to introduce David Sturman, who will remember Darren Myers."

I hurried through the crowd and stood beside Geoff. He put his arm around me and patted my shoulder, and I dug in my pocket for a Kleenex.

David Sturman was a heavyset, balding man in his fifties, whose face burned from the exertion of climbing onto the platform. His voice was soft and did not carry well, and I moved forward with the crowd to hear what he said.

"I offer my condolences to the friends and families of the six victims of Nine Nine November. I am here today representing the loved ones and coworkers of Darren Myers, the owner and operator of Uyak Cannery." He paused and looked at a note card he held in the palm of his right hand. "Darren was the second-to-last passenger to board the Beaver on Wednesday. He was on his way to Japan for cannery business."

Sturman glanced again at his note card. "How can I sum up Darren's life in a few short sentences?" Sweat streamed down Sturman's forehead, and he wiped his brow with his shirt sleeve. "Darren was a man of vision. He convinced a few investors that he could resurrect a defunct salmon cannery and turn it into a thriving business, producing both a canned and frozen product. The investors that had the foresight to believe in Darren have not been disappointed. In six short years, Uyak Cannery has become the fourth most productive cannery on Kodiak."

I thought his speech sounded more appropriate for a shareholders meeting than a memorial service, but perhaps Mr. Myers had been all business.

"Darren was well respected by his employees, and in his honor, the cannery has stopped operation and is holding its own memorial service today. Darren wouldn't want us to sit idle too long, though, so we will resume production tomorrow, and we will attempt to meet the high standards Darren set for us."

After another peek at the card in his hand, Sturman continued. "In addition to being a fine businessman and visionary, Darren was an honest friend and a loving father. His two children, Sandra and Peter..."

"Liar! These are all lies. Darren Myers was horrible and a lousy father!"

The woman's voice screeched from the back of the crowd, and as I turned to see who owned the voice, a large body rammed into me and sent me sprawling. I was so surprised by the blow that I wasn't even able to put out my hands to break my fall. My right cheek slammed into the gravel parking lot, bounced, and then landed on the small rocks. I felt strong hands grasp me around the waist and pull me to my feet.

"Are you okay, Doc? Your face is a mess." Geoff pulled a handkerchief from his pocket and began wiping gravel and blood from my face.

My face stung, and I felt dazed. "What happened?"

"Those stupid people from the TV station trampled you so they could get footage of Mrs. Myers."

"That was Darren Myer's wife who yelled?" I reached a hand to my cheek and lightly touched the damage.

"That's what someone said."

I looked toward the back of the crowd. "Where'd she go?"

Geoff followed my gaze. "She must be in the upper parking lot. See the TV cameras?"

I didn't see the woman, but I saw the camera crews grouped around someone in the upper lot.

"I guess she wanted to be on television."

"My dear, are you okay?" Glenda walked toward me. "Oh my goodness. You should go to the emergency room and get that looked at."

"It's nothing, Glenda. Just a little road rash." Cool air stung the abrasions, and I blinked back tears.

"Can I have your attention, please?" Sturman's voice wasn't loud enough to cut through the chatter of the crowd.

"Excuse me!" Steve yelled. "If we could please return to our service."

The crowd in the lower parking lot hushed, but the television crews did not interrupt their interview.

Sturman's face had faded to a pale white, and perspiration dripped from his chin. I hoped he wasn't about to have a heart attack.

"I guess that's all I have to say. Darren will be missed. And now I would like to introduce…" he checked his note card… "Martin Shires, who will remember Richard Simms."

I barely heard Marty's self-serving speech. He must have been very disappointed that Mrs. Myer's outburst diverted the attention of the television crews. The cameramen didn't return to the lower parking lot until near the end of his talk, and even then, they stayed at the back of the crowd. I wondered what Mrs. Myers had told the reporters. *Maybe Peter had been right. Perhaps she had hated her husband badly enough to blow up a plane full of people.*

The service ended with another prayer by Father Ivanof. A light drizzle began to fall as we walked up the road toward our vehicles. I held my right hand over the side of my face to keep the rain out of my cuts. The television crews milled around, uncertain what to do next. The cameramen shot footage of the passing mourners, and I looked away from the cameras, irritated at their invasion of the service.

I didn't turn when someone tapped me on the shoulder and said my name. Powerful masculine cologne engulfed me, and I knew I had never met the man who was trying to get my attention. I was afraid he was a desperate news correspondent wanting an interview. Geoff, my protector, came to my aid.

"Can I help you, sir?" Geoff said, taking my arm, and stepping between me and the stranger.

"I want to introduce myself to Dr. Marcus," a deep voice said.

Curiosity prevailed, and I looked at the man. He was not a reporter, and he did not belong in a parking lot on Kodiak Island. He wore an expensive, dark-grey suit and a conservative maroon tie. His shoes were Italian leather and soon would be ruined when the rain turned the road into a mud pit. He sported a deep tan that set off his sapphire eyes. His short, dark hair was combed neatly, and his smooth face looked as if he had shaved only minutes earlier. I suspected that the body beneath the suit was lean and fit, and I had to admit that he rivaled Peter for good looks. I gawked unashamedly at the handsome stranger, and then I realized why he had sucked in his breath and diverted his eyes as soon as he saw my face.

"Hello," I said. "I was trampled by a news crew, but I'll be fine."

"It looks painful." He held out his manicured hand. "I'm Jack Justin."

"A relative of the senator?" Geoff asked.

"Her son."

"I'm sorry for your loss," I said.

Jack nodded. "Thank you."

"Why didn't you speak today?"

"The reporters haven't figured out who I am yet, and I want to keep it that way as long as possible."

"Of course." I introduced Geoff to Jack, since Geoff was hanging on every word we said.

Jack nodded and then turned his back to Geoff and lowered his voice. "I understand that you found the crash site."

"I was in the plane with the pilot who found the wreckage."

"I'd like to talk to you."

"Sure."

He put his hand on my arm and stopped walking. Geoff stopped for a moment and then awkwardly continued up the road. "Not here," Jack said. "Can I buy you dinner tonight?"

*Boy, this guy smelled good.* "Sure." *Never turn down a free meal with a handsome, aromatic man.*

"You say where and when."

"Henry's at seven?"

"I'll find it."

"It's in the middle of town; you can't miss it."

"Okay, then." He nodded and walked down the hill.

I wondered why Jack Justin wanted to talk to me, and I dreaded him asking about the remains of his parents. The troopers must have told him their condition, but maybe he wanted to question an unofficial source.

Geoff stood in the rain by my Explorer. I hurried to the vehicle and unlocked it, and Geoff slid in and slammed the door.

"What did he want?"

"To meet me tonight and ask me something." I pulled slowly onto the road and turned on my windshield wipers. The light mist was progressing into rain.

Geoff was quiet until we turned into the marine center parking lot. Then, he said in a low voice, "Be careful with this guy, Doc. I don't trust him."

I nosed into my parking space and turned off the key. "What's this weather supposed to do?"

"We're in for a big storm."

# Chapter Five

I changed my clothes three times before I decided on black jeans and a dark green sweater. Jack Justin might wear a suit and tie to Henry's, but there was no need for me to overdress just to match my dinner companion. Besides, I didn't want to look too eager. I hadn't been out to dinner with a man in a long time, but Justin didn't need to know that. I reminded myself that the guy was probably married with five kids, and he only wanted to eat dinner with me to learn the gruesome details of his parents' deaths. *So why was I putting on extra eye makeup and lipstick?*

I hadn't worn lipstick in so long that I forgot how to apply it, and when I smeared it, I had to wipe it off and start over. I hoped the lipstick and eye makeup would draw attention away from my scabbed and pitted right cheek. I dabbed liquid powder over my injuries, but it only seemed to enhance rather than diminish the damage.

Geoff's warning rang in my ears. Easy-going Geoff was usually not judgmental, but I doubted Geoff trusted anyone in a suit and tie.

I still could smell Jack's cologne, and I hoped the evening would be pleasant. Despite the subject of our meeting, I was looking forward to this diversion to get me out of my apartment and away from my obsessive guilt.

I arrived at Henry's a few minutes before seven. The dimly lit sports bar and restaurant was only half full. With most of the fishing fleet away from port, Kodiak had become a sedate, small town.

In two weeks, though, when the salmon fishery closed for a few days, the bustle would return; Henry's would be packed, and the beer would flow. I enjoyed the current peace of quiet Kodiak, and as I stepped into Henry's, I sensed the lowered testosterone level of the establishment.

Jack Justin sat at the bar, sipping a beer. He'd caught on to the Kodiak dress code and now wore faded blue jeans and an ecru cable-knit sweater. The light sweater set off his tan, and I tried not to stare.

"Doctor Marcus." He stood and held out his right hand.

He still smelled great. I usually didn't mind my celibate lifestyle, but this man was a powerful reminder of what I had been missing. "Please, call me Jane."

He nodded and motioned for me to walk ahead of him. I chose a booth next to the wall toward the rear of the restaurant. As long as we kept our voices low, no one would be able to overhear our conversation.

The waitress handed us menus, and Jack asked me what I recommended. I suggested the prawns, and he nodded in agreement. I ordered a glass of Chardonnay, and he asked for another beer.

"What do you think of Kodiak?" I asked

"It's wet," he said.

I laughed. The rain had been relentless all afternoon, and now a driving wind was turning the weather from unpleasant to nasty. The low ceiling cloaked the emerald mountains in a coat of grey, making mud and asphalt the most prominent features of the town.

"When did you get here?"

"This morning."

"You haven't seen Kodiak at its best, then. When the sun shines, there's no place like it."

Jack shook his head. "I'm a city boy. I would go stark-raving mad isolated like this."

I recalled Jack's reason for visiting the island and silently reprimanded myself for my thoughtlessness.

"Did your parents enjoy the wilderness, or was this trip strictly business?"

Jack propped his elbows on the table and steepled his index fingers in front of his nose and mouth. "A little of both, I think. I don't believe my father planned to come until the last minute. Knowing Mom, she gave him an ultimatum, but I'm sure he would have preferred to remain in his office." Jack paused and gazed over my left shoulder, his eyes unfocused. I said nothing but waited while his thoughts drifted. I couldn't imagine how difficult it would be to lose both parents at once. He must still be in shock, and perhaps he had traveled to Kodiak to force himself to accept the reality that his parents were gone.

His eyes returned to my face. "Mom liked the outdoors. When I was young, we used to take camping trips. Dad and I hated sleeping outside and getting eaten by insects, so eventually, Mom gave up. She gave away our camping gear, and from then on, when we traveled, we stayed at five-star hotels."

*Poor you, and your poor mother having to give up something she enjoyed and sacrificing quality family time.*

"Why did they come to Kodiak, then?" I asked.

Jack leaned back in the booth. "As I'm sure you know, my mother was a U.S. senator. She was on the Senate Finance Committee." His voice drifted away, and I waited for him to continue.

The waitress set our drinks in front of us. "Sorry," Jack said. "I was just thinking. I've been so involved in my own life that I haven't thought much about why my mother became a senator, but lately I've realized what a fanatic she is—or was—about the environment. Dad and I talked about it not long ago." Jack laughed, as if his mother's love of nature embarrassed him, and I thought I must have misunderstood him.

"Anyway," he continued. "I think her sole purpose for getting on the Senate Finance Committee was to ensure that more money gets spent on environmental causes." He laughed and shook his head.

"A politician that believes in an issue," I said. "What a refreshing change of pace."

He cocked his head and looked at me as if I had missed the point. Then he nodded and smiled, his eyes sparkling like gems. "I guess anyone who enjoys living here would agree with my mother." The statement sounded like an insult.

"So, your mother was here on business?"

"More or less. The Department of the Interior has her visiting wildlife refuges all over the country. She's gone on most of the trips by herself, but Dad said when she was invited to Kodiak, she was so excited that she insisted he come with her. Dad didn't want to go, but..." Jack shrugged.

"I gather you were closer to your father than you were to your mother."

"Oh yes. Dad and I lunched together at least twice a week. I hadn't seen Mom in months."

The waitress set our salads in front of us, and I wondered what had happened to my appetite. We ate in silence. After a couple of bites, I pushed my bowl away and tried not to stare at Jack, who was shoveling lettuce and tomatoes down his throat as if he hadn't eaten in weeks.

"I guess I'm hungry," he said, as he used a spoon to scrape the last of the dressing out of his bowl.

"Do you want mine?" I pointed to my salad.

He grinned. "Better save room for the prawns."

As if on cue, the waitress deposited huge plates of fried prawns and baked potatoes in front of us. My stomach burned at the smell of the fried food, and I wasn't sure I would be able to eat any of it. Jack fixed his eyes on his plate, picked up his knife and fork and began devouring the meal.

"Aren't you going to eat that?" He looked at my plate after he had cleaned his own. I'd eaten two prawns in the time he'd consumed his entire meal.

"I guess I'm not hungry," I said.

"Can I eat it?"

"Sure," I pushed my plate toward him and laughed. "Do you always eat like this?"

He smiled. "I have a high metabolism. I used to drive Mother crazy. She could never keep the refrigerator stocked."

I was beginning to feel sorry for his mother. In her son's eyes, it didn't seem as though she had done anything right.

I watched Jack eat my prawns and half my baked potato. Finally, he leaned back in the booth and exhaled. The waitress swooped in, picked up the empty plates, and inquired about dessert.

I looked expectantly at Jack, but he declined and asked instead for a cup of coffee. I nodded my head when she asked if I also would like coffee.

Jack asked about my job, and I briefly explained what I did. When the coffee arrived, we sipped for a few minutes in silence.

"The FBI thinks someone planted a bomb on the plane," Jack said, his voice low and serious.

"I don't think anyone has said that yet. I believe they're looking into that possibility."

Jack shook his head. "Their expert examined the wreckage today. The blast was caused by an explosive device."

"How could they determine that so quickly?"

Jack leaned forward, forearms on the table. "I don't know, but the expert seemed certain." His eyes burned. "They think my mother was the intended target."

"Do you agree?"

He sipped his coffee and then sat over his cup, staring into it. "I don't know. It's true the election was turning ugly, but I don't think Eaton would have her killed."

"Eaton was her opponent?"

"Yes, and I know him. He's not a bad guy."

I studied the dark blue eyes and bronzed face and wondered who Jack would have voted for. I suspected Jack's political views lay miles right of his mother's.

"Does the FBI think that Eaton flew to Kodiak and planted the bomb?" I asked.

"Of course not, but Mom claimed that Eaton had drug ties, and not long before she left on this trip, she announced that soon she would be able to prove he had connections to a certain Mexican cartel." Jack shrugged. "The FBI thinks that's more exposure than the Mexicans wanted."

"But you don't agree?"

"I think she was bluffing. Eaton was beginning to pull ahead in the polls, and Mom panicked. Dad said it was an act of desperation, and I think he was right."

*You would*, I thought.

"Dad had more enemies than Mom," Jack said, and he sounded proud of his father for this feat. "He made his living by taking companies away from people, and he considered death threats a sign of success." Jack laughed and sat back. "I remember once when I was in high school, a guy whose company Dad had just stolen called the house and told my mother she would soon be a widow. Mom was inconsolable, but Dad thought it was funny."

"What happened?"

"What?" He shrugged. "Oh, nothing. That's just it, though. Dad never took threats seriously."

"And maybe this time he should have?"

"Exactly."

"Was he involved in a takeover at the time of his death?"

Jack cleared his throat and spoke in a low voice, as if anyone at Henry's would care about his dad's corporate raiding. "He was in the early stages of acquiring stock in two or three different companies, but there was one in particular he had his eye on. I don't know much about it, but the last time we lunched, he had that predatory look in his eye, and I knew something big was about to happen."

"When was this?"

"What?"

"When did you last see him?"

"Two days before they flew up here. He was complaining that he'd be away from his office at the worst possible time, and he was worried that my mother would make him camp in the wilderness away from his fax and phone. He looked into it and said there are places here that don't have cell-phone access." Jack spread his hands and looked at me for confirmation.

I laughed. "Believe it or not, there's no cellular coverage for most of the island. As you said, this is the wilderness."

"I know."

"But did anyone know he was coming to Kodiak?"

"Anyone who reads the paper would know. Everything my mother did was publicized."

"Yes, but you said she usually traveled alone. Did the news articles say your father was flying to Kodiak with her?"

Jack nodded. "My parents did things together so rarely, that whenever they did, her campaign manager made sure it was publicized. I don't think it would have taken a genius to find out her schedule here in Kodiak."

"Have you told the FBI your suspicions?"

The waitress appeared with the coffeepot. Jack shook his head, but I accepted a refill.

"Not yet," he said.

"Don't you think you should let them know about the company your father was interested in acquiring?"

Jack twisted sideways in the booth and stretched his legs and then sat forward again and looked at me.

"I need to find something that belonged to my father before I can discuss his business dealings with anyone."

We were finally approaching the reason for this meeting. I waited and watched Jack struggle with the words.

"I wonder if...Well, maybe you can't help me, but you were the first on the scene of the crash. My father usually carried his briefcase with him, and I can't find it."

"I'm going to save you some pain and trouble," I said. "If your father had his briefcase with him on the floatplane, there is nothing left of it."

"But I thought maybe you or the pilot saw it."

I remembered the foot in the boot, and I felt my face grow hot. "Did the troopers tell you what condition the bodies were in?" This was a cruel question, but I felt Jack needed to be slapped in the face with the facts. If he thought someone picked up an intact briefcase from the wreckage, he needed a clearer picture painted for him.

"I know, I know." He waved his hand as if dismissing the point. "Bits and pieces. But this briefcase was made of high-gauge metal. I gave it to him as a present, and it was supposedly indestructible. Dad loved it. He said if the house burned down, at least his papers would be safe."

"It was metal, like a camera case?"

"That's right." Jack nodded his head.

"I remember seeing a small piece of metal that looked like part of a camera case. Maybe you can talk the FBI into letting you look at the wreckage, and you can see if that's it."

Jack frowned. "Just a piece of metal?"

"I don't think they build briefcases strong enough to withstand a bomb blast."

"This one should have."

I didn't like the way Jack studied my face. I felt as if he didn't believe me. *Did he think Steve or I had walked away with his father's briefcase?* I looked at my watch. "I should be getting home."

Jack stared at me but didn't say anything. I motioned to the waitress for the check and didn't argue with Jack when he withdrew a credit card from his wallet.

When we reached the glass door leading out of the restaurant, I saw large raindrops pelting the pavement. I zipped my raincoat and pulled the hood over my head and then smiled at Jack and thanked him for dinner. I put my hand on the door handle and was bracing myself for the storm when Jack's hand closed around my right forearm.

"Just a minute," he said.

I pushed my raincoat hood back, so I could hear him.

"I don't want you to think I'm being callous. I've just lost my parents, and it has been a terrible shock to me." He lowered his face close to mine and whispered, "I have to think about the future, though. I need that briefcase, so please, if you know where it is or you see it, let me know. There's nothing valuable in it, but I will pay a reward."

I jerked my arm from his grasp and pushed open the door. I forgot to pull up my hood, but I barely noticed the driving rain. *This nightmare kept getting worse.*

When I got home, I dried my hair with a towel and made a mug of hot chocolate. *Why did I only meet men like Jack Justin?* The men in my life always wanted something from me. Would I never have a normal relationship? My marriage had ended in betrayal and bitterness, and I'd help put the only guy I'd been attracted to since then in jail. I was beginning to believe that people like me were not supposed to have relationships, but my hormones refused to accept this notion. I kept banging my head against the wall, repeating the same stupid mistakes over and over.

I chuckled. Oh well, I'd only wasted two hours on Jack Justin. I'd known shortly after he began talking about his mother that I didn't like the man. *What was he after? What had been in that briefcase that was so valuable? George Justin wouldn't have carried the only copy of a valuable document with him. I* dropped into the soft cushions of the couch. *Unless, he obtained the document after he left New York. Perhaps it had been faxed to him.*

I put my feet on the coffee table and sipped the cocoa. *But how would Jack know about some document or correspondence his father had received after he left New York?* Jack told me the last time he spoke to his father was two days before the Kodiak trip. Of course, there was no reason I should believe that Jack had told me the truth. I was certain the man could lie without blinking an eye.

I pushed myself off of the couch, filled my cup with water, and set it in the sink. *How could one small planeload of people have so many enemies?* Poor, innocent Craig, sharing a plane with a bunch of cobras.

I thought about Jack Justin for several moments and then pulled my cell phone from my purse and checked my messages. I had three messages, and the first was from my father.

"Jane, are you there? I just saw you on CNN. What's going on? I'm waiting to hear from you."

I checked my watch. It was after midnight in Kansas. I would call him in the morning.

The second message was from Dana Baynes. "Hey, small-screen star, that was some crazy memorial service. Call me tomorrow. I want an autograph."

Message number three was from Steve Duncan. "Hi Jane, I need to talk to you about something. Can you meet me at Bayside Cafe for coffee in the morning at 9:00? Call me back if that's a bad time."

I grabbed the remote and clicked on the television. I had forgotten about the news crews at the memorial service and the possibility that my image might be broadcast on national television. I should have remembered to call my father and warn him that he might see me on TV. Even if he'd heard about Senator Justin dying in a plane crash on Kodiak, he would have no reason to think I was connected to the accident. I hated to have him worry about me; I should have called him sooner.

Since my mother's death three years ago, my father had found it difficult to reenter the mainstream of life, and I wasn't sure he wanted to build a new life for himself. Instead, he had become more interested in his children's lives, and since I was the only female, the only unattached child, and the only member of my family to live three-thousand miles from him on a godforsaken island in the North Pacific, I was his biggest concern. I tried to call him frequently, and he had been to visit me once. He found Kodiak intriguing, but didn't understand why I wanted to live here. He never said he worried, but I knew he did.

I watched CNN for twenty minutes, before the anchorwoman began talking about Senator Justin's mysterious death.

A photo of Senator Justin with short-cropped, grey hair filled the screen as the reporter said, "An FBI source informed CNN this afternoon that preliminary forensic tests from the plane crash that took the lives of Senator Margaret Justin and her husband, financier George Justin, indicate that the crash was the result of a midair explosion." The photo of Senator Justin disappeared, and the anchor's huge, blue, slightly-crooked eyes blazed unblinkingly. "Furthermore, FBI experts believe the explosion was caused by the detonation of an incendiary device."

She paused, turned, and looked at a different camera. "Today, in the village of Kodiak on the island where the crash occurred, a memorial service was held for the pilot and the three local passengers of the de Havilland Beaver." The screen cut to images of the memorial service. As I expected, the first image was of Father Ivanof in his sweeping black robe offering a Russian Orthodox prayer. This was followed by a brief shot of Steve Duncan proclaiming Bill's faultlessness in the crash. I gritted my teeth when I saw myself on the screen, telling the world that it would be a darker place without Craig. My eyes looked swollen, as if I had been crying and was about to cry again. I had and I was, but I'd hoped no one else could see that. *What must my father have thought when he watched this?*

The newswoman stared from the set again. "Trouble broke out at the service when the widow of passenger Darren Myers screamed at the man eulogizing her late husband."

The camera cut to a shot of David Sturman mumbling his eulogy, and then Maryann Myers screaming from the back of the crowd. Confusion followed as the cameras swung toward Mrs. Myers. I touched my cheek, remembering that this was when I had been knocked to the ground. I'd been too busy warding off trampling feet to catch this part of the service.

The cameras zoomed in on a small, red-haired woman, who was screaming about how horrible her husband had been. She then turned and ran up the road to the parking lot. The next shot was a close-up, and I couldn't help but feel sorry for Mrs. Myers. Mascara smeared her pale cheeks, and her shoulder-length red hair hung in tangles. Her eyes were red and puffy, and I suspected that she was confused and frustrated by her grief at the loss of her husband.

"Mrs. Myers," a journalist said through wheezing breaths, "tell us about your husband."

I snorted. What a stupid question. The reporters were so desperate for news or scandal that they chased down this poor woman and then didn't even know what to ask her.

Maryann Myers rubbed her eyes and nose with both hands. No one bothered to interrupt filming long enough to hand her a handkerchief, and her rubbing only served to further smear her mascara.

She drew in a deep breath, pursed her mouth, and stared at the camera. Her eyes looked glassy as if she either had been drinking or had taken medication. If she had taken tranquilizers, they hadn't worked.

"My husband cheated on me, and he deserves to be dead."

The reporters waited for her to say more, but when she stood tight-lipped, a female journalist said, "But Mrs. Myers, what about the other five people on the plane?"

If Mrs. Myers responded to that question, the reply wasn't worthy of the national news. Instead, the blue-eyed anchor's concerned visage returned to the screen. "In Cincinnati today, a gas leak . . ."

I turned off the set and leaned against the oak cabinet. What a day this had been, and I knew things would get worse before they got better.

# Chapter Six

I didn't sleep well. I had nightmares about my mother and about Craig. I awoke at five, drenched in a cold sweat, and climbed out of bed. I considered jogging until I looked out the window. The fog had lifted, but a strong wind and heavy rain tortured the Sitka spruce trees, which seemed to bend their heads to avoid the beating. The high winds were unusual but not exceptional for late June, and I hoped the storm abated before my planned collection trip. I would need all my courage to crawl into a floatplane, and I didn't think I could do it unless the weather was perfect.

I showered, dressed, and because I couldn't think of anything else to do, I drove to work. The marine center was quiet, and I spent the two hours before my appointment with Steve catching up on paperwork and making notes for the journal article I hoped to publish after I analyzed the results from this summer's work.

At 8:45, I grabbed my purse, shut off my office light, and locked the door. The marine center was never noisy, but this morning it was a morgue. The hallway was dark, all the office doors were closed, and my footsteps echoed on the tile floor. I peered at my watch in the gloom to make sure it was still running, and then I realized with a start that it was Saturday. *How had I forgotten the day?* I usually was well-organized, but I hadn't been able to concentrate.

I was still replaying the week in my mind, trying to figure out how it already could be Saturday, when I arrived at the double glass doors that led outside. I pushed hard on the lock bar to open the door and heard a muffled cry. Betty dropped her key ring and jumped back.

"I'm sorry, Betty. I didn't see you there." I stooped to retrieve Betty's keys, but she plucked them from beneath my fingers.

She stood straight, pushed her rubber rain cap away from her eyes and said, "Perhaps you should be more careful. Maybe Craig would still be alive if you weren't so careless." She turned, bent, and inserted her key into the keyhole of the door, which by now had slammed shut. I watched her unlock the door and march stiffly through it.

*What a bitch!* She never had been friendly to me, but I had no idea she disliked me so much. *What had I done to her? Or maybe everyone at the marine center felt that way.* I was not the only one who blamed me for Craig's death.

Sleet pelted the asphalt, and I pulled the hood of my raincoat over my head and ran for my Explorer.

The Kodiak Air Services van huddled alone in the Bayside Café parking lot, and as I crawled out of my Explorer, I pulled my hood tight and bent my head against the wind and rain. I understood why most of the citizens of Kodiak had chosen to stay in their cozy homes on this Saturday morning.

The aroma of coffee and fried bacon slapped me in the face when I walked through the door. Steve sat in the far corner of the small café, a steaming cup of coffee in his right hand and the *Kodiak Mirror* in his left.

"Anything interesting in the paper?" I asked as I approached the table.

Steve glanced up at me and smiled; his hazel eyes looked bloodshot from lack of sleep. He tossed the paper aside. "Nothing new on the crash, at least nothing in the paper."

I pulled out a chair and sat down. "Did you see CNN?"

"Oh yes, and every other news channel. My mother called me in a panic."

"Thanks for reminding me. I need to call my dad back this morning."

The waitress arrived, and I ordered black coffee. She returned a few moments later with a large mug of strong brew. I inhaled the thick aroma and tried to relax.

"So, the FBI thinks someone planted a bomb," I said.

"I don't think they'll know for certain for a few days. They have to run some tests on the debris at their lab in Virginia, but they're leaning that way."

"What do you think?" I asked.

Steve sat forward and pinched his mouth with the thumb and index finger of his left hand. "That's why I want to talk to you, Jane. I need to run my thoughts past someone, and I can't say this to anyone at the office. My wife is a wreck over this, so I don't dare talk to her, but I trust you, and I know you'll be discreet."

Steve had my attention. I gripped my coffee cup and leaned across the table toward him.

"Like I told you before," he said. "I don't see how a stranger could know what plane we would be using for that flight. No one at the office remembers anyone inquiring about that flight. You called to find out what time it was scheduled to arrive in Kodiak, but that's the only interest anyone showed in it. We could have used any of our planes for that flight." He shrugged. "I didn't know what plane we would use until we made out our daily flight plan that morning. I looked at our books and saw three separate trips to the same part of the island, so I combined them. That's just smart business for us."

"I've been wondering about that," I said when Steve paused. "I'm surprised Simms didn't request a separate charter for his special guests."

Steve shook his head. "No. The refuge is always looking for ways to cut back on their flying bill. A combined charter is cheaper for them. Simms jumped at it."

"Why is that better for you, then? Don't you lose money when you combine trips?"

Steve shrugged. "Depends on the circumstances. If those flights had been all we'd had booked for the day, then yes, we would have lost money. But, we had more business than we could handle that day, and when we charge separately for seat fares and water stops, we make more money than when we charge our standard charter rate."

I nodded. "That makes sense, but no one except you and Bill knew you had decided to combine the trips?"

"I called Simms to make sure he didn't mind. The plan was that Bill would stop at Bradford with the Justins and Simms, and then would take them flight-seeing, make the other stops, and return to town. Simms agreed to that arrangement, but I didn't tell him who their pilot would be or what plane we would use for the trip. None of the other passengers knew the trips would be combined."

"What about your employees? Did they know what plane you'd use?" I thought Steve might be offended by this question, but he seemed to be expecting it. He played with his coffee cup and looked down as he answered.

"Cheryl, our dispatcher, certainly knew what plane we would use, and any of the other employees might have known. It was no secret." Steve looked into my eyes. "But I've questioned them all, and I trust them. They're as sick about Bill's death as I am, and they all swear to me that they didn't tell anyone anything about the flight. Cheryl says you are the only one she talked to about that trip."

"You said it was a busy day," I said quietly. "Could someone have forgotten mentioning it?"

Steve sighed. "Of course. I've thought of that, and I've also thought that if someone did inadvertently say something about the trip, he or she might feel too guilty to admit it." He sipped his coffee. "I can't rule out those possibilities."

We were quiet for a minute, and then Steve leaned forward again. "Assuming only my office staff and pilots knew about the flight, I don't understand how a stranger could have plotted and placed a bomb on that plane." Steve's voice was barely above a whisper.

"What are you saying? Do you think someone in your office planted a bomb on one of your planes?" I didn't understand how Steve could trust that his employees would tell him the truth and at the same time suspect that one of them was a murderer.

Steve exhaled and shifted in his chair. The waitress appeared with the coffeepot, and we both accepted refills.

"I hate to even say this, because I have no proof to back it up. I know you'll think this is crazy, but there was one person who knew what plane Bill was flying that day."

"Who?"

Steve rubbed his nose, glanced at the table, and then returned his gaze to my face. "Bill's girlfriend, Toni Hunt, knew. I saw her hanging out with him on the dock that morning."

"You think she might have told someone?

Steve paused for a long time before saying, "Maybe."

"What's up, Steve? What aren't you telling me?"

"I shouldn't say this." Steve gripped the edge of the table, and I thought he was going to stand.

I reached across the table and patted his hand. "Tell me what you're thinking."

"I think Toni may have planted the bomb." The words poured out in a rush.

I sat back in the chair and frowned. "You're talking about the cute little girl I saw at the memorial service?"

"I think that cute little girl is psychotic. She played some nasty games with Bill, and I think he was afraid of her."

"Oh, come on, Steve."

He nodded. "I'll tell you a story. Several months ago we had a bachelor party for one of the other pilots. Bill and Toni had been dating for a few weeks, and Toni told him he couldn't go to the party." Steve smoothed his short hair. "We gave Bill crap. You know, guy stuff, and he told her he was going to the party and that was final." Steve paused. "When the party was over, and we left the bar to walk to our vehicles, there was Bill's truck: The windows had all been broken and the hood smashed with a sledgehammer. Bill told me the next day that Toni admitted she did it."

"What!"

"Yeah, that cute little girl has a short circuit."

"Still, what would she know about planting a bomb?"

"That's the thing I can't get out of my head. Toni grew up in the bush. Her dad is a guide and a pilot, and one day when she was at the office, she told me how she helped her dad excavate an area for a ramp for the plane." Steve thumped the table twice with his fist. "They used dynamite for the excavation, and Toni enjoyed the job. I can remember her wide, excited eyes as she explained the properties of dynamite to me. This young lady knows about and probably has access to explosives."

"But why would she kill Bill? Even if she was angry with him, do you think she's crazy enough to kill him?"

Steve shrugged. "I don't know. They were having a screaming match when I saw them on the dock that morning. I didn't hear what it was about, and frankly, I didn't care. I was tired of their fighting, and I'd told Bill more than once not to fight in front of passengers; it's unprofessional. Whatever it was about, though, they must have made up." Steve lowered his voice. "Or, at least Bill thought they had. I asked him if he could work late, and he said he couldn't, because he had promised Toni he would take her out to dinner." Steve raised his eyebrows and shook his head. "Maybe Toni was still mad, and perhaps her mind is so sick that she thought this was the best way to get even. I'm not a psychologist. I don't know."

Steve paused for a moment and then said, "Think about how easy it would have been for Toni to put explosives on that plane. She could have wrapped up a few sticks of dynamite and a timer, put a bow on the package, handed it to Bill as he was getting in the plane and told him not to open it until he got back to town. Bill would have done as he was told."

The door creaked as another customer entered the cafe. I watched the elderly man sit in a booth near the door. The waitress approached him with a mug and a pot of coffee.

"I think you should tell the FAA inspector or the FBI what you just told me," I said.

"How can I? Does it sound rational to you?"

I shrugged. "I hope you're wrong about Toni, but she has to be considered as a suspect, and the FBI should understand that only a few people knew what plane you were planning to use for this flight."

"I told the FAA inspector that, but he shrugged it off. Said there were ways for people to find out these things."

I stared at Steve. *What a mess this was. Had this disaster been caused by the jealous young girlfriend of the pilot?*

"I tell you what," I said. "Why don't we talk to Toni? We should be able to sense if she is unbalanced enough to blow up an airplane."

"I don't know." Steve sat back and crossed his arms over his chest. "She's clever."

"Come on, Steve. She can't be a day over twenty. I think the two of us can handle her."

"You didn't see the pickup truck." Steve blew out a loud breath between slightly-parted lips. "Okay. Are you free this afternoon around 4:00? I won't be flying in this weather, but I need to do some engine work on the 206."

"4:00 is fine," I said. "Do you know where she lives?"

"I know her parents, and they live in town now. I think Toni still lives with them, but maybe I should call and check that she will be there this afternoon."

"No," I said. "Let's not give her any time to think up answers."

Steve paid for the coffee, and we left the cafe. The day was still dark, and the fierce wind drove the rain at a forty-five-degree angle. I sprinted for my Explorer, started the engine, turned on the windshield wipers, and cranked up the heater. I stared through the rain-spattered window at the boat harbor and pitied the poor fishermen working on their boats in this weather. A man in a thin, blue windbreaker walked down the dock, his shoulders hunched against the unsympathetic elements, hands tucked deep in the pockets of his Carharrts. At least he was in the boat harbor. I wouldn't want to make my living at sea in this weather.

Three cars occupied the marine center parking lot when I arrived, and I was relieved I wouldn't be alone with Betty in the big building. One of the vehicles was Peter's Audi, and the other, a small compact, belonged to David Miles, one of the chemists at the lab.

The front door was unlocked, and I hurried down the hallway, hoping to avoid Betty. I took two steps past the door of the central office, when Betty's shrill voice pierced the silence. "Doctor Marcus!"

I stopped and stepped back to the office door. "Yes, Betty?" I was pleased to hear the sharpness of my tone.

Betty was not contrite. Her own words dropped the temperature in the already-cold building another two degrees. "You had a call from an FBI agent."

I waited for her to say more, but she simply stared at me as if waiting for me to react to this news. "What did he want?" I finally asked.

She looked down at her desk, picked up the small pink message slip, and held it out for me. "He didn't say, but he wants you to return his call."

I walked toward her and plucked the slip from her fingers. I wished I had the power to fire marine center employees, but both Betty and I knew I lacked that authority.

I waited until I was locked securely in my office before I looked at the message slip. In Betty's neat, cursive handwriting, it read: Agent Nick Morgan. A local telephone number followed the name, so I picked up the phone and dialed it. A young woman informed me that I had reached the Kodiak Police Department, and I asked for Agent Morgan.

A moment later, a deep voice said, "Agent Morgan."

"Hello, this is Jane Marcus. I have a message to call you."

"Yes, Dr. Marcus. Thank you for returning my call. I'd like to meet with you and ask you a few questions about Nine Nine November."

"Okay." I felt my heart pound.

"Do you have any free time today?"

"Now would be fine."

"I can be there in twenty minutes."

"Do you know where the marine center is located?"

"No, but I have a local policeman for a chauffeur."

Twenty-two minutes later, a sharp knock rattled my office door.

"Come in." I stood.

The door opened smoothly, and the man that walked through it held out his hand to me.

My previous association with the FBI had left a bad taste in my mouth, and I found it difficult to trust any FBI agent. As Agent Morgan grasped my palm in a firm handshake and stared squarely into my eyes, however, I decided to reserve judgment.

I notice a man's eyes and teeth; hairline and physical build are secondary considerations. Nick Morgan rated high in all four categories. He had grey-blue eyes that reflected his intelligence. I also thought I saw honesty and sincerity in the sparkling depths, but I know eyes can lie about honesty. A man's honesty cannot be determined so easily.

"I have a few questions for you, Dr. Marcus."

"Please, sit down." I gestured to the chair sitting against the wall, and Morgan pulled it in front of my desk and eased himself into it. He folded his hands in his lap, and I noticed the gold band gleaming on his left ring finger.

"I don't know what I can tell you that I haven't already told the FAA inspector," I said.

"I'm sure you know that our bomb experts have concluded that the explosion was no accident." He must have worn braces when he was young. His white teeth were perfect. His smile would be dazzling, but I doubted that many people saw it.

"In other words, someone planted a bomb on the Beaver."

"We think so."

"Well, sir, I don't think you can consider Craig a valid terrorist target. From what I've heard, some of the other passengers were much more likely than Craig to attract powerful enemies. Craig was just a college kid with his entire future ahead of him. He was an innocent bystander."

Morgan bit his lip and nodded his head. "I know," he said in a quiet voice. "My deepest sympathies for your loss. I don't believe that someone blew up this plane to kill your assistant, but my job requires me to interview the associates and families of all the victims." A light speckling of grey tinged his short, black hair at the temples, and fine lines creased the corners of his eyes. I wondered how old he was.

"I should have been on that plane." The words fell unwillingly from my mouth.

"What?" He cocked his head to one side.

I laughed and pushed my chair back from my desk. "Oh, nothing. It's just that I sent Craig alone at the last minute, and I feel guilty about that. I don't like to fly, so I found an excuse not to go."

I saw Morgan struggling to form his next question, and I realized what he must have been thinking. "I don't think the bomb was meant for me, either," I said. "I don't know many people in Kodiak, and everyone at the lab knew I didn't fly out to Uyak with Craig. A fish biologist does not attract many violent enemies."

An embarrassed grin played across Morgan's face. "No angry ex-boyfriends?"

"My life should be so exciting."

"What about Craig? Did he have a girlfriend?"

"Craig attended the University of Washington, and I think he had a casual girlfriend there. I kept him too busy for a social life here in Kodiak. He bunked with some students from the marine center, but we've been working seven days a week since this paralytic-shellfish-poisoning crisis began."

"That's what he was doing in Uyak Bay?"

"Yes. He was collecting clams from a site where a lady was poisoned. He could only dig for the clams at low tide, and only the early morning tides were low enough to get a proper sample. He camped for two nights, so he could make two collections."

Morgan paused for a moment. "Will you have to take more samples, now?"

I nodded. "Yes, I'll have to repeat the collection procedure on the next series of extreme-low tides. The results won't be as valuable, because so much time has passed since the poisoning, but they'll be better than nothing."

Morgan stood. "You're a busy woman, Dr. Marcus. I won't take any more of your time. Thank you." He held out his hand, and I shook it.

The warm flesh of his hand distracted me. I had questions for this man, but I couldn't remember what they were. I drew my hand away. "Have you already talked to the relatives and associates of the other people on the plane?"

He stretched his neck and frowned at me. "I've talked to some, but we're still in the early stages of our inquiries." He folded his arms across his chest. "Why?"

I smiled. "You know how it is in a small town. I've heard rumors. I'm sure ninety percent of them are false, but I don't think the senator and her husband were the only people on the plane with enemies."

"I would be happy if you would tell me everything you know, Dr. Marcus. I would appreciate information about any of the people on that plane."

I pulled my chair up to my desk and folded my hands in my lap. "That's the problem," I said. "I don't know anything but gossip, and I don't think I should be repeating gossip to you."

"Sometimes that's all we have to go on."

I didn't know what to say, so I held his gaze and said nothing.

"Well," he said. "Thank you for your help, and if you think of anything else you want to tell me, I can be reached through the Kodiak Police Department, or here's my card with my cell number."

I nodded, and Agent Morgan left my office, shutting the door behind him.

I stared at the smooth, white door for several minutes. *What kind of person could kill six people just because he or she wanted one of them dead?* I read about monsters like that each day in the paper, but I associated such psychopathic behavior with cities, not with the wilderness. I wanted to believe that this evil had come from the outside, that the killer was from some other place, and that his reasons for killing had nothing to do with the people of Kodiak or the island itself. The more I learned about the pilot and passengers of Nine Nine November, though, the more I believed that the murderer and the intended victim could be local.

I pushed my chair away from the desk, stretched, and stood. I was wasting my time here and was really in no mood to interact with my colleagues. I grabbed my jacket and purse, shut off the light, and locked my office door. I hurried quietly down the hallway, rushing past the office door holding my breath in fear that Betty would call my name. I felt as if I were back in high school, skipping class.

I drove to the grocery store and bought some fruit, fresh vegetables, and a two-pound can of coffee. The hostile weather was keeping shoppers away from the large Safeway store, and I hurried through the checkout with no wait. I was cruising to my apartment when I remembered I still hadn't called my father.

As soon as I got home, I dumped my sack of groceries on the counter and called my dad in Kansas. The phone rang three times before he answered with a breathless, "Hello."

I assured him I was okay and tried to play down the fact that Craig had been my assistant. He wasn't fooled, and my clumsy attempt at trying to protect him only served to irritate him.

"Tell me the truth, Jane. Are you in any danger?"

I sighed. "No, Dad, I don't think so. The FBI doesn't know who planted the bomb or why they did it, but I'm sure the motive had nothing to do with Craig or me."

"They said on the news that Senator Justin's political opponent ordered someone to plant the bomb."

"That's just one theory."

"No," my dad said. "Haven't you heard the latest? A member of Eaton's election campaign staff came forward and says he believes Eaton was behind the bombing."

I pulled the stool away from the counter and sat down. "When did you hear this?"

"A few minutes ago. I turned on CNN as soon as I got home, and it was on the news."

I tried to change the subject, but all my dad wanted to talk about was the bombing and my safety. The conversation depressed me, so I told him that someone was at the door and that I would call him soon.

I flipped on the TV, and while I listened to the news around the world, I cut up bananas, grapes, apples, and oranges for a salad.

"Startling news from New York today, where a former staff member on Alfred Eaton's campaign came forward to finger his ex-boss in the bombing in Alaska of the small plane on which Senator Margaret Justin was a passenger."

I laid the knife on the counter, wiped my hands on my jeans, and hurried to the living room.

The grey-haired male anchor stared grimly through wire-rimmed glasses at the camera. "Eaton and Justin were fighting a brutal campaign battle for the senate seat, and while polls just before her death gave Eaton a slight edge, Justin promised to reveal damning evidence against Eaton, linking him with the importation of drugs into the United States."

File footage of Eaton giving a speech flashed on the screen. "According to an FBI source, the ex-staff member, whose name is being withheld, says Justin's allegations against Eaton were true, and he believes Eaton took steps to silence Senator Justin. The FBI is taking the accusation against Eaton seriously and their spokesman says they will follow up every lead."

A commercial came next, and I turned off the television and returned to the kitchen. I was skeptical. The mysterious source who reported Eaton's involvement with the bombing was an ex-employee, no doubt disgruntled. *Why would the FBI report such obviously biased, unsubstantiated information?* I wondered if they released this tidbit to the press to quash criticism that the investigation was not moving forward.

I ate my fruit salad and then stretched out on the couch, planning only to rest for a few minutes.

I sat up straight when the phone rang. I looked at my watch: 3:45. I hurried to the phone.

"Hi," Steve said. "Do you want me to pick you up at your place?"

I sat on the bar stool and rubbed my forehead with my left hand, slowly recalling that I'd made plans with Steve to visit Toni Hunt. I recited my address to Steve, washed my face, grabbed my jacket and purse, and walked down to the parking lot to wait for him. The weather hadn't improved, and I huddled under the protection of the roof near the stairs, watching the rain splatter off the pavement in front of me.

A red Ford pickup turned into the parking lot ten minutes later and stopped beside me. I opened the passenger door and climbed in beside Steve.

"You sounded out of it when I called," Steve said, as he nosed his truck onto Spruce Cape Road. "Did I wake you?"

"I fell asleep on my couch this afternoon and slept better than I have in days."

Steve nodded. "I know about insomnia. The last few days have been one long nightmare."

"I wish I didn't feel so responsible," I said. "I can't get over the fact that I sent Craig to his death."

Steve slowed the truck to make the turn-off and looked at me. "How do you think I feel?" I studied his face. His red-rimmed eyes looked yellow and his skin was drawn and sallow. He looked years older than he had a few days before, and I realized what a strain this had been on him. I had been so caught up in my own grief, guilt, and self-pity that I hadn't thought about how terrible Steve must feel. He bore the weight not only of one death, but six. No matter how this turned out, he always would feel that he should have been able to protect his pilot and passengers.

We turned left onto Rezanof, and I watched two kids ride their bikes down the sidewalk, heads bent against the driving rain. Steve pulled up in front of the large, one-story, cedar home, whose beautifully landscaped lawn I had admired since I'd moved to Kodiak. Brightly colored lilies framed an emerald lawn, and rhododendrons skirted the house. White, yellow, sapphire, and fuchsia plants hung from beams above the porch.

"These plants are taking a beating in this rain," Steve said.

"This is where Toni Hunt lives?"

"This is her parents' home. She still lives with them, and I guess she will awhile longer now," Steve said. "She was trying to convince Bill to let her move in with him, but I don't think he was crazy about that idea."

Steve sprinted to the front door, and I hurried after him. He pushed the ivory doorbell, and we waited only a few moments until a plump, middle-aged woman wearing a lacy apron over her sweater and jeans opened the door.

"Hello," she said, scrutinizing our faces. "Well, hello, Steve. What can I do for you?"

"Mrs. Hunt, uh Marge, this is Dr. Jane Marcus from the marine center." Marge smiled at me, wiped her right hand on her apron, and then held it toward me. I gripped her damp, soft hand and smiled back. "Jane lost a coworker in the crash the other day, and we were talking and thought we would stop by to see how Toni is doing."

Marge looked a little confused, as if she didn't understand what the loss of my colleague had to do with her daughter. She stepped back into the hallway. "Forgive my rudeness. Please come in out of the rain."

We stepped into the tiled entryway, and Steve shut the door behind us. Marge Hunt was silent for several moments. "Toni isn't doing so well," she said. "I'm not sure she is up to visitors."

"I know this has been difficult for her," I said.

"Yes, it has. She and Bill were very close."

"We won't tire her out," Steve said. "I just want to let her know we're here if she needs us."

Marge didn't know what to say to Steve's persistence, and I was glad and a little surprised that Steve hadn't meekly backed out the door. He hadn't been crazy about approaching Toni, but apparently once he decided to do this, he planned to carry it through.

"Well," Marge shifted from one foot to the other, burying her hands in her apron pocket. "I guess you could talk to her for a few minutes, if she will see you. She won't come out of her room, so you'll have to talk to her there."

Steve and I pulled off our rain gear and shoes and left them in the entry hall. We followed Mrs. Hunt through a large living room and up a flight of stairs. The upstairs hallway was dark, and Marge didn't bother to turn on a light. Through the gloom, Steve and I followed her to the end of the hall.

She stopped in front of a closed door and knocked twice. When nothing happened, she knocked again. She cracked open the door and called Toni's name. Nothing. She shouted louder, and I heard a muffled, "What do you want?"

"You have visitors," Marge said.

"Who?"

"Steve Duncan and a friend."

I didn't hear Toni's reply, but she must have agreed to see us, because Marge held the door open and motioned for us to enter. The dim light from Toni's room revealed Marge's down-turned face as she slowly shook her head.

Toni's room was black and in the process of becoming blacker. A black rug, a black bedspread, and dark grey walls that Toni was in the process of covering with a coat of glossy black paint sucked up light filtering through shrouded lampshades.

"Wow," Steve said. "This is a black room."

"I'm in mourning," a petite brunette said. She placed the paint roller in its pan and covered it with a cloth. Headphones drooped around her neck over her black T-shirt, and I wondered what dark music she had been listening to.

She sat on the end of her bed and stared up at us. She had painted her pretty face with black makeup: black eyeliner, black mascara, and even black lipstick. The combined effect of the makeup and the dim lighting in her black bedroom made her skin appear sickly white, and I was struck by her resemblance to Morticia from the old television show, *The Adams Family*. You didn't need to be a psychologist to know this girl had problems.

"Who are you?" Toni asked as her dark eyes squinted toward my face. Steve had been so distracted by the sight of her bedroom that he hadn't remembered to introduce me.

"I'm sorry," he said. "This is Jane Marcus from the marine center. One of the passengers on Bill's plane was her assistant."

"The crash wasn't Bill's fault." Toni stood and stalked to the head of her bed, sitting by her black-shrouded nightstand.

"I know that, Toni," I said. "We're just here to see how you're doing, how you're holding up under all this."

"Bill loved me." She stuck her chin in the air and folded her arms across her chest.

"Toni," Steve said, walking around the end of her bed and sitting beside her. "I haven't had a chance to talk to you since the crash." He paused for a moment, and I knew he was choosing his words carefully. "You talked to Bill after I did that day. Did he tell you anything? Was anything wrong?"

"What do you mean?" Toni pushed against the headboard of her bed, and I thought Steve was brave to sit so close to her. I kept my distance.

"I don't know what I mean. That's just it. Someone planted a bomb on that plane. Did Bill tell you if he saw anyone suspicious, or did he have an argument with anyone?"

"No," Toni said as soon as Steve stopped talking. "I've been thinking about that, and everything was normal. He asked me out to dinner, and I know he was going to propose to me. I know it." Her words trailed into sobs, but instead of comforting her, Steve backed away from her. I didn't blame him. She wasn't the kind of person you wanted to put your arms around.

"At least no one else will have him now." The words escaped between sobs.

"What?" I said.

She lifted her face and looked at me, two black lines of mascara defining the trails of her tears down her cheeks. She thrust back her shoulders and puffed her cheeks. "Bill died mine. He will be mine through eternity. No other woman will ever have him."

Steve muttered something and stood.

"That's one way to look at it," I said. "But I'm sure you'd rather have Bill alive."

"Well of course." She spat the words at me.

"Listen, Toni," Steve said. "You can't think of anyone who would have wanted to hurt Bill?" He enunciated each word of the question as if talking to a child.

"Why are you asking me these questions?" Toni said. I thought the senator was the bomber's target. No one would want to blow up Bill."

"The FBI doesn't know that the senator was the target, they are just guessing. Steve and I are checking out other leads."

Toni looked from Steve to me and back to Steve again. "No one would want to kill Bill. I would murder anyone who tried to hurt him."

We left Toni huddled on her bed, hugging her knees against her chest. I had moments when I regretted that I didn't have children. This was not one of them.

We called our goodbyes to Mrs. Hunt, who was in the kitchen baking cookies. The rain didn't seem quite as brutal when we stepped off the Hunt's front porch.

"What do you think?" Steve asked as we cruised down Rezanof.

"Unstable is a good description. I don't think we can rule her out. If she knows about explosives, and you say she does, then yes, I think she has the personality to blow up her boyfriend and five other people and then feel sorry for herself the next day, because she lost the love of her life. The girl has problems."

"Yeah," Steve said. "That's what I think too."

Steve asked me if I would like to stop and grab something to eat, but I said no. I had an overwhelming desire to be alone, locked in my apartment, away from the crazy world.

As soon as I got home, I hung up my raincoat and dug my cell phone out of my purse to check the messages.

The temperature in the room dropped when I heard Jack Justin's voice. "Hi, Jane, this is Jack Justin. I'd like to meet with you again at your convenience." There was a short pause. "I don't want you to get the wrong idea about me; let's start over. Call me at the Baranov Inn, room two twelve. Bye."

I pushed the rewind button and wished I'd gone to dinner with Steve. I suddenly did not want to be alone.

# Chapter Seven

I went to bed at 8:00 and didn't sleep at all. I tried all the tricks, but my mind raced, and I couldn't slow it down. Anyone who knew anything about the passengers and pilot of Nine Nine November was reluctant to talk to the FBI. No one wanted to spread gossip, and neither did I, but Agent Morgan wasn't from this community. *How would he learn alternative motives for the explosion unless someone relayed the rumors to him? Yes, he would question innocent people, but maybe he also would find the monster who planted the bomb.* I hated to violate confidences, but my first commitment was to Craig. I'd vowed I would find out how and why he had died, and I still planned to fulfill that promise.

I rolled over and looked at the illuminated dial of my alarm clock: 11:15. I wondered if Dana had told the FBI about George Wall, the renegade guide who had threatened Dick Simms. I picked up my phone and dialed Dana's number.

"Hello," Dana panted between breaths.

"What were you doing? You're out of breath."

"Stair climber."

"I'll wait while you catch your breath."

"What's up?" she said a moment later. Her gasps had mellowed to light wheezes.

"Do you exercise like this every night?" I asked.

"If I did this every night, I wouldn't be in such bad shape. I ate a whole pan of brownies tonight, and now I'm feeling guilty."

I laughed. "Sorry to interrupt your penance, but I was just wondering if you've talked to the FBI about George Wall."

There was a long pause, and I worried Dana had passed out. Her tone was cool when she replied. "Listen, Jane, I shouldn't have said anything to you about Wall. I've thought about it, and he's not a viable suspect."

"What do you mean? You convinced me that he was violent and that he had a murderous grudge against Simms." I heard my voice rising in pitch, and I slowly exhaled.

"Look, Dana. I'm not sure the senator was the target of this disaster, but the FBI is focusing all their attention on the senator and her husband. They're not looking at the other passengers. You need to tell the FBI what you know. I met the investigator today, and he seems like a nice guy; he's easy to talk to."

"No way, Jane, and don't tell him to call me. I don't want to get involved in this."

"But Dana."

"Did you hear me? I'm serious. Keep me out of this."

I couldn't believe the hostility in her voice. *What was her problem?* "Fine, Dana. Thanks for your help," I said, and disconnected.

My heart thudded as I slammed my head against my pillow. The dial of my alarm clock finally blurred and faded at 4:30. I slept for two hours.

When I awoke, my sinuses were clogged and my head pounded. I pulled back my bedroom curtain and stared at the sky. The weather had improved. It was still drizzly, but only a slight breeze rustled the spruce needles. I pulled on my sweat suit and jogging shoes. My arms and legs ached from a restless night, but I forced myself out into the damp morning.

After two blocks, my muscles began to loosen and my head cleared. The rain-soaked air was tinged with the pungent aroma of spruce and the sweet scent of wildflowers. Church bells clanged in the distance, but the streets were quiet.

I jogged for twenty minutes and then turned around and retraced my steps home. I stepped into the shower and turned the water as hot as I could stand it. Sometime in the middle of the night I had decided to talk to Morgan and tell him every rumor I had heard. I reviewed this decision as the steamy water flowed over my head. I wouldn't tell him who had told me the information, and I would stress that I was only repeating rumors. Then, at least he would have something new to investigate, and he could look at other possible targets besides the Justins.

The phone was ringing when I stepped out of the shower. I wrapped a towel around myself and hurried into the bedroom. "Hello."

"Jane, it's Steve."

I sat on the edge of the bed and waited for him to continue.

"Toni Hunt's mother called me last night, and she was pretty upset."

"What happened?" I pulled the towel tightly around me to ward off the chill.

"Toni was hysterical after we left, and Mrs. Hunt is afraid she'll get sick again."

"Get sick as in attempt suicide?"

"She didn't say that, but that's what she meant. She wants us to stay away from her daughter."

A flash of heat rushed through me. "I don't plan to go anywhere near her daughter," I said, "but I will tell the FBI agent everything Toni Hunt told us."

"Do you think that's a good idea?"

"Yes I do, Steve. Six people were murdered. I don't think we can afford to protect anyone's feelings, reputation, or even sanity. If Toni Hunt placed that bomb in the airplane, that may be the reason why she is suicidal."

A loud sigh sounded in my ear. "What a mess," Steve said. "I'll call you if I hear anything else."

I told Steve goodbye and then found my purse, dug out the card Morgan had given me, and dialed his number. I was expecting voicemail and was surprised when his deep, rough voice came on the line.

"Dr. Marcus. What can I do for you?"

"After a restless night, I've decided to tell you every rumor I've heard about the passengers and pilot of Nine Nine November."

"Well, that's a nice change of pace. I was beginning to think every resident of this town had taken an oath of secrecy. When can we meet?"

"How about 3:00 this afternoon?"

"At the police station?"

"My office."

"I'll be there."

I hung up the phone and immediately felt lighter. This seemed like the first good decision I had made in weeks. I might not win any friends by talking to Morgan, but I might provide information that would help catch Craig's murderer.

I dressed in blue jeans and a sweatshirt, walked into the living room of my apartment, and surveyed the scene. I opened the hall closet, dragged out the vacuum cleaner, grabbed a dust rag, and went to work. After I had cleaned the floors, furniture surfaces, countertops, and washed the dishes, I felt better. Next, I tackled the mountain of dirty laundry, and once the washer was humming, I turned on the television, grabbed the remote, and stretched out on the couch. I flipped quickly past the news channels and settled on a tennis match, which distracted me for an hour.

At 2:00, I drove to the marine center, and was relieved to see an empty parking lot when I arrived. I left the front door unlocked and turned on a few lights for Agent Morgan. I went to my office and sat for a while, but at 2:45, I returned to the front lobby and waited for Morgan. He was five minutes early.

I was glancing through a marine center brochure and didn't know he was there until I heard the front door scrape open. I stood, walked out of the carpeted reception area, and intercepted him in the tiled entryway. He was unbuttoning his black raincoat, and I saw that he was dressed casually in blue jeans and a navy turtleneck. The shirt emphasized his compact, muscular physique.

"Dr. Marcus." He held out his right hand, and I took it.

"Let's go back to my office." While the reception area was more comfortable, I felt more secure in my office. Should any of my colleagues arrive for some Sunday afternoon office work, I did not want them to overhear me sharing my ideas with an FBI agent.

Morgan nodded and followed me down the long hall. When we arrived at my office, I held open the door for him and then shut it behind us. Morgan sat in the straight-back chair in front of my desk, placing his briefcase on the floor beside him. I opened the window blinds, revealing my view of the dark, Sitka spruce forest.

"This is a beautiful place," Morgan said. "I've never been to Alaska before." He crossed his left leg over his right and cupped his interlaced fingers over his left knee.

I sat in my desk chair and smiled at Morgan. "The weather has been dreadful since you've been here. I'm not sure anyone could think this is beautiful."

A grin flickered across his mouth, and I caught a glimpse of straight, white teeth. "Maybe I should say that I'm sure it is beautiful on a nice day."

"That it is." I looked away from Morgan's eyes, certain that they would hypnotize me if I stared too long. I plucked a pen from my desk and devoted my full attention to it.

Several moments of silence elapsed, and then Morgan said, "Dr. Marcus, we appreciate your help."

I didn't look up from the pen. "Craig was a good person. He didn't deserve to die." I felt tears form in the corners of my eyes and brushed them away. "I will do whatever I can to help find those responsible for his death. My only obligation is to his memory." I put my pen down and looked up. Morgan was nodding.

"I understand," he said. "If the explosives were placed to kill someone other than the senator or her husband, then we need local help to understand the dynamics of the relationships of the other passengers."

I put my elbows on the desk and rested my chin on steepled hands. "I saw the news last night. Does the FBI believe Eaton's ex-staff member? Do you have strong evidence that Eaton was behind the blast?"

Morgan tilted his head to one side and kept his eyes locked on my face.

"I know," I said. "Confidential FBI information. You want me to tell you every rumor I've heard about the passengers, but you aren't going to tell me a thing."

Morgan shrugged. "That is what I'm supposed to say, but I'm not very good at playing by the rules." He uncrossed his legs and shifted in the hard chair. "I have not been briefed on every aspect of this investigation, but I don't believe there is any hard evidence against Eaton. Our source is questionable."

"But you still think Eaton might be responsible?" I asked.

"At this point, Eaton or his associates are our strongest suspects."

I leaned back in my chair. "I'm sure you're aware that only Kodiak Air Services employees knew which plane would be used for the senator's flight."

Morgan nodded. "I know that Steve Duncan believes that, but," he shook his head, "in my experience, that type of information has a way of leaking. The flight schedule wasn't a secret, and even Mr. Duncan cannot say for sure how many of his employees knew the plan for the day." He put his right hand on the edge of my desk, and I watched his strong fingers.

"Do you know why Mr. Duncan told me something that points the blame at his own employees?"

My face grew hot. "Steve wants to get to the bottom of this as badly as you do." I sucked in air and forced myself to calm down. "That's one of the things I want to tell you. The pilot, Bill Watson, had a girlfriend named Toni Hunt. Steve introduced me to Toni, and we both think she is unstable."

Morgan reached for his briefcase, clicked open the locks, and extracted a notepad and pen. I waited for him to begin writing before I continued to tell him about Toni. I related the story about her smashing Bill's truck and then told him that she knew how to use dynamite and probably had access to it.

When I finished talking, Morgan looked up at me and nodded his head. "I appreciate this," he said. "We haven't talked to her yet, and now we can prepare for a more intense questioning."

"Be careful," I said. "She's fragile. She may not be guilty of anything, but she is a very disturbed young woman."

Morgan squinted his eyes, and the lines in the corners wrinkled. "Is there anyone else?"

"George Wall," I said.

"We know about him and his threats to Dick Simms."

I picked up the pen from my desk and began playing with it again. "Did you know that he was arrested for blowing up a man's truck in Colorado?"

Morgan wrote something on his notepad. "Yes. We plan to talk to him as soon as we can find him."

"Is he missing?"

Morgan shrugged. "We haven't tracked him down yet, but we just began looking."

"If you're looking for the target of this crime," I said, "you might want to spend some time looking at Dick Simms' enemies."

The corners of Morgan's mouth turned up. "I understand Mr. Simms was not popular. Did you know him?"

"Oh yes, and I didn't like the guy. He was arrogant and ineffectual in a job that I consider to be extremely important." I put down the pen and pushed my chair back from my desk. "No one I knew liked him."

"But did anyone dislike him enough to murder him along with a plane-load of people?"

I wrapped my arms around myself. "That's what keeps bothering me. I understand hating someone enough to murder them, but what kind of sick mind could blow up five other people in the process of killing his target?"

Morgan shifted and stood. He walked behind me and stared out at the forest. I twisted in my chair and waited for him to speak.

"When you've been doing this job as long as I have," he said, "you stop asking those questions. There's no shortage of people out there who think that sacrificing a few innocent lives is necessary to further their cause or to protect their way of life."

"That's why you think this was some sort of terrorist act?"

Morgan turned toward me and sat on the edge of my desk. He was so close that I could smell the subtle fragrance of his aftershave.

"I didn't say that I thought this was a terrorist act, Dr. Marcus. Most bombings are personal crimes. Bombs may soon be the lethal weapon of choice in this country. The number of bombings per year is escalating at an alarming level, and often the inexperienced bombers don't realize how much damage their weapon will do."

"I think anyone who places a bomb on an airplane knows what the result will be," I said.

"Yes," Morgan said and stood again. "But maybe the bomber didn't think about the pilot or the other passengers. If it was a personal vendetta, the killer could have been mentally imbalanced or too focused on his prey to think about all the consequences of his actions."

I nodded. "I think Toni Hunt could be that imbalanced, and she knows how to use explosives."

Morgan sat in the chair across from me again. He leaned forward. "We consider everyone in this country a capable bomb maker."

"That's ridiculous," I said. "I don't know the first thing about building a bomb."

"Because you've never wanted to blow up anything," Morgan shrugged. "If you wanted to build a bomb, you wouldn't have any trouble finding the instruction book and the raw materials."

"I've heard you can learn how to build a bomb on the Internet," I said.

"Yes, and bomb-making manuals as well as videos have been available for years. A guy from Arkansas made a fortune with his series of bomb-making manuals. The most popular is called *The Poor Man's James Bond*. His books show you how to make a bomb with items that most people have in their homes."

"Really," I said. "That's unsettling."

"It isn't difficult to get dynamite," Morgan continued. "Most places you just have to fill out a couple of forms and show identification. Anyone can buy it."

"I had no idea. I associate bombs with sophisticated or fanatical terrorists."

"I hope this was a personal vendetta," Morgan said. "A crime committed by one person against one intended target is much easier to solve than a crime committed by members of a large organization. I'll take one lunatic over a group of fanatics any day."

"Have you spoken with Jack Justin?" I asked.

"Yes," Morgan said. "Why?"

"I think he believes that someone found his father's briefcase at the crash site. I tried to explain to him that everything was blown apart in the explosion; his father's briefcase would not still be intact if it was on that plane."

Morgan folded his arms across his chest. "Mr. Justin described the briefcase to me, and I checked with our explosives experts. They think the case would have survived."

"I didn't think anything was that tough."

Morgan was quiet for a moment, and then he seemed to phrase his words carefully. "Did Jack Justin tell you why he is so interested in finding that briefcase?"

"He said he wanted his father's business papers."

"Hmm."

"He did seem more concerned about the briefcase than his parents' remains," I said, "but I just met the man. Maybe that's the way he is."

"I don't think Mr. Justin has told us everything, but I doubt he knows anything about the bomb. I plan to question him further, though."

"Has the FBI taken over this investigation?" I asked.

"We're in charge, but there are several agencies involved, including the Alaska State Troopers." He dropped his pen and notepad back into his briefcase. "The FBI has an excellent laboratory and one of the best explosives experts in the world. He only had to look at the plane wreckage for a few minutes to determine that the small pockmarks in the metal were the result of high-speed particle penetration."

"I don't understand."

"When a bomb explodes, it hurtles tiny fragments of itself and anything in its way at speeds of thousands of feet per second. The fragments stick to their depth in whatever they hit. A piece of luggage can become embedded in part of the plane. A really good investigator can also pick out craters left in the metal by hot gasses given off in the explosion. These craters are unique and are not found in any other kind of impact."

"And the FBI has the best explosives expert?"

"One of the best. There's a guy with the FAA who is also very good, and he's been brought in on this, too. This was a small plane crash, but because explosives were used, and I won't lie to you, because a U.S. senator was on the plane, it's a big deal. Homeland Security, CIA Counterterrorism, and the State Department Bureau of Intelligence and Research have their fingers in this, too."

"With all that expertise," I said, "someone should be able to get to the bottom of this."

Morgan smiled. "I think we will."

"Well, I can't think of any more gossip for you."

"What about Maryann Myers? Do you know her?" Morgan stared at my face while he asked the question."

I shook my head. "No, I don't know her at all." I remembered what Peter had told me about the Myers' divorce, but I didn't think the gossip of a bunch of poker players bore repeating to an FBI agent. "Have you talked to her?" I asked.

"No. She's out of town until Tuesday, but we'll speak to her then."

Morgan stood and held out his hand. "Thank you, Dr. Marcus. You've been very helpful."

"As I said, I'm just repeating gossip, but for Craig's sake, I want to get to the bottom of this." Morgan's hand was dry and warm. I reluctantly released it. "Please, call me Jane. Dr. Marcus makes me feel old and much wiser than I am."

Morgan nodded and grinned. "I'm Nick."

Morgan's scent lingered behind him after he left my office, and as I slowly inhaled it, I hoped this man would be able to figure out who was responsible for Craig's death.

A thudding noise like a book dropping brought me to my feet. I remembered that the front door of the center was unlocked, and I grabbed my purse, turned off my office light, slammed the door shut, and hurried down the hall. I fumbled in my pocket for my keys. I heard a clicking noise that sounded like footsteps on the hard-tiled floors.

I pushed through the front door, sucked in air to steady my hand, and locked the door. I ran to the parking lot and my Explorer. There were no other vehicles in the lot. Should I call the police, or had I imagined the sounds in the large building?

# Chapter Eight

Dense fog smothered Kodiak Monday morning. I usually found fog mysterious and exciting, but as I drove to my office, I longed for sunshine. The fog only served to deepen a nightmare I felt never would end.

I parked in the lot at the marine center, entered the building, and walked down the hall toward my office. I slowed at the main office and looked warily through the door—no sign of Betty.

"Hello, dear," Glenda said, looking up from a pile of paperwork on her desk. "Are you feeling any better today?"

"A little, Glenda, thanks. Do I have any messages?"

"Not a thing." Her voice was high and pleasant, and a bright smile lit her face.

I turned to leave, but then swung around. "Glenda," I paused. I thought for a moment about what I wanted to say. "Why doesn't Betty like me?" The question tumbled from my mouth and seemed to surprise me more than Glenda.

"Oh, dear," Glenda said. I expected Glenda to deny that Betty disliked me, but she didn't. "Betty is my friend, but sometimes I don't understand her. She is usually so generous and caring, but once in a while she takes a dislike to someone, and there's no changing her mind. Don't take this wrong." Glenda leaned forward across her desk toward me, her small, round glasses perched on the end of her nose. "Betty has old-fashioned ideas. I don't think she believes a woman should have your position, and she has trouble respecting a younger woman." She waved her hand dismissively and sat back in her chair. "Now, please don't tell Dr. Wayans I said that. I don't want to get Betty in trouble. She is very good at her job, and maybe I'm wrong. She hasn't confided in me about her feelings for you, but I see the way she treats you."

"She was very rude to me Saturday," I said.

"Oh my. Try to ignore her, dear. I'll talk to her."

I sighed. "I don't want to get Betty in trouble, but I feel she thinks I'm responsible for Craig's death, and that bothers me. I'm carrying around enough guilt already."

Glenda stared at her desk, her mouth pursed. Finally, she looked up at me. "Betty was very fond of Craig, and she did tell me once that she felt you worked him too hard."

I felt a sudden rush of temper. "That's none of her business."

Glenda looked at the floor. "You're right," she said, "and I've said too much. I'll speak with her, Dr. Marcus."

I turned and fled down the hall before I said something to Glenda that I would regret. By the time I reached my office door, the anger already was dissolving into guilt. *Had I worked Craig too hard? Should I have given him a few days off and gone on the collection trip myself?*

I inserted the key into the lock on my doorknob, and was surprised when the knob turned freely in my hand. I stepped back from the door and then remembered my hasty retreat from the building the previous afternoon. I'd been so anxious to get out of the building, I had forgotten to lock my door.

I turned on my office light and looked around. Everything was how I had left it. I shook my head and shut the curtains, blocking out the dismal fog. I now was certain that I had imagined the noises in the building. If I hadn't imagined the sounds, I knew if I looked long enough, I would find the logical sources for them. I had to get a grip on myself; I was losing control.

I sat in my desk chair and forced myself to think about my day. I needed to prepare the exam that I was scheduled to give my class on Wednesday. I usually spent a week making up an exam, but I hadn't even thought about this one. I opened the class folder on my desk and tried to concentrate. The class had performed badly on my last test, so I planned to make this one a little easier. I couldn't understand why these brilliant chemistry students had difficulty with biology, a subject I considered infinitely more understandable than chemistry, but they seemed to struggle with my class. Maybe it was me. Somehow, I hadn't captured their interest.

A sharp knock rattled my door. "Hey, Doc. It's Geoff."

The door opened a crack, and my spirits rose at the site of smiling blue eyes and long red hair. "Come in, Geoff."

Geoff lumbered into my office and sprawled in the chair in front of my desk. He studied my face. "How you doing, Doc? You look tired."

"I'm better, Geoff. I talked to the FBI yesterday, and I think they'll figure this out."

"I almost called you the other night to find out how your meeting with that Justin guy went. I was a little worried about that."

I smiled. "You have good people instincts, Geoff. I wish I could say that about myself."

"What happened?" Geoff sat forward.

"I think the guy believes I stole his father's briefcase from the plane wreckage."

"Are you kidding me?"

I shrugged.

"Did he threaten you?" Geoff asked.

"Not really, but I don't think he believed me. I probably haven't seen the last of him."

"Be careful, Doc. You don't know what you're into here." Geoff stood and leaned over my desk. "I understand that you want to know why Craig died, but there's at least one and maybe several very dangerous people involved in all of this. Keep your distance from it."

I'm not sure if I said anything else to Geoff, and I was only vaguely aware of him leaving my office. His words chilled me. *Was I in danger?*

I couldn't concentrate on preparing exam questions and turned instead to my lesson plan for the day. At 10:00, I headed downstairs to the classroom and unenthusiastically delivered a lecture. Whether they were picking up on my mood, or they were still thinking about Craig, the students seemed listless and asked few questions. At the end of the class, I watched them file out of the room and felt as if I had failed them.

I wandered slowly back to my office, staring at the floor, wondering when I would get back on track. As I turned the corner by the central office, I saw a man standing in the hall. I didn't look up until a familiar voice said, "Hello, Jane. I need to talk to you."

My heart began to race even before I placed the voice, and when I glanced up and saw Jack Justin, I stepped back against the wall. He looked as if he hadn't slept since the night we had dinner together. His hair was uncombed, and dark stubble covered his face. His blue eyes were rimmed with red, and the tan had faded to a mustard color. He wore blue jeans and a stained sweatshirt.

"What happened to you?" I asked. I thought maybe he had been in an accident.

He didn't answer my question. Instead, he walked toward me, hands outstretched. "Jane, you've got to help me." He lowered his voice to a whisper, and I noticed scratches on his right hand. "I need my father's briefcase. I'll give you whatever you want for it."

I wrapped my arms around myself and backed two steps down the hall. "I told you, I don't have it."

"Please," he said, continuing toward me. "It contains some very important documents. They won't do you any good, but they could incriminate some powerful people. Don't you understand?" His eyes pierced through me. "Those people want them back."

"Listen to me, Jack." I spoke slowly, hoping it would sink in. "I do not have your father's briefcase. I did not see it at the crash site. I would give it to you if I had it."

David Hihn, an associate professor of nutrition, opened his office door and stared at us. "Is everything all right, Jane?"

"Fine, David. Thanks."

I turned to Jack. "Maybe we should go into my office." I wasn't anxious to have a conversation with this man in the confines of my office, but I didn't want to make a scene in the hall. My colleagues didn't need more cause to gossip about me.

"Please, sit down." I pointed at the chair in front of my desk. I pulled the door part-way shut, leaving it open far enough so that I could call for help if necessary. Justin sat and then stood again. I leaned against the closed window blind.

Justin took a deep breath, and I could see him strain to talk in a level tone. "Jane, dangerous people want this briefcase. You have no idea what they will do to get it."

"Then tell the FBI about them," I said.

He kicked the chair, and it crashed to the floor. I edged toward the door.

"Don't you get it? These are the people who planted the bomb on the plane. They will do anything to get what they want. They will kill me if I talk to the FBI. They're dangerous, Jane."

I sidestepped to my chair and sat down, hoping the move would calm Justin. "I believe you," I said. "You have my full attention, but please listen to what I'm saying. I don't have your briefcase. I think it's in a million pieces, and you're not going to find it. You say it is indestructible, and maybe it is, but I saw the wreckage of that plane, and everything was blown to bits."

His eyes were glazed, and I didn't believe he'd heard a word I'd said. "Either you or Steve Duncan has that briefcase. I know that."

"Why? Why would we keep your briefcase and not tell you or the FBI we had it? Think about it, Jack, you're not making any sense. We'd either give the briefcase to the authorities, or we'd blackmail you for it, and we're not doing either."

Chapter Eight

"You know as well as I do why," Jack said.

I waited for him to elaborate, but he didn't. I didn't know what else to say. There was no reasoning with the man.

He leaned over my desk, lowering his head to mine. He didn't smell like the same man I'd met a few days ago. The pungent aroma of sweat cloaked any lingering cologne.

"Listen to me," he said, breathing stale breath in my face. "If you don't give me what I want, I will tell these people that you have the briefcase and you can deal with them, instead of me. I'll tell them that I believe you plan to blackmail them."

Sweat trickled down my forehead. "Who are these people? Are they part of a drug cartel?" Jack pulled back, stood upright, and began to pace. "Jack," I searched for reason in his face, but didn't see any. "If you know who planted the bomb, tell Agent Morgan. He can help you. I'm sorry, but I can't."

Jack turned toward me. "I've been to the crash site," he said. Now I understood why he and his clothes were such a mess. I wondered how long he had crawled through the thick brush looking for the briefcase. "It wasn't there, so you must have it."

There was no getting through to this guy. "Maybe the FBI or the troopers have the briefcase, Jack." My head was beginning to ache. "Speaking of the authorities, how were you able to wander around the crash site? Isn't it secured?"

"It's taped off, but no one is guarding it. I had a pilot drop me off and camped there overnight. I searched for ten hours but didn't find any part of that briefcase."

I shrugged. "I can't help you, Jack."

Jack slapped the door frame and then rushed across the office toward me. I wheeled my chair toward the corner of the room. His face burned crimson and his eyes bulged. He stopped on the other side of my desk and leaned across it again.

"This is no game," he said. "If you know where that briefcase is, tell me. You're going to get us both killed." His red eyes danced back and forth, focusing on nothing. He punched my desk with his balled-up fist and then turned and hurried from my office. I could hear my heartbeat in the silence that followed.

I believed Jack Justin. His thoughts were muddled to the point of derangement, but he had said that his life and now mine were in danger, and I didn't doubt the veracity of this. Either he had been taking mind-altering drugs, or he truly was frightened. I believed it was the latter.

93

My hand was shaking as I lifted the telephone receiver. I dialed Agent Morgan's number. I was sent straight to voicemail and left a message for him to call me as soon as possible.

Next, I tried Kodiak Flight Services and was informed that Steve was at the dock. I grabbed my purse and jacket, locked my office door, and hurried from the building. I felt too edgy to sit around. I needed to talk to someone.

The fog was thinner than it had been when I'd driven to work, but the visibility was still less than a mile, and the ceiling was no more than eight-hundred feet. *What was Steve doing at the dock? Certainly he wasn't flying anywhere.* I wondered who Jack Justin had found to fly him to the crash site. The weather had not been flyable for the last several days.

Steve was the only person at the floatplane dock, and he was fueling a blue-and-white Beaver. I parked my Explorer and trotted down the ramp toward him. He waved at me, and I stood back until he finished filling the fuel tanks. Then, he coiled the hose and walked toward me, wiping his hands on his black jeans.

"What are you doing?" I asked. "You're not flying in this, are you?"

"No, I'm just getting restless. The forecast is good, and we're backed up, so I want to be ready to go as soon as the weather breaks."

"Have all the airlines been on hold the last few days?"

"Pretty much." He slid his hands into his back pockets.

"I just talked with Jack Justin, and he said someone flew him out to the crash site, dropped him off, and then came back out the next day to get him. Is that possible?"

"Adventure Air," Steve said, and shook his head. "Their motto should be, 'Each flight with us is an adventure.'"

"They've been flying in this crap?" The thought made me shudder.

"I heard they took a few flights out. I also heard they got stranded on the other side of the island. Maybe that was Justin's flight."

"Has Justin talked to you?" I asked.

"He called me two days ago and asked about a briefcase. He thought maybe I'd seen it at the crash site."

"He's convinced that either you or I have his father's briefcase."

"That's insane."

"I couldn't reason with the man. He says his and my lives are in danger, unless I give him the briefcase." I felt tears in the corners of my eyes. "He scared me, Steve"

Steve reached toward me with oily hands and embraced me. I fought to keep control over my emotions. "I thought I should warn you," I said. "He's distraught, and he'll probably try to contact you next."

"If that briefcase was on the plane, there wouldn't be anything left of it," Steve said.

"That's what I thought, but Agent Morgan thinks this particular briefcase could have possibly survived the crash."

Steve released me. "I didn't see a briefcase."

"You and I know that," I said, "but I can't seem to convince Justin that we didn't walk off with it."

"I wonder what was in the case that is so important."

"Justin believes that the people who planted the bomb are after the briefcase. He says they will do anything to get it back."

Steve stepped back. "We've got to tell the FBI this."

"I called Morgan, but he was out, so I left a message."

"Why hasn't Justin told the FBI?"

"He claims he'll be killed if he says anything, but I think there's more to it than that."

"Like what?"

"I don't trust Jack Justin, and I don't think he's an innocent bystander."

"You think he blew up his parents?" Steve whispered the question.

I thought about my answer for a moment. "I think he knows more than he's saying. Just be careful, Steve." I turned and retraced my steps up the ramp.

"You too!" Steve yelled after me.

My stomach growled with hunger, but I had no appetite. I considered stopping someplace for coffee, but I didn't want to deal with people, so I drove slowly back to the marine center.

I passed Peter Wayan in the lobby of the marine center. He wore his biggest smile and was acting as tour guide for an elderly couple. He undoubtedly smelled money and was going for the kill. I felt sorry for the couple; they didn't stand a chance. I could almost see Peter's fangs. Peter gave me a curt nod and then looked away. He usually introduced me to future, possible grant-givers as one of the center's assets, but today, he must not have thought I would help his cause. *Avoid infection by scandal, Peter.* I liked Peter, but I knew he would not be my closest ally if my troubles involved the marine center. I was not even certain he would stick by his own wife if she did something to hurt his precious center.

I was thinking about Peter as I walked down the hall, and didn't notice the note taped to my door until I was in front of my office. Then, it assaulted my senses like a neon sign.

"YOU WILL BE NEXT BITCH" was written in red, felt-tip pen on white, lined notebook paper.

I snatched the note from the door and looked around. My first thought was one of embarrassment. I wondered who else had seen the note. *What must my colleagues think of me?* Then, I began to shake. I dropped my keys and fell to my knees to retrieve them. Had Jack Justin returned and left this note? The childish threat seemed out of character for the man, but he had been unreasonable and desperate. Maybe he thought fear would motivate me if his promise of a reward did not.

I stood, stuffed the keys in my pocket, and hurried toward the main office. A dull pressure pounded behind my eyes. I trotted through the door of the office and screeched to a halt in front of Glenda's desk. She wasn't there.

"Can I help you?" The crisp enunciation of each word caused my spine to stiffen. I wasn't prepared to confide my problems in Betty; she was the last person I wanted to smell fear on me.

"Did you see any strangers walk past the office in the last hour?" I asked.

She hissed, and I knew I was wasting my time. "I'm too busy to sit here and stare at the hall," she said.

"As always, Betty, thanks for your help."

I stomped out of the office. We weren't likely ever to become friends, but at least her sarcasm had served a purpose. Anger mediated my fear, and as I walked toward my office, reason began to prevail. I looked at the note I still gripped in my hand. The neat, block letters looked like something a teenage girl would write. This was probably just a childish prank; the work of Toni Hunt's disturbed mind. If I could believe Jack Justin, the people who wanted his father's briefcase had planted the bomb on the plane. Toni might be innocent, but she was distraught and confused. If Steve and I had upset her as much as her mother said we had, then this might be her way of striking back.

I convinced myself I was right and wondered if I should call Mrs. Hunt and tell her what her daughter had done. My purse buzzed twice, and I fumbled my phone from it. "Marcus," I said after the fourth ring.

"Jane, this is Nick Morgan. I got your message."

I felt my muscles unlock and realized how tense I had been.

"Agent Morgan, I need to talk to you again."

"Are you okay?" Morgan asked. "You sound out of breath."

"I'm fine," the words rushed out, "but I've been threatened twice this morning."

"By whom?"

I heard talking in the background, and then Morgan's muffled voice, as if he'd put his hand over the mouthpiece. "I'm on the run," he said. "Can I stop by your office around 5:00 this evening?"

"That will work." I hoped my disappointment didn't transmit over the phone. I wanted him to drop everything and come now. I wanted a knight in shining armor, but I reminded myself that they only exist in fairy tales.

I sat at my desk and began sorting through the pile of papers, but I couldn't focus. *Was my life in danger? What had I done to become a threat to someone? Had I asked too many questions, or was it just that confounded briefcase? What could I do to convince Jack Justin that I did not have, nor had I ever seen his father's briefcase?*

I pushed the papers aside and stood. My collection trip was Thursday, and I could begin getting my gear ready. I went down to the lab and flipped on the light switch. Fluorescent lights lit up the space, and I stood staring at Craig's computer and personal gear. An unexpected flood of grief washed over me, and I sat on one of the lab stools. After a few minutes of tears, I wiped my face and stood. I had to move on. I searched through the basement labs until I found two large boxes. Then, I began packing Craig's gear into the boxes.

I turned on the computer and checked the hard drive for files relating to our research, and when I saw the file labeled, "Cycek Collection," I struggled against more tears. I brought up the file and smiled at Craig's careful work. He had mapped the beach and plotted where he would dig his bivalve samples. In practice, this was good scientific technique, but I knew from years of experience that a large rock sitting in the middle of a plotted collection grid could screw up the whole plan. Nevertheless, I printed a copy of Craig's grid and decided that in memory of him, I would do my best to follow his collection plan.

I finished boxing up Craig's gear and wrote his parents' address on the outside of the boxes. Now at least I could look around the lab, without being bombarded by reminders of him.

I made a list of the gear I would need for Thursday. Since my equipment all had been lost in the crash, I would have to scrounge replacement gear from the other researchers in the building. I decided I would keep the trip simple. I needed a tent, radio, and a battery, but I could do without cooking gear, and even decided to forgo the kerosene stove. As long as I dressed warmly and took a good sleeping bag, I would be warm enough without heat.

I considered borrowing a satellite phone but dismissed the idea. On Kodiak, with its mountainous terrain and thick vegetation, it often was impossible to get a satellite signal when camped at sea level. A sideband radio was more reliable, and on it, I could receive as well as make calls. I had plenty of collection containers and a spare shovel. I would need little else. Digging for bivalves was not a complicated scientific procedure, and I planned to collect what I needed and get back to town as quickly as possible. I would fly out to Uyak Bay on Thursday, make one collection on the low tide Friday morning, and a second collection on the low tide Saturday morning. I'd set up the charter to return to town for noon on Saturday.

I left the lab and walked upstairs to the main office. I was relieved to see Glenda sitting at her desk, and turning my back to Betty, I asked Glenda to check around for a spare battery, radio, and tent for me. She made a note and assured me that she would have the gear by the following morning. I told her I had boxed up Craig's personal effects.

"Don't worry," honey," she said. "I'll get one of the graduate students to mail those for you." She nodded her head. "I'll get them out of here this afternoon."

I smiled at Glenda, resisting the urge to look at Betty. I returned to my office and began making a list of the personal gear I would need for the collection trip. I was in my office for less than fifteen minutes when my cell phone buzzed. Dana Baynes' contrite voice greeted me.

"Are we still friends?" she asked as soon as I answered the phone.

"Of course."

"I was a bitch when you called the other night. I want to apologize."

"It's okay, Dana. I understand."

"You were being a Good Samaritan, and all I wanted to do was stick my head in the sand."

"I became involved in this disaster the minute my assistant was killed," I said. "You don't have that responsibility."

"Maybe not, but I owe it to you to help. You're my friend."

I thought about the threats I had received that day and wasn't sure I wanted a friend's help. I didn't need anyone else's blood on my conscience.

"There's not much we can do now, Dana. It's in the FBI's hands," I said.

Dana paused, and I listened to her shallow breathing. "I hope you're letting the FBI handle this investigation, Jane. The person who planted that bomb is a cold-blooded murderer. If you aggravate the killer, one more life isn't going to bother his conscience."

"I'm being careful."

Chapter Eight

"I did find out something," Dana said. "But please, pass this on to your FBI agent. Don't look into it by yourself."

"What?" I stood and paced behind my desk.

"I've been feeling guilty about the way I treated you the other night, so I asked a few questions about George Wall."

"And?"

"I was surprised to learn that he's here in town, working as a freight hauler for Afognak Air."

"Afognak Air, the airline that services the logging camps on Afognak Island?"

"Right," Dana said. "I thought he was in jail, but he must be out on bail?"

"And he's still here?"

"Since the explosion, you mean? I don't know. I didn't call Afognak Air, and I don't think you should either, Jane. Call the police."

"I understand," I said. "I'll be careful."

"Don't get involved," Dana said.

I didn't tell her that I already was involved in this mess, and I was in over my head. "Thanks, Dana."

"Let's go out for dinner soon."

We didn't make plans, but I promised I would call her in a few days. I sat and stared at my desk for a few seconds and then grabbed the phone book and looked up the number for Afognak Air.

Dana's warning as well as the two previous threats of the day hung in my head. I didn't give the Afognak Air dispatcher my name when I asked if George Wall worked for the air charter company.

The lady paused. "Yes," she said. "He isn't here right now, but if you give me your name and number, I'll tell him you called."

"Where is he?" I asked, and then quickly added, "When do you expect him back?"

"He's loading a plane. He should get back to the office in an hour if everything goes well."

So George Wall—a man who hated and had promised revenge against Dick Simms, a man who had done time for blowing up a pickup truck—worked on the floatplane dock, where he had access to any of the planes tied there. Was I missing something? Agent Morgan hadn't seemed that interested in George Wall, but I believed the man wore a big red banner that said, "Number One Suspect."

"Ma'am?" The dispatcher's voice startled me. "Would you like me to have George call you?"

"No thanks. I'll call back later."

99

*If Wall had planted the bomb, why hadn't he left the island? Then again, why should he? It didn't seem the authorities were that interested in him.* I didn't know George Wall, but from what Dana had told me, I believed the man was dishonest and possibly quite dangerous. When Morgan arrived, I would talk to him again about Wall.

As if in response to my thoughts, a sharp knocked cracked on my door. "Yes?" I called.

The door pushed open and Nick Morgan looked into my office. "I'm a little early. Are you busy?"

I was reclining in my desk chair, feet propped on the corner of the desk. I swung my feet to the floor and sat straight. "Not very," I said. "Come in."

He shut the door behind him, placed his briefcase on the floor, and sat in the chair by my desk. Today, Agent Morgan was dressed in a black trench coat, a charcoal suit, a white shirt, and a maroon and grey pinstriped tie. His eyes appeared dull, and the creases at their corners were more pronounced. This case was beginning to wear on the FBI agent, but his fatigue made him no less attractive. I forced myself to look at his left ring finger. The gold band helped me to focus. I wondered again how old Morgan was. Before, I would have guessed mid-forties, but today he looked fifty.

He regarded me with a weary smile. "I was concerned about you after we spoke earlier. What happened?"

I told him about Jack Justin's visit. Morgan sagged in the chair and rubbed the bridge of his nose.

"Justin thinks he knows who the bombers are," I said. "Do you have any idea who he's talking about?"

"I think he believes his father was the target of the bombing." He spread his hands and placed them on the desk. "And, right now, I would have to agree with him. Unfortunately, Mr. Justin has not provided us with any details. We've been looking all day for Jack but haven't been able to find him. I don't suppose he told you where he was going."

I shrugged. "No, and he was frantic. I know he believes his life is in danger unless he finds that briefcase. He even flew out to the crash site to look for it."

Morgan sighed and stared over my head, his gaze unfocused. "I wonder how Jack knows his father had the briefcase with him." He paused. "And if George Justin did have the briefcase, I wonder what happened to it."

"I still don't believe it survived the explosion," I said.

"Our experts assure me it would have."

Blood began to pulse in my temples. "I hope you aren't suggesting that Steve or I took the case from the crash site." I folded my arms across my chest and watched Morgan's face.

"No, no." He shook his head. "I don't think anyone took the briefcase from the crash, but an object the size of the briefcase might be hard to find in the thick vegetation near the wreckage. The debris from the explosion was scattered over a large area. If we could find that briefcase, we might be able to answer a few questions."

"There is something else," I said. I opened my desk drawer and retrieved the note that had been taped to my office door. I handed it to Morgan. "I'm sorry. I was so upset when I saw it that I handled it before I thought about fingerprints."

He grasped the note by the corner and held it up. "When did you get this?"

"Just before I called you today. A little after noon."

"Do you think Jack Justin left it?"

"Maybe," I said, "but it doesn't seem like his style. I think an anonymous note is too subtle for him. And," I added, "there's the writing."

"Mmm." Morgan squinted his eyes, considering the penmanship. "I'm no expert, but it doesn't look like a man's handwriting."

"No. It looks like something a teenage girl might do."

"Of course, if this note was from Justin," Morgan said, "he could have gotten someone to write it for him by convincing them it was a practical joke."

That possibility hadn't occurred to me, but I still didn't believe the note was Justin's handiwork.

"He was too upset to do something like this," I said. "I don't think he would have bothered with it." A thought suddenly occurred to me. "Do you think the people he's frightened of could have left the note? If he told them about me as he threatened he would, maybe they left the note on the door."

Morgan's eyes dropped to my desk, and he was silent for a moment. "Did anyone here see a stranger in the hall?"

"I asked at the office, but the secretaries said they hadn't seen anything unusual."

Morgan put his hand over his mouth and yawned. "This is probably nothing more than a sick prank. I'll send it to the lab, and maybe they can pull some prints off of it. We'll need to get a set of your prints so we can eliminate them."

"Okay." I offered a sheepish smile. "I'm sorry I touched it."

Morgan shrugged. "There's no reason you should think like a cop."

I cleared my throat. "My first intuition when I saw the note was that it looked like something Toni Hunt might do."

Morgan nodded. "I spoke with Miss Hunt today, and she is unstable. I don't know that she's capable of planting a bomb, but this note would be within her realm. Even though I didn't mention your name, she probably suspects you told me about her, and this may be her way of revenge."

I remembered the story about Bill's smashed pickup. "I'll watch my back if she's mad at me. I don't trust that little girl. There's something else I just found out," I said. "George Wall, the guide with the grudge against Simms, is here on the island. He's working as a freight handler for Afognak Air."

"Yes," Morgan said. "We haven't had a chance to question him."

I sat forward and leaned across my desk. I locked eyes with Morgan. "This guy has a violent past and a job that gives him access to all the commercial floatplanes."

Morgan matched my look of intensity as he bent his head toward mine. "I understand, Dr. Marcus, and we will question him. At this point, he is not our primary suspect, but we won't ignore him."

I sat back. Morgan had made his point by using my title. I was not an FBI agent and not Morgan's boss. I had no right to second guess him.

"Sorry," I said. "I guess I'm a little tense. My friend tells me that I shouldn't be so involved in this."

"Your friend is right." His face broke into a broad smile, and my apprehension dissolved. "Of course, I have appreciated your help." He stood. "Tell you what. If you aren't busy now, why don't we go by the police station, get you fingerprinted, and drop off this note? Then, I'll take you to dinner."

"Dinner?"

"No shop talk. We'll just relax for a couple of hours."

I thought about the gold band on his hand and knew I should say no, but his smile weakened my thin resolve. After all, it was only dinner. I grabbed my jacket and purse, locked my office door, and followed him out of the marine center.

Morgan explained that a city policeman had dropped him at the center, and he was supposed to call when he wanted to be picked up. *Had he planned to catch a ride with me,* I wondered, *and if so, what else did he plan? Did I look like an easy mark, someone he could seduce? Was I this assignment's R & R?* The muscles in my neck tightened. This man was attractive, and I was lonely. However, I wasn't desperate, and I had no desire to get burned again. I would go no further than dinner and conversation.

I expected an ink pad and a fingerprint card, but I should have known that my fingerprints would be recorded electronically. Nevertheless, the process unsettled me and left me feeling like a suspect.

I looked up at Morgan as we walked out of the police station. "You took my prints so you could eliminate them from the note, right?"

Morgan stopped walking. "Yes, of course. Why?"

"I don't know. I guess I feel like a criminal."

Morgan smiled, and this time I could see a gleam in his eyes. "You've been watching too much *CSI*."

"*SVU*," I said.

"Whatever."

"I want to know if I become a suspect."

Morgan's eyes widened, but the smile stayed on his lips. "Should you be?"

"I feel guilty about sending Craig on that collection trip instead of going myself, but that is the extent of my guilt."

"Good. I make it a practice never to take a suspect to dinner."

*Was he joking or flirting with me, and why couldn't I judge the difference?* Other people seemed to understand the nuances of human relationships, but I never had been good at that—the price I paid for being a science nerd.

Morgan wanted to return to his hotel to check his messages, so we decided to dine at the hotel restaurant. I didn't complain. The restaurant at the Baranov Inn was one of the best in town.

I waited in the bar while Morgan went to his room. I downed a glass of Merlot too quickly and decided to wait until Morgan arrived before I ordered a second glass. The muscles in my neck and back relaxed as the wine worked its magic. It had been a bad day, and the end to this nightmare was not in sight. *Why couldn't I simply take Dana's advice and stay away from the investigation? It didn't matter now; it was too late. I already was involved.*

I watched Morgan walk through the door of the bar, and his attire surprised me. He had changed from his suit and wore a dark blue sweater, jeans, and hiking boots. Even though I had seen him wear jeans before, he struck me as the kind of man who was more comfortable in a suit.

He gestured at his clothes as he approached the table. "I hope this is okay for this restaurant."

I laughed. "You're fine. Kodiak doesn't have many dress codes, and since this restaurant is near the harbor, it's a favorite of fishermen. I once saw a guy eating here whose hands and clothes were black from diesel fuel." I shrugged. "No one cared."

"Maybe I'm overdressed." Morgan pulled out the chair opposite me and began to sit. He stopped halfway down. "Are you starving, or do I have time for a drink?"

"I think I'll survive a few more minutes."

Morgan ordered scotch and water and I got another Merlot. We watched the bartender pour our drinks and then sipped in silence for a few minutes.

"I needed that," Morgan said.

"You look tired."

Morgan nodded. "It's important to solve a case like this quickly, because the trail cools down fast. We have several leads, but nothing feels right."

"What do you mean?" I asked.

Morgan gripped his drink with both hands. "Oh, nothing. I shouldn't have said that much. We need to talk to Jack Justin. I hope we'll find him tonight."

"Okay," I said. "You said no shop talk, so why don't you tell me a little about yourself."

Morgan's gaze drifted from his glass to my face. I couldn't read his eyes. The lighting was dim in the bar, and a shadow fell across his face.

"My job is my life," he said slowly.

"That sounds like something they teach you to say at the academy."

Morgan chuckled. It was a low, musical sound that caused me to feel warm inside. "That's right," he said. "The J. Edgar Hoover Oath."

"You're married," I said, my voice low. If he was trying to hide this detail from me, he should have taken off his ring.

His eyes dropped to the table. "Yes," he said.

"Any children?"

"No children. Angela says I was never home long enough for that."

I nodded. "Your work keeps you away from home."

Morgan gripped his glass in both hands and swirled the ice cubes. "I like my job; it's challenging." His eyes lifted to my face. "But it's difficult to have a family when you're away from home more than you're there."

His face flushed, and I felt I was prying. "So tell me about work," I said.

I saw the tension melt from his shoulders as he sat straight and smiled. "Thousands of hours of frustration hopefully followed by ten minutes of triumph," he said.

"Why did you choose the FBI?" I asked.

"Good question. One I ask myself at least once a day." He leaned back and took a long sip of his drink. "Believe it or not, I started out as a scientist. I have a bachelor's degree in chemistry, a master's degree in psychology, and a PhD in forensic science from George Washington University. An FBI recruiter approached me when I was working on my doctorate." He shrugged. "I had nothing planned, and I was tired of being broke. The money and job security sounded good to me."

"And you work with the Behavioral Science Unit?"

Morgan nodded. "It's called CASKU now. That's Child Abduction Serial Killer Unit. Most of the time I'm there, but I specialize in terrorist behavior, so I spend a lot of time with the Counterterrorism Unit." He drained his glass. "Or on location at a crime scene."

"Are you ready to eat?" I asked.

Morgan pushed back his chair and stood. He waited for me to stand and collect my purse and wine glass and then followed me into the dining room. The hostess seated us by one of the three large windows that offered a view of the bay and the boat harbor. The evening was grey, but the fog had lifted.

I pointed out the window. "Maybe we'll get a weather break."

"That would be nice," Morgan said, as he eased himself into the chair across from me. "I'd like to get back out to that crash site."

"I don't know how Jack Justin managed to get out there," I said. "Steve Duncan told me that a few pilots made trips during this storm, but it's nothing I'd fly in."

Morgan shook his head. "It's been below minimums since I've been here."

The waitress brought us menus, and Morgan ordered another drink. When she returned, I ordered grilled salmon, and Morgan chose beer-battered halibut.

When the waitress left, he smiled at me. "Fish is healthy, right?"

"Yes," I said, "when it's prepared any way except the way you ordered it."

"I can't get the hang of eating right."

Did he have a dimple, or was that just a shadow in the low light? I decided I would not have more wine.

"I'm impressed," I said. "You have a much stronger chemistry background than I do, and I work in a chemistry lab."

"I don't do much forensic work anymore," Morgan said. "When I first started out I did that, but now I investigate and profile suspects. I know just enough about explosives to know when I should call the experts, and when I should send something to the lab." He rubbed his chin. "I'm usually the only profiler on a case, and I like that. I don't like being second-guessed by other profilers. This job is hard enough, but when you begin doubting yourself, it's impossible."

"Where do you live?" I asked.

Morgan took a sip of his drink, put it on the table, and played with his glass. A minute passed.

"I'm sorry," I said. "Did I say something wrong? Am I getting too nosy?"

"No, no. I'm sorry." He didn't look up. "Right now, that's not an easy question to answer. My wife and I have recently separated, so I don't have a home. We lived in Virginia, about forty-five minutes from Washington D.C. I work at Quantico."

"I'm sorry," I said again.

"My wife would tell you it's my fault, not hers." Morgan looked up at me and tried to smile but failed. "We're trying to work it out. Maybe after this case."

He looked at the table, and I could see he was thousands of miles away. The waitress arrived, as if on cue, and set our salads in front of us. We ate in silence, and I noticed how much better my appetite was tonight than it had been when I'd eaten with Jack Justin.

As soon as we finished the salads, our dinners arrived, and except for intermittent comments about the food, we didn't talk during dinner. The quiet was relaxing, and the only thing that bothered me was how comfortable I felt with Nick Morgan. *Keep your distance*, I warned myself. *You're too old to make this mistake again.*

We both ordered coffee after the meal, and the restaurant's strong brew helped clear my head. "I've read a little about you FBI profilers," I said. "You've done some amazing things."

Morgan set his coffee cup in the saucer. "When the profiles work, they're impressive." He shrugged. "Lately, though, I've been investigating more than profiling. I like to be out in the field, and profiling is depressing work. Day after day, you are bombarded with cases of depraved crimes, and you only have time to help a fraction of the law enforcement agencies who need your help."

"It must feel good when something you've told the police helps them catch a serial murderer or a terrorist, though."

Morgan nodded. "Sure, there are some good, ego-building moments, but those are interspersed between hours of looking at mutilated bodies and listening to tapes of young girls being tortured. It warps your everyday life. The world becomes one big crime scene, and everyone is either a victim or a predator. I was no picnic to live with."

"And this is easier?" I asked.

A smile lifted the corners of his mouth. "A little. At least I'm involved in one case at a time and will hopefully see it through from beginning to end."

"Profiling," I said, not wishing to drop the subject quite yet. "How do you learn it? I've heard some amazing predictions about a criminal, based on only a few facts."

Morgan took another long sip of coffee. "All we do is offer educated guesses based on common sense. You'd probably have trouble doing it, because our guesses don't require the scientific proof you're used to dealing with. We base our assumptions upon past trends and what little physical evidence we have."

"Like Sherlock Holmes."

"Exactly, although I'm not as smart as he was." Morgan shifted in his chair and then gestured with his right hand. "There are certain clichés that are true, such as a criminal often returns to the scene of his crime. You'd be surprised how often that happens, and how often that's what traps the criminal."

I felt chilled and pulled my jacket around my shoulders. "Knowing how to profile must be a great help to you when you're investigating."

"It is, if I can keep it in the back of my mind. The facts must come first, and when they are lacking or aren't getting me anywhere, then I begin using my profiling skills."

"And what do your profiling skills tell you about this case?" I asked as I lifted the coffee cup to my lips.

The waitress arrived with the coffeepot, and both Morgan and I accepted refills.

"I thought this conversation was off-limits." He smiled, and then the smile faded. "This isn't an easy case. As you have pointed out, most of the people on that plane could have been the target. Our experts in the Explosives Unit believe the bomb was crude, with a simple timer. An unsophisticated device doesn't rule out a terrorist group, but it does make personal revenge a more viable motive."

I rubbed my finger across the surface of the table. "Wouldn't it be smart for a terrorist group to use a simple bomb to mislead you?"

Morgan shrugged. "That's possible. As I said, this isn't an easy case. The media thinks that because the blast occurred in a remote corner of the world, we should be able to solve the case quickly. But, by the time we got here, the trail was already cold, and now all this weather has kept us from thoroughly investigating the crime scene."

The waitress brought the check, and Morgan tossed the credit card on the cash tray. I objected to him paying for my meal, but he waved away my protest. "This has been the most relaxing evening I've had in months," he said.

I felt the same, but I didn't tell him that.

"I've been talking about myself all evening," Morgan said. "How about an after-dinner drink in the bar? I have a few questions for you."

*Don't do it*, I told myself, and then said, "Sure."

Morgan signed the credit-card receipt and then we moved back to the same table we had occupied earlier. He ordered a brandy, but I only allowed myself another cup of coffee.

I watched his face as he sipped his drink. The muscles looked looser now, the lines around his eyes and mouth relaxed and faint. The alcohol and conversation had served to lessen his reserve.

"Tell me about your job; it sounds interesting."

I smiled. "Now you're just being nice. Most people's eyes glaze over when I begin talking about toxic dinoflagellates."

He laughed. "You're solving a mystery, much like I am."

I nodded. "That's the way I look at it, and I feel good about my work most of the time."

"Why only most of the time?" Morgan asked.

"I usually feel as though I'm trying to save lives," I said, "but then reality slaps me in the face, and I know I will probably never develop a simple field-test kit for measuring paralytic shellfish poisoning toxins. I think the best thing to come out of this study is that we are slowly educating the public and convincing people not to eat bivalves from untested beaches."

"Explain the problem to me." Morgan settled back in his chair with his brandy.

"It's complicated. PSP toxins are called saxitoxins. There's not just one toxin to worry about, but at least twenty-one different molecular forms."

"Twenty-one related molecular forms?"

I nodded. "You're beginning to see the problem. These twenty-one forms undergo transformations that change one toxin into another. The forms vary in toxicity."

"Doctor Marcus," a low, deep voice said.

I looked up into the square face and thick-lensed glasses of Doctor Barry Gant, one of my associates at the marine center.

"Doctor Gant." I smiled at him and hoped etiquette would not force me to introduce Special Agent Nick Morgan to my coworker. I had never thought of Gant as a gossip, but the marine center was a small place, and rumors spread like the plague. I did not want my colleagues to think that the FBI was investigating me.

Gant paused for a moment, looking uncertainly from Morgan to me. "I've been wanting to tell you that I'm sorry about your assistant. I know how I would feel if something like that happened to one of my assistants."

I was touched. I could tell that Gant was not comfortable sharing his feelings, which made his offer of condolence all the more special. Only a couple of my other colleagues had said anything about Craig's death, and now it struck me that maybe they hadn't said anything because they didn't know what to say or how to say it.

I reached up and grasped Gant's left hand. He started to step back, but stopped himself. His palm was sweaty. "Thank you," I said. "I appreciate you saying that."

I dropped his hand and he stepped away. His wife, a small woman whom I had met at the marine center Christmas party, smiled at me and then grasped her husband's arm and pulled him toward the restaurant. I watched them walk away and then returned my gaze to Morgan. His head was tilted, and he was watching me curiously.

I wiped my eyes, embarrassed when I realized they were wet. "I'm sorry," I said. "Where was I?"

"Twenty-one different toxins," Morgan said. He sat forward, reached across the table, and squeezed my hand. I lingered under his touch for a few seconds and then slowly withdrew my hand and gripped the handle of the coffee cup.

I cleared my throat. "Twenty-one toxins that can change forms, much like a chameleon changes color as it moves from one background to the next." I sipped the coffee. "For example, a person's stomach acid can change the original saxitoxin to another form that is six times more toxic."

Morgan's eyebrows lifted. "Wow," he said.

"That's the main problem, but not the only problem that's keeping us from developing a field-test kit." I folded my hands on the table, feeling as if I were giving a lecture. "Some species of bivalves are able to hold higher levels of toxin than other species are, and some species, such as butter clams, have the ability of binding the most highly toxic forms of saxitoxin. Butter clams can also hold the toxins for up to two years after initial ingestion." I took another sip of coffee. "That's why I think it's so important to get out to the small villages and communities in Alaska and educate people. If someone insists on digging and eating clams, at least the person should know which species of bivalves are the least likely to be toxic."

"And do you know what species those are?" Morgan asked.

"Well," I smiled, "a steamer clam would be a better choice than a butter clam, and mussels should be avoided at all costs."

"I'm not sure I understand. Why is a steamer clam less toxic?"

"For some reason, a steamer is able to transform saxitoxin into one of its less toxic forms."

Morgan drained his brandy. "This is beyond me," he said.

"Sometimes it's beyond me, too. It's a complicated puzzle, and I love puzzles. But, I'm not a chemist, and understanding the intricacies of a complex organic molecule requires all my brainpower."

The waitress appeared to refill my coffee and asked Morgan if he would like another brandy. He shook his head and asked instead for coffee.

"If people know the bivalves are dangerous, why do they eat them?"

I looked into my steaming cup of coffee. "For some reason, the incidences of PSP have increased in recent years. Native Alaskans who grew up eating clams and mussels are suddenly getting sick. Everyone knows there's a risk, but until recently, the risk was small. Until someone dies in their own village or town, people don't believe there's a problem."

"Is that what happened in the most recent case?" Morgan stirred a heaping teaspoon of sugar into his coffee.

"Doris Cycek," I said, nodding my head. "She and her husband, Jim, lived in a remote cabin in Uyak Bay. Doris was sixty-four." I sipped my coffee while I thought about the case.

"I think the Cyceks used to fish, but for the last few years, they've lived like hermits, rarely coming to town." I shrugged. "It's a simple story, really. Doris loved clams and Jim didn't. He dug clams for supper, Doris ate them, and about twenty minutes after supper, her lips began to feel numb and her fingers and toes started to tingle. Soon, she was dizzy and sick to her stomach, her breath coming in short gasps. Jim called the Coast Guard, and forty-five minutes later when they arrived, Doris couldn't walk or talk and was barely breathing. She stopped breathing on the way to town and was pronounced dead at the local hospital. I was called to the hospital, where I met Mr. Cycek." I shook my head. "The poor guy was in shock; it all happened so fast."

"Was there anything he could have done to save her?" Morgan asked.

I shook my head. "Other than talking her out of eating clams, no. Maybe if they'd lived closer to town or Mrs. Cycek had been younger and stronger...." I shrugged. "It's hard to say. Most people survive paralytic shellfish poisoning, but Mrs. Cycek was the third person to die this year, and extremely high levels of toxins were found in the bivalves that provided the final meals for the other victims. The first death was a young man near Kodiak, and the level of saxitoxins in the mussels he ate was the highest ever recorded. The second case happened only a few miles from the Cyceks', but that's the interesting part of all of this."

"What?" Morgan asked.

"The second victim, a forty-five year old fisherman, dug his clams in an enclosed lagoon that had four freshwater streams emptying into it. The small organism that carries saxitoxin blooms under those conditions, and we've known for a long time that stagnant lagoons are hot spots for PSP. We warn people that if they must eat bivalves, dig on beaches that face the open ocean."

I leaned toward Morgan and lowered my voice, as if imparting a secret. "Jim Cycek's beach faces the open ocean. It should be one of the safest beaches on the island. If the bivalves are toxic on his beach, they could be toxic everywhere on the island, or everywhere in this part of the state. Now, we have to figure out why, what's causing this bloom."

"Is the water red?" Morgan asked. "I haven't noticed it."

"There's a slight red tint in places, but we've found that red tides are not the best indications of high PSP levels."

"I see why you're anxious to get out and collect more samples."

"Yes," I said, "and then I need to gather bivalves from as many locations on the island as I can. We could learn a great deal about paralytic shellfish poisoning this summer. My boss at the marine center wants me to hire another assistant to help me, but I don't think I will. I don't have the heart for it."

"You can't blame yourself for this, Jane." Morgan's voice was low and soothing. *Why couldn't I find somebody like him to lean on?* I wanted to be taken care of, and I wanted to be held. I gulped hot coffee.

"You're flying out to Uyak on Thursday?"

"Yes," I said. "On the third."

"Will you stay at Cycek's?"

I laughed. "No, although Mr. Cycek did offer to let us stay with him when we collected samples."

"You'll take a tent, then?" Morgan frowned.

"Sure," I shrugged.

"And stay by yourself?"

I smiled at him. "I'm used to that."

"Aren't you afraid of bears?"

"I'm more afraid of strange people. I think I'm safer in a tent on Kodiak Island than I would be in an apartment in New York."

Morgan's frown dissolved into a smile. "Point made," he said.

The waitress returned with her coffeepot, but I put my hand over my cup and Morgan shook his head. I looked at my watch and was stunned to see it was ten fifteen. I couldn't remember an evening passing so quickly or pleasantly.

Morgan insisted on paying the bar tab, and then he walked me downstairs and through the lobby of the hotel. I thanked him for a nice evening, and he held out his hand. I hesitated and then gripped his warm, firm flesh.

"Thank you." His voice was low and husky. "Be careful, Jane. I'm not certain what's going on here yet, but I think you should take any threat seriously."

I nodded, concentrating more on the heat of his hand than on his words.

"Call me any time, day or night, if you need me."

He let go of my hand, and I smiled as I backed toward the door. I didn't trust my voice to speak, so I waved at him, turned and trotted toward the parking lot. I barely noticed that the rain had stopped.

I felt lighter as I drove home. Hours had vanished while Morgan and I had talked. It had been better than a therapy session. I had unburdened myself by sharing work and personal problems with a man who truly seemed to listen. Okay, I was physically attracted to the guy, but I could handle that. He was a married man, and I would not have an affair with a married man, no matter how tenuous his relationship with his wife. I thought we could become friends, though, and right now I needed a friend more than a lover.

Beneath the bubbling in my head, something nagged at me. Something Morgan said had alerted all my senses, but we'd talked about so much, I couldn't pinpoint the comment that tugged at my mind. I shook my head. I would remember when the time was right.

I parked in my allotted space and walked up the stairs to my apartment. I unlocked the door, thinking about the way Morgan folded his arms across his chest and tilted his head as he listened to me.

I flicked on the light. *Why, why, why couldn't I find an unattached guy like Nick Morgan?*

I walked toward the kitchen and dropped my purse on the counter and then pulled it toward me and removed my phone from the front pocket, I turned it on and called voicemail. *Maybe things wouldn't work out between Morgan and his wife. Yeah, right, and then he'd quit his job and move to Kodiak.* I laughed out loud and started to take a step away from the counter, but then I froze and slowly turned around. A computer-printed note sat on the end of the counter. The note hadn't been there earlier.

# Chapter Nine

I reached a trembling right hand toward the page and then remembered fingerprints and pulled back. Instead, I leaned my face toward the note to read it.

> *Please place Mr. Justin's briefcase on the backseat of your car and leave your car unlocked tomorrow morning when you go to work. We know everything about you. If you do as we say, you will not be harmed. Do not contact the police.*

Too many cups of coffee burned in my stomach. Sweat streamed down my face as I ran toward the bathroom, and I wasn't sure I was going to make it. I stumbled through the door, grabbed the edges of the porcelain bowl, bent forward, and retched. I sat on the floor for several minutes, forcing myself to breathe slowly. I then pushed the handle and watched as the remnants of an enjoyable evening twirled out of sight.

*How had someone gotten into my apartment?* I looked up. *Could the intruder still be here?* I sat for a moment, listening, and then pulled myself to my feet.

I felt shaky and unsteady, and I kept a hand on the wall as I wandered through the rooms of my living space, flipping on lights as I went. I checked closets, behind curtains, and under beds. When my search was finished, I latched the deadbolt on my door and sat stiffly on the couch.

My head pounded. Someone had invaded my home. I didn't know whether to be angry or frightened. Tears poured down my cheeks, and I fought to gain control. I knew I should call Morgan, but I couldn't until I calmed down. The author of the note warned me not to contact the police, but what else could

I do? I didn't have a briefcase to leave on the backseat of my car. My life was in danger no matter what I did.

I closed my eyes, leaned back, and concentrated on breathing evenly. Jack Justin apparently had offered up my name to the people who had threatened him. *Did he really believe I had his father's briefcase, or had he panicked and blurted out my name so they would leave him alone?* When I'd seen him that morning, he had been terrified of someone. He believed the people who wanted the briefcase were responsible for the bomb. I was beginning to believe he was right.

Suddenly, I remembered what Morgan had said during dinner that had bothered me. At the time, it was an unformed idea that my mind didn't want to accept, but now the full force of it smacked me in the face.

I sat forward and wiped my eyes with the toilet tissue I still gripped in my right hand. I stood, wobbled a couple times, and then marched toward the telephone.

I called Morgan's cell. By now, I had the number memorized. He answered after three rings. His voice sounded groggy and muffled.

"Did I wake you?" I asked. I couldn't believe he had gone to sleep so quickly. I looked at my watch and was surprised to see it was almost midnight.

"Jane, what's wrong?" His voice was suddenly alert and clear.

"I'm sorry to bother you; I know you're tired."

"What is it?"

"A note," I said. "Waiting on my kitchen counter when I got home."

"Don't touch it. I'll be right there." The phone clicked in my ear and then went dead.

I wondered how he would find my apartment. I hadn't told him where I lived, and I wasn't listed in the phone book. I expected him to call back and ask directions and then remembered he didn't have a car.

I walked to the bathroom, brushed my teeth, washed my face, and combed my hair. My bangs were pasted to my forehead with sweat. I fluffed them until they dried, and then went to the bedroom and slipped into an oversized sweatshirt and jeans. I returned to the living room couch and sat hunched over, elbows on my knees. A few moments later, my door buzzer sounded.

I pulled open the door and fought for control when I looked into Nick Morgan's worried eyes. He set down his briefcase and opened his arms. I accepted his comfort, and then he grasped my arms and gently held me in front of him, studying my face.

"Are you alright?"

"Fine." I pulled away and hugged myself. "I didn't touch the note."

"Good. Where is it?"

I led him to the counter and pointed at the printed page. He read it and studied it for a few minutes. Then, he opened his briefcase, pulled a latex glove onto his right hand, slipped the note into an evidence bag, and then dropped it into his briefcase.

"Was there any other sign that an intruder had been in your apartment?"

"No."

He walked to the door and opened it, examining the lock and the door frame. "You should get a better lock," he said. "This would be easy to open."

Fatigue poured over me. What was happening to my life? I lived in a small, safe community in Alaska, not New York City or Los Angeles. Would I have to chain myself in to stay safe at night?

"If the author of this note wants to harm me, locks won't keep me safe," I said. "I don't have the briefcase, but I can't seem to convince him of that."

Morgan sat on a kitchen stool. Under his long black coat he wore a dark-blue-and-white FBI sweatshirt and blue jeans. "Why did you say he?"

I perched on the other stool and took a deep breath. "Tonight at supper, you said that the criminal often returns to the crime scene. That bothered me, but I didn't know why. After I got home and saw the note, I remembered that Jack Justin braved terrible weather to fly out to the crash site."

"Are you saying that you think Jack Justin planted the bomb that killed his parents?"

"Yes." Morgan's disbelieving tone irritated me. "It wouldn't be the first time a child killed his parents, and anyone callous enough to kill his own parents wouldn't blink an eye at taking out a few more people in the process."

"Maybe."

"It makes perfect sense," I said. "There's no conspiracy or terrorists running around threatening him. "There's just one guy who wanted to bump off his parents and now needs to get ahold of the documents his father was carrying with him. Maybe the Justins disinherited their son, and Jack wants to get his hands on the latest copy of the will."

Morgan rubbed his eyes.

"You don't think that's possible?" I asked.

"Oh yes. It's possible."

"But you don't believe it," I said.

"I didn't say that." He held his hands up. "You may be right, but I don't think we can afford assumptions at this point. We need to be careful."

"So what should I do?"

Morgan remained motionless for several minutes while he thought. "Drive to work tomorrow. Park the car in the lot, and go to your office."

"And then what? Justin, or whoever wrote this note, isn't going to be happy when he doesn't see a briefcase on the backseat."

"Place a note on the car seat saying you don't have the briefcase." Morgan's voice was low and calm. "With the help of the local police force and a few other agents, I will stake out your vehicle and watch who approaches it."

"What if he sees you?"

"We'll be careful, Jane. We've done this before."

The knot in my chest loosened. *It couldn't be this easy, could it?*

"What time do you get to your office?" Morgan asked.

"I'm usually there by 8:30, sometimes earlier."

"Go in at 9:00 tomorrow. It may take me awhile to get this organized."

I nodded.

"Will you be alright here?" he asked as he stood.

I wanted to say no; I didn't want him to leave. I could see he was exhausted, though, and I had too much pride to let him see my fear.

"I'll be fine. You need to get some sleep."

Morgan nodded and started toward the door.

"Did you drive here?" I asked.

He turned his head toward me and smiled. "No. I hitched a ride with one of Kodiak's finest."

"That explains how you found my apartment so easily."

"Lock the door after me," he said, as he stepped into the hallway.

It was unnecessary advice. I planned to lock it and then sleep on the living room couch, where I could keep an eye on the door.

I was more tired than I ever could remember being, but I couldn't sleep. The couch was not as comfortable as my bed, and every noise required examination. My usually quiet apartment seemed alive with unfamiliar sounds. I tried to read, but couldn't concentrate. I paced, but that only heightened my apprehension. Sometime after four, exhaustion finally won out, and I slept for three hours.

I awoke slowly to my buzzing alarm. My head throbbed and my neck felt stiff. I was confused. *Why was I sleeping on the couch? Was it the middle of the day?* It seemed so bright. I'd shut the curtains, but sunlight streamed through them. Slowly, I remembered the events of the preceding night, and my headache worsened. I swallowed two aspirin and stumbled into the shower.

As my senses returned, so did my unease. I had planned to take a long, hot shower, but I thought I heard noises through the pounding water. I scrubbed my head and body as quickly as I could and stepped out of the shower stall. The apartment was quiet; I had imagined the noises.

I dressed in black jeans and a grey sweater. I didn't have a class today, and except for two appointments with students, I planned to spend the bulk of the day closed in my office, catching up with paperwork. I liked to wear comfortable clothes when I planned a day of sitting at my desk.

I made coffee and ate a bowl of cereal. The morning seemed to be crawling by. I wanted to get going and get this over with. After eating, I went to the spare bedroom that I used for an office and rummaged until I found a marking pen. On a piece of computer paper, I wrote in block letters: I DO NOT HAVE MR. JUSTIN'S BRIEFCASE.

I looked at my watch. It was only 8:30, but I couldn't sit still any longer. I took my purse, jacket, and the note, and walked downstairs to the parking lot. The temperature was only in the sixties, but the day felt warm and inviting. A few fluffy clouds dotted the brilliant blue sky. I inhaled crisp air. The sight of the sun after several stormy days was a relief, and my spirits rose despite all the threats and apprehension over what I was about to do.

I unlocked my Explorer and climbed in. I knelt on the front seat and carefully placed the note on the backseat. The Explorer's windows were tinted lightly, so a person could see through the windows only by walking up to the vehicle and cupping his hands to the glass. If Morgan was watching, he couldn't miss seeing someone do that. *But why would Justin or whoever had left me the note be so foolish?* The person must know he would be observed approaching my vehicle.

Maybe he or she believed I wouldn't contact the police, or perhaps the person was so focused on getting his hands on the briefcase that he wasn't thinking clearly. Justin had not been rational when he had approached me at the marine center the previous morning. I could believe he would plan something this careless, and I hoped he would follow through, and Morgan would catch him. I was ready for this to be over.

I drove slowly through the streets of Kodiak. The sidewalks hummed with activity. Kids played, skated, and bicycled, and two young mothers walked together, each pushing a baby stroller. I drove past a baseball field, where a girls' softball team practiced on the sodden diamond. After the long, stormy stretch, islanders embraced the sun, determined to enjoy every minute of it. As I sat at a stop sign, I saw one ambitious man stirring paint, a ladder propped against the side of his house. It was no wonder paint jobs deteriorated so quickly here. The wood never had a chance to dry out.

If only I could shed my fear and enjoy the beautiful weather. I took a deep breath and looked around me. The colors were vibrant, as if a veil had been whisked away to reveal a sparkling gem. On a day like this, it was no mystery why Kodiak was nicknamed the Emerald Isle. Verdant mountainsides gleamed beneath the lapis sky, and the ocean glinted, reflecting sunlight like a diamond. Beautiful flowers, both wild and cultivated, were struggling to recover after being battered by the wind. I saw a few broken tree limbs, but the Sitka spruce are hardy trees and used to storms much worse than the one we just had experienced.

My heart thudded when I pulled into the parking lot of the marine center. I parked at the edge of the lot, hoping my vehicle would be easier to watch there. I checked the note again, making sure it was still propped in the rear seat. I gathered my briefcase and purse and climbed out of the Explorer. I fought the urge to lock the doors, and after one quick look back, I hurried away from the vehicle and into the building.

I stopped at the office, and Betty, in an awkward attempt to be cordial, informed me I had no messages but that my box to Craig's parents had been mailed. I walked to my office, unlocked the door, turned on the light, and closed the door behind me. I stood with my hand on the doorknob and felt as if the room was closing in on me. I pushed the door open; I didn't want to be alone today.

I looked at my appointment book. Except for 10:00 and 2:00 meetings with graduate students, the day was my own. I wished for a change that I had a crowded schedule, anything to get my mind off Jack Justin and his briefcase. I wondered if Morgan and his assistants were in place, watching my Explorer. I hadn't seen any sign of the police when I entered the building, but I wasn't supposed to see them; their goal was to remain hidden.

I grabbed my coffee cup and returned to the central office, relieved to see that neither Glenda nor Betty were at their desks. I filled my cup with the thick black brew and retreated down the hall. I set the cup on my desk and began sorting through papers. I read, sorted, and made notes for the next forty-five minutes. I was beginning to settle into a routine when my 10:00 appointment knocked on my door.

"Hi Cassie. Come in." Casandra, a petite, shy, first-year graduate student entered my office and edged onto the chair in front of my desk. She held her head down, her long black hair nearly covering her eyes.

"Sorry about Craig," she mumbled, her voice so low that it took me a moment to decipher what she had said.

"Thanks, Cassie. It was quite a shock. I'm going to miss him." My voice cracked, and I shook my head. "Let's see, we need to go over your class schedule for next fall."

The meeting lasted for thirty minutes, and after Cassie left, I summoned the energy to work on the exam I had scheduled for my class the following week. I had trouble mustering enthusiasm for summer classes. The students were tired and less focused. For the most part, they weren't interested in learning what I had to teach and only wanted to get the class over with before the fall semester. The temptation to give them a test from a previous semester was strong, but I knew I couldn't do that. Copies of all my earlier exams were out there floating around. I had to devise something new and original.

A gurgle from my stomach caused me to look at my watch. It was 11:55. I had forgotten to bring something with me for lunch, and I couldn't go anywhere. I was certain Morgan would tell me as soon as they apprehended someone peering through the windows of my Explorer. Until then or the end of the day, I had to stay put.

I stood and stretched. I wandered out of my office, shutting but not locking the door. I took several steps down the hall and stopped. I returned to my office, grabbed my purse, and locked the door. This was no time to be careless.

I looked for Geoff in his lab, but he must have been at lunch. I flipped on the light in my lab and began reviewing the procedure and making certain the equipment and chemicals were ready for the high-performance liquid chromatography I would perform on the bivalve samples I collected from Uyak Bay. Lab preparation had been one of Craig's jobs, and he had been so good at it that I hadn't supervised him closely. I took inventory of my supplies, making certain I knew where he kept everything.

At 12:40, I was making notes in a spiral notebook, when a muffled blast shook the building. Bottles of chemicals rattled in the cabinets and a stack of books slammed to the floor. *An earthquake.* I'd felt tremors before, but nothing like this.

Two Korean graduate students peered into my lab, their eyes wide.

"I think it was an earthquake," I said. "Are you okay?"

A second loud thud sounded from the floor above, and this time I knew we weren't dealing with a force of nature. "Get out of here!" My voice shook.

The two young men stared at me. "Go!" I yelled. "Something is wrong. Get out of the building!"

They paused only a moment and then they both ran. I was on their heels.

# Chapter Ten

We sprinted up the stairs and through a thin layer of smoke that became thicker when we reached the lobby. Two of my coworkers barreled through the lobby doors in front of us. I pushed outside after the graduate students and sucked gratefully at the fresh air.

I stopped, hands on my knees, head up, gulping air.

"Keep moving!" someone yelled. "Get out of here!"

I wasn't certain the order had been directed at me, but I didn't question it. I ran toward the parking lot, panic closing over me. The world became a blur around me, as I concentrated only on moving my arms and legs.

I stopped when someone grabbed my arm and held me.

"Thank heavens! Are you okay?" Morgan asked.

I wanted him to let go so I could keep running. I never had been so scared in my life.

"Calm down," he said. "Come on, I'll walk with you."

"What happened?" I spit out the question between gasps.

"We don't know yet," Morgan said. There were two explosions in the building. As soon as it's safe, we'll send in a team to investigate."

I turned and looked at the marine center. I felt my knees buckle, and only Morgan's firm grip kept me from falling. A large hole gaped in the wing of the building that housed the offices, and the section where my office had been was the most badly damaged. *If I'd stayed in my office over the lunch hour, instead of going down to the lab... .*

"Did everyone get out?" I asked.

Morgan dropped my arm and shook his head. "We don't know yet. Luckily, the explosion happened over the noon hour, so most of the staff and students were out to lunch."

I felt sick to my stomach and light headed. *I wouldn't have been here if I could have moved my vehicle.*

Someone called Morgan's name, and we turned around. A police officer approached him. "I'll be back in a minute," Morgan said to me, and walked toward the policeman.

My senses were numb. I wandered toward my Explorer, not knowing where else to go. When I reached my vehicle, I leaned against it for support, as if receiving the consolation of an old friend. I opened the driver's door and glanced at the backseat as I climbed in. I froze and backed out of the vehicle. The note was gone.

I saw Morgan still talking to the policeman. I hurried toward him, but he seemed so far away, and I couldn't make my legs move fast.

He finished his conversation and looked around for me. When he saw me, he ran toward me. "Are you okay, Jane? You don't look well."

I reached him and leaned against him. He put his arms around me. "What happened?" he asked.

"The note," I said. I closed my eyes and gritted my teeth. I felt as though I was falling apart, and I couldn't allow that to happen. I pushed away from Morgan and stood, feet apart. I was determined to be strong.

"What about it?" Morgan glanced toward my Explorer.

"Did you see who took it?"

"It's gone?"

I nodded my head

Morgan leaned his head back and stared at the blue sky. "Dang it!" he said. "I assumed that focusing our attention on your vehicle was an attempt to divert our gaze from the marine center, but now it looks like the explosion was the diversion." He sighed. "We rushed the building and forgot about your vehicle."

"So you mean all of this," I gestured at the ruined structure, "was caused so that Jack Justin, or someone, could look in the back of my car?"

Morgan nodded. "And he didn't find what he was looking for."

My head thudded. *Was this somehow my fault, too?* I'd only done what I'd been told, but I felt responsible. I prayed that no one had been hurt in the blast, but as I looked at the damage, I knew that anyone who had been in an office near mine could not have come through this unscathed. I tried to recall if I'd seen anyone's office door open when I'd walked to the lab. I remembered seeing a couple of people in the hall, but they were headed toward the lobby.

Morgan walked me to my Explorer. "Don't touch the rear door handles," he said. "I doubt our friend was careless enough to leave fingerprints, but we have to check."

I opened the front door and sat in the driver's seat. "I don't know what to do," I said.

"I want you to stay here, and I'll assign a police officer to keep an eye on you." Morgan's voice was firm, discouraging dissent.

I nodded, because I did not want to go anywhere else until I knew if any of my coworkers had been harmed or killed in the blast.

"I don't want to scare you more than you already are," Morgan continued, "but I'm sure you know your life is in danger. You can't go home, and you can't stay alone."

I felt my head nodding in agreement again. I was exhausted and my brain screamed. I'd lost my capacity for fear, burned it out. I watched Morgan walk away and then leaned back against the fabric seat. I needed an aspirin, but I'd left my purse in the lab. I thought about my office and knew everything would be gone: all my files, my briefcase, and my computer. At least I'd backed up most of my computer files on my home computer, so I still had my research. Only the work I'd done in the last week would be gone. My class would get a reprieve from their exam.

A young policeman, dressed in blue, took up his position a hundred feet from me and stood staring at me. Morgan must have given him strict instructions, because he stood nervously at attention, hands crossed in front of him. His gaze did not waver from my Explorer.

I closed my eyes and tried to think. *Who usually stayed in their offices during the lunch hour?* I didn't know. I didn't have many friends at the marine center, so I rarely socialized when I was there. I had meetings and conferences with my associates, but I paid little attention to their work schedules.

*The secretaries.* My eyes burned from the smoke. *At least one of them would have stayed at the center over the noon hour.* They rotated their lunch schedules so that the main office was always open during office hours.

I looked at the damaged section of the building again, smoke still billowing from it. My trachea sizzled and my sinuses closed up, reinforcing my already pounding headache. If the secretary had been sitting at her desk, she might have escaped with only minor injuries. The focus of the blast appeared to be near my office, which was fifty feet from the main office. I wondered which secretary had been on duty, and then shook my head and tried to banish the wish that it had been Betty and not Glenda. Betty and I did not get along, but I did not wish her injured.

I gripped my temples in my left hand and leaned forward on the steering wheel. Distant sirens came closer, and I lifted my head to watch as three lime green fire engines pulled into the parking lot. The fire crews moved with speed and efficiency, grabbing equipment and rushing into the building. I hadn't seen flames, and the smoke seemed to be thinning. I wondered how much of the building would be damaged by smoke. Peter would have a heart attack when he saw this.

Where was Peter? I stretched my neck to see if I could see his car in the parking lot, but the lot was too crowded, and my head ached too much to make sense of it all. News travels fast in a town the size of Kodiak, and in addition to citizen gawkers, newspeople and their cameras were beginning to arrive. I'd hoped that most of the national reporters were gone, but apparently the networks and larger newspapers had left crews behind, just in case anything else happened. They hadn't been disappointed.

More police cars arrived, sirens wailing. They set up a barricade at the entrance to the parking lot and announced that everyone except police or emergency workers would have to stay outside the secured area.

A police officer saw me sitting in my vehicle and began to approach but was intercepted by my guard. After a brief discussion, the older officer nodded to my guard and left.

I heard more sirens that I assumed were either additional police cars or fire engines, but when two white-and-blue ambulances pulled to the front of the lot, I sat forward, heart thudding.

I yanked open the car door and left it gaping as I hurried toward the front of the center.

"Ma'am, excuse me. Where are you going?" My guard stepped in front of me.

"Someone must have been in there." I pointed at the building.

"I'm sorry, you can't go in there," he said.

"I have to." I took two steps and was stopped by his firm grasp on my arm.

"No ma'am. I have direct orders."

I could see there was no point in arguing with him. I turned slowly and returned to my Explorer, feet dragging with each step. My arms, legs, and head all felt numb, and I had the odd sensation I was floating and that none of this was real. I wanted to sleep.

I crawled into the Explorer and slammed the door. I sat still, eyes fixed on the ambulances. Time crawled. Sirens and yells faded together into the background, replaced by a loud humming in my ears.

Out of the corner of my eye, I watched the clock in my Explorer. Twenty minutes passed, and then thirty. *Why didn't Morgan come out and tell me what was happening?* Firemen and policemen continued to rush in and out of the building, but still the ambulance crews did not return. Perhaps the scene was still unstable, and the EMS crews had not been allowed inside yet. Maybe there was no hurry, because no one was seriously injured...*Or, maybe there was no hurry, because the victims hadn't survived.*

Finally, I saw a gurney, and I sat forward, squinting to see who was on it. I couldn't make out the patient, but I thought I saw one of the emergency workers look down, say something, and then nod her head. I rubbed my eyes. If the injured person was conscious, maybe he wasn't seriously injured.

A few minutes later, a second gurney rolled through the front doors, and I watched as the emergency crew lifted the second patient into the same ambulance where they had lifted the first victim. The door slammed shut and the ambulance sped away, lights and sirens blaring.

The second ambulance stayed, and I wondered how many more victims there were. The third gurney exited the building at a slow pace. The two young men pushing it didn't look down at their patient. I held my breath, squinting to make out details.

The man at the head of the gurney stopped and opened the rear door of the ambulance and then he and the other man lifted their charge inside. I only got a brief look as they lifted their bundle, but it was enough. A sheet concealed the form beneath it. The sheet had been pulled over the victim's head.

I pushed out of my Explorer and began running. My sudden action startled the young policeman assigned to watch me, and he had to tackle me from behind to stop me.

My head smacked into the soft, wet earth, and I lay there dazed, the wind knocked out of me.

"Ma'am, are you okay?" The policeman was also on the ground and crawled beside my head.

I looked at him as I gasped for breath.

"I'm sorry, but I'm supposed to keep you away from the building." He rolled me over onto my back, stood, and then pulled me into a sitting position.

"Are you okay?" he asked again.

I fought for air and thought I was going to pass out. My jeans and sweater were wet and muddy from my fall. I wondered for a moment what had happened to my jacket and then remembered that it too had been in my office.

"Jane!" Morgan's voice boomed behind me, and the young policeman quickly stepped away.

"Are you okay?" Morgan asked. "What are you doing down there?"

"I'm fine." I stood, brushing clumps of mud off my jeans.

I nodded toward the ambulance that was driving slowly through the parking lot. "Who?"

Morgan grasped my right forearm, looked into my eyes, and said, "Barry Gant."

"Oh no." The image of Gant with his wife in the restaurant the previous evening floated through my mind. Gant had been one of the few colleagues who had told me he was sorry about Craig's death. *How could he be dead?* I hadn't seen him that morning at the marine center, but he'd been alive and enjoying himself at the restaurant the previous evening.

"We have to tell his wife," I said.

Morgan shook his head. "Someone has already taken care of that." He gripped my shoulders. "This isn't your fault, Jane."

The words bounced off of me. I felt responsible for everything. "Who else?" I asked.

Morgan knew what I meant. "Steve Carole is unconscious and Glenda Wayne suffered burns and abrasions. There are a few people with minor injuries, but it could have been a lot worse."

*Not Glenda.* I gripped my pounding head in my hands and began walking toward my Explorer. Steve Carole was a biochemist who had been at the marine center for only three months. I didn't even know if he was married, but now he might die because someone had planted a bomb in my office. Glenda was a lifelong resident of Kodiak, a happily-married mother of two and grandmother of four. I thought of the photos of her grandchildren that decorated her desk. She had to pull through this.

I couldn't speak for several minutes. I climbed into the driver's seat and gripped the steering wheel. Morgan stood by the open door, and when I looked at his face, I saw that it was streaked with dirt and soot, the lines in his skin accented by sweat and grime.

"The blast originated in my office, didn't it?" I was certain I knew the answer to that question.

Morgan nodded. "It looks that way, but we won't know for sure until the bomb squad picks through the debris."

"Why?" The word came out as a sob.

"I don't know," Morgan said. "I won't lie. I think the bomb was meant to kill you and divert our attention away from your car."

"Jack Justin," I said.

"He's at the top of our list, and we're looking for him. He hasn't been in his hotel room since yesterday morning, and he hasn't left the island on any commercial flights."

"He didn't get what he was after," I said.

"Jane, we don't know that Jack Justin did this, but you are right. The person who planted this bomb did not get the briefcase, and you are still alive."

"I know my life is in danger," I said. "I just wish I understood why."

A man in a charcoal grey suit walked across the lot toward us. "I'll be back in a minute," Morgan said, and walked toward the man. They met, conversed for a minute, and then walked briskly toward the building.

I looked for my police guard, but he wasn't there. I felt useless, alone, and frightened. *Why was all this happening to me? Was I somehow being punished for Craig's death?* I knew the idea was absurd, but I couldn't shake it. At this rate, I soon would be joining Craig.

Morgan returned a few minutes later and sat in the passenger seat of the Explorer.

"Do you feel like driving?" he asked.

"Where are we going?"

"I'm late for a 2:00 appointment with Maryann Myers," he said.

"What does this have to do with her?"

"Nothing that I can see," Morgan said, "but the evidence crews are here now, so I might as well keep my appointment. Mrs. Myers is not an easy lady to find, and I don't want to miss my opportunity."

I reached for the key and then remembered it was in my purse in the lab. I pointed toward the glove compartment. "I have another set of keys in there," I said.

"This isn't a good place to keep keys," Morgan said, his head bent to the small compartment as he searched for the keys.

"Yes, I know," I said, and took the keys from his hand.

I backed out of the space and drove to the entrance of the lot. The policeman guarding the lot unhooked the rope barricade and allowed us to leave.

"Where does she live?" I asked.

"Twenty seven hundred Willow Creek Drive. Do you know where that is?"

"I think it's in Bell's Flats. It will take us about fifteen minutes to get there."

Morgan sighed. "I hope she'll wait."

"I don't understand why you're bothering with her." I nosed the Explorer onto the Near Island Bridge. I'd never seen so much traffic on the long bridge before, and all of it was coming toward us.

"I learned early in my career not to let one incident divert the entire focus of the investigation."

I was certain this field trip was a waste of time, but I wasn't the expert. I waited for a long line of traffic before turning left onto Rezanof. It looked as if everyone in town was driving over to Near Island to check out the explosion.

"You might remember," Morgan said, "just a few days ago you called me, concerned that we were limiting the scope of our investigation to the Justins and their enemies."

I depressed the accelerator as we left the city limits. The island dropped away to our left, but I was in no frame of mind to appreciate the stunning beauty of Chiniak Bay. "Yes," I said, "but that was before Justin threatened me and then blew up my office."

"We don't know he did that." Morgan's voice lacked conviction.

"The bomb in my office is directly related to George Justin's briefcase. My scientific mind won't allow me to believe otherwise."

Morgan didn't respond but stared straight ahead as we sped past Boy Scout Lake, Lake Louise, and Coast Guard Housing. We rounded Barometer Mountain and the Kodiak National Wildlife Refuge Office, where Dana Baynes worked. We crossed the Buskin River Bridge and were buzzed by a plane landing at the airport.

He turned his head at the next group of large buildings. "What's that?"

"The largest Coast Guard base in the world."

Morgan nodded his head slowly as he watched the buildings whiz by.

We followed the road around Women's Bay and past the fairgrounds on our right. We reached the Sargent Creek Bridge, and I slowed.

"I think we turn right on the next road," I said. "I'm not very familiar with Bell's Flats."

I eased onto Russian River Road and drove half a mile before I saw the green street sign for Willow Creek Drive.

"There it is," Morgan said, and I turned left onto a gravel road. Twenty seven hundred was a cedar, ranch-style house on the right. I turned into the long, muddy driveway.

The Myers' attempt at landscaping had resulted in thin, patchy grass and scraggly daffodils, and I wondered why weeds and wildflowers hadn't taken over the yard. Perhaps someone had gotten carried away with weed killer, or maybe the horse that watched us from a fenced-off section of the yard occasionally was allowed to roam free.

Seven-foot, square, king crab pots dominated the backyard. Row after row of the metal cages stacked twenty feet in the air either awaited the slim possibility of another king crab season on Kodiak or would be loaded onto a crab boat headed to the Bering Sea in the fall. I wondered if Darren Myers had been a king crab fishermen before becoming a cannery owner.

Two large black labs rushed at us, greeting us with loud, low barks. I eased my door open.

"Hi guys." The lead dog jumped up on me, adding his muddy paw prints to my stained jeans. I rubbed his ears, and he whined with pleasure. The second dog clamored for his share of affection

"Bruno, Titus, get down. Come here." Maryann Myers stood in the front doorway, motioning to the dogs. They looked at me, hesitated, and then obeyed their master.

I'd forgotten how small Maryann Myers was. She stood under five feet and could not have weighed more than ninety-five pounds. Today, her flaming red hair was combed and curled around her face, accenting her delicate features. Her blue eyes burned bright, not glassy like they had been at the memorial service. Her gaze jumped from Morgan to me and then back to Morgan again.

Morgan stepped in front of me and withdrew his I.D. from his inside coat pocket. He held out his hand. "Mrs. Myers, I'm Special Agent Nick Morgan, and this is Dr. Marcus from the marine center. I'm sorry I'm late. There was an explosion at the marine center, and I lost track of time."

"Oh my!" I noticed a trace of a Southern accent in her voice.

"Come in," she said, and she somehow magically ushered us into the house at the same time she shooed the dogs out the door.

The interior of the house surprised me. Everything was decorated in white: white carpet, white curtains, white furniture, and white walls. White—especially white carpet—was not a practical choice for muddy Kodiak. I kicked off my shoes in the entryway, and Morgan followed my example.

"Can I get you anything to drink?" Maryann Myers asked.

"No," Morgan said, and I shook my head. We followed her through the hall and turned right into a bright, airy living room.

Open curtains framed two large picture windows, and the sun's rays danced on the white surfaces. Maryann motioned for us to sit on a white couch, and I looked down at my jeans. "I think maybe I should stand."

"Hold on just a minute," she said, and hurried from the room, returning a moment later with a large bath towel. She spread the towel on the couch and I sat on it, feeling like one of her dogs.

She sat across from us in a rocking chair. She folded her hands on her lap and looked at Morgan. "Now, what can I do for you?" she asked. "I'm not sure I understand why you want to talk to me."

"Mrs. Myers," Morgan began.

"Please, call me Maryann."

"Maryann, we're speaking with everyone we can who was related to or a friend of any of the passengers on Nine Nine November."

"Why is she involved in this?" Maryann nodded at me. "She's not an FBI agent."

Morgan smiled. "She's my chauffeur. She knows the island, and I don't." His explanation made me feel very unimportant, but it seemed to appease Maryann Myers.

She nodded. "Okay. I said some things at the memorial service that I regret. I was upset and very emotional that day." She crossed her legs and slowly rocked the chair. She looked down at her hands. "Every word I said was true, but I shouldn't have made a scene. What I did was disrespectful to the other victims and their families."

"Tell me about your late husband, Mrs. ... Maryann."

She glanced up at the ceiling and began to rock faster. "Darren was soulless. He had absolutely no conscience, and he did whatever it took to get ahead." She leveled her gaze at Morgan. "All he cared about was himself and making money. I hated him." Her voice cracked, and she licked her lips.

Morgan remained silent, nodding his head sympathetically and studying Maryann as her hands tightened around the arms of the rocking chair.

She looked from Morgan to me. "I'm glad he's dead." Her tone was hostile, but tears streaked down her face. "Now I don't have to worry about a messy divorce, and everything he owned is mine. I only wish he could know I got it all." She laughed and wiped her face. "That would bother him more than knowing he was dead."

I wondered if Mrs. Myers knew she was not doing a good job of clearing herself as a suspect in this matter. She didn't seem to care about that.

"You want to know if I hated my husband enough to kill him, don't you?" She sat forward, jutting her chin toward Morgan.

Morgan remained silent.

"Well, I did." She fell back in the chair and suddenly looked very weary. "But I could never kill innocent people just to get rid of him." If he'd died from eating a strychnine-laced cinnamon roll, I'd be your woman, but I could never do this. I'd never plant a bomb and blow up a planeload of people." She began to sob and pulled a tissue from her sweater pocket.

"Can I get you some water?" I asked.

She waved her hand. "No, I'll be all right," she said, and the sobs began to subside.

"Did your husband have any enemies?" Morgan's voice was softer but still insistent.

"Besides me?" Maryann shrugged. "He had plenty of business competitors among the canneries here in town, but I don't know that you could call any of them enemies." She shook her head. "You need to talk to David Sturman. He's the superintendent of the cannery, and he can tell you more than I can about Darren's business deals."

"Yes, I plan to speak with him," Morgan said. He shifted on the couch. "What about the day of the accident? Did you know your husband was flying to town?"

Maryann dabbed her eyes with the tissue. "Yes, I knew. He called me and asked me to drop off some freezer parts at Kodiak Flight Services. The large flash freezer had broken, and they needed the parts right away. He said they could come out on the same flight that he was going to catch back to town." She shrugged. "We were divorcing, but he still ordered me around."

Morgan sat forward in his chair. "And you took the parts to the hangar or the dock?"

She paused. "I don't remember. To the hangar, I guess. That's where I usually take things."

The tears started again, but this time Morgan didn't wait for them to stop. "Did you know who the pilot was going to be for that flight, and what plane he was planning to use?"

If Maryann Myers understood the implications of this question, she didn't let on. She sniffed. "I didn't think about it. I knew all the pilots well, but Bill...." She pulled her sweater around her and began rocking again. "That's the worst part," she said. "The thing I can't get out of my mind. I don't think I'll ever be able to forget."

"What?" I asked.

Her eyes glistened when she looked at me. "Every time I think about that plane exploding, I see Bill as he was the last time I talked to him. He looked so young and handsome." She rubbed her forehead and then stared at the ceiling. "He wore a teal sweatshirt that looked brand new and was the same shade as his beautiful eyes and the bill on his Kodiak Flight Services cap." Her voice caught. "His face was bright. He had his entire future in front of him."

We were all quiet for several moments. "That's what I remember when I think about that explosion, Agent Morgan. I don't grieve my husband's death, but I mourn the loss of that handsome young man."

I was on the verge of tears myself, fighting for control over my emotions. This day was beginning to wear on me, and I suddenly wanted to be out of this house.

"Mrs. Myers," Morgan asked, "had you planned to meet your husband when he arrived in town?"

Maryann dropped her hands to her lap. "Oh no, we tried to avoid being in the same town, let alone the same car."

"Do you know what his plans were?"

Maryann shrugged. "Not really. For some reason, I thought he was planning to catch the evening jet to Anchorage. I don't know if he told me that or if I just assumed it. He didn't spend much time in Kodiak. When he came to town, he was usually on his way somewhere else."

Morgan stood and held out his hand to Maryann, and I felt the knot in my stomach untwist. We finally were getting out of this place.

"Thank you, Maryann. That's all I have for now, but I hope I can call you if I think of anything else."

She grasped Morgan's hand and stood. "Of course, but like I told you before, I don't know anything that can help you with this investigation."

"Sometimes, people know more than they realize."

Maryann followed us through the house, and when we stopped in the front hall to put on our shoes, she opened the front door and ordered her barking dogs to sit. They didn't want to, but they obeyed the order, tails wagging while they watched us walk to the Explorer.

I started the motor and backed slowly out of the muddy driveway. I reached for my purse to find my sunglasses and then remembered it was still in my lab at the marine center.

"Where to?" I asked.

"Let's drive back to the marine center and see how the investigation is going."

"My purse is in a downstairs lab," I said. "Can we get it?"

Morgan nodded. "I think so."

"What was your impression of Maryann Myers?" I asked, as we cruised along Russian River Road.

"Interesting lady," Morgan said. "She's cooperative and doesn't hide her feelings about her husband, but she's a little unstable."

"Who isn't?" I asked.

Morgan looked at me. "How are you doing?"

"I'll be okay. I just wish this was over."

Morgan looked out his window and didn't say anything for several minutes. We were driving past the airport, when he said, "I think you should cancel your collection trip."

"No," I said. "Why should I do that?" I was beginning to look forward to the collection trip. I would get away from town, violent threats, exploding offices, and Jack Justin's confounded briefcase.

"Someone is after you. Until now, threatening you was good enough, but today they tried to kill you."

"Only because Jack Justin thought he could kill me and get his father's briefcase. Now that he knows I don't have the briefcase, maybe he'll leave me alone."

Morgan massaged his temples. "I don't believe that, and neither do you. I don't know who or what we're dealing with, but the person is dangerous. You've made no secret about your field trip, and once you're in the wilderness by yourself, Jane, the police and I can't protect you."

"I'm not asking for your protection," I said. "I can't put off the collection trip. I've already waited too long to get those samples."

Morgan sighed and stared straight ahead. We continued our trip in silence. When I pulled onto the Near Island Bridge, I couldn't believe my eyes. The bridge was packed with vehicles. Crashing waves and gulls' cries had been replaced by blaring horns and angry voices, and I felt as if I suddenly had been teleported to Los Angeles during rush hour. I was certain there were more vehicles on this bridge than there ever had been before, and I hoped it could support the weight.

"Alright," Morgan said. "The police should be out here clearing this. It will take us an hour or more to get to the marine center."

"Why don't you get out and walk? It's not far."

"What about you?" he asked. A car was beginning to pull onto the bridge behind me, so I jammed the Explorer into reverse and edged backwards. The car retreated and allowed me to back off the bridge.

"I'll go back to my apartment to get cleaned up."

"No, I can't leave you alone," Morgan said.

I looked at Morgan. "I'll be fine. Call me later."

Morgan looked at the bridge and back at me. "Be careful," he said, and slid out of the Explorer, slamming the door behind him.

I knew I'd frustrated him, but I refused to be treated like a helpless woman. I'd been taking care of myself for a long while, and this wasn't the first time I'd run into dangerous men. I drove toward my apartment, feeling self-sufficient, but the closer I got to home, that feeling began to dissolve into apprehension.

I parked in my usual space and watched the stairs for a few minutes. Two teenage boys bounced down them, laughing at some private joke, and my mood lightened.

I looked for my purse and again remembered it was at the marine center. I didn't have my apartment key. I thought about walking to the manager's office and getting a duplicate key, but then decided to check first to see if I'd forgotten to lock the door or had left a window open. I had been so worried about intruders that I doubted either of these two possibilities was likely.

I eased up the concrete stairs, my chest and stomach bunched into knots. I rounded the corner, took two steps toward my apartment, and nearly bolted. The front door was cracked open two inches.

I didn't know what to do. Should I run and get help? My mind screamed, *flee*! However, my body kept inching toward the door. I couldn't seem to stop myself.

I wiggled my fingers through the crack in the door and gently pushed it open. When I saw my home, rage usurped fear. Every inch of it was totaled. Through tears that were distorting my vision, everything I saw was broken. The furniture was slit, and my stuff was strewn everywhere.

*Not my computer*! I rushed through the apartment, mindless of danger. I threw open the back bedroom door and waded through papers, computer disks, and shattered drawers that apparently had been flung against the walls. I switched on the computer, and the screen bounced to life. I sank into the desk chair and cried, but this time, the tears were tears of relief. If the vandal had destroyed this computer, my research, a year and a half of my work, would have been gone.

I rummaged through the wreckage of my home office until I found a jump drive, and then I began the lengthy process of backing up everything on the computer hard drive. I'd kept three copies of my research. The original was on the hard drive of my computer at the marine center. I copied that onto jump drives, and once a week brought the drives home to copy onto the hard drive of my home computer. Unfortunately, I then took the jump drives back to the office, where they were stored. When my office blew up, I lost two copies of my research, and if the vandal had destroyed my home computer, I would have lost it all.

All I could think about was generating another copy of my work. I didn't worry that someone might still be in my apartment or that I had left the door wide open. Nothing mattered until my research was safe.

Forty-five minutes later, everything was copied. I put the drive in my pocket and found my passport, which was stashed in my travel backpack.

I hurried into the kitchen, where I kept a spare set of house keys in a small drawer. Luckily, that drawer was still in place, the keys in the far rear corner where I had left them.

I ran from the apartment, slamming and locking the door behind me, jumped into the Explorer, and drove to the bank. The lady in charge of the safety deposit boxes peered curiously at me over her reading glasses, and I remembered I still was wearing my muddy clothes. I explained that I needed to get into my safety deposit box, and supplied my passport for identification. She nodded and led the way to the back of the bank.

Once I had locked the jump drive in my box, I collapsed in a chair. Overwhelming relief soon was replaced by fear and uncertainty. I wanted to call Morgan, but I knew he would send the police to my apartment and insist I not return there. It was bad enough that an intruder had pawed through my things; I didn't want a squad of police searching through everything, too. My privacy was valuable, and I hated the person who had invaded it. I would not allow him to keep me out of my home.

I felt stronger and more in control as I strode from the bank and climbed into my vehicle, but my resolve began to dwindle when I parked in the lot at my apartment complex. My hands trembled as I pushed the key into the lock on the doorknob. I held my breath and then pushed the door inward.

The mess was just as I had left it. I shut the door and stood quietly for a moment, listening. I was just about to relax, certain I was alone, when my telephone buzzed and a scream escaped my throat.

I was breathing hard when I answered. I expected to hear Morgan's voice, and I was trying to decide whether or not to tell him the truth, when my father surprised me by saying, "Jane, are you okay? You sound out of breath."

"Dad!" I wanted to cry and tell him everything, but I knew better. There was nothing he could do to help me with this problem, and I didn't want to worry him any more than I already had.

"I'm fine," I said. "Why are you calling in the middle of the day?" I squeezed my head in my hand and prayed this already bad day wasn't about to get worse. I had answered too many awful phone calls during my mother's long, horrible fight against ovarian cancer, and even for a while after she had lost that battle, I cringed each time I heard a ringing phone. Now, my dad was calling me at my apartment during work hours, and his voice sounded strained.

"The bombing at the marine center is all over the news," he said. "They said one person is dead and at least three have been injured. I've been trying to get ahold of you on your cell phone, at your office, and at home." I looked at the blinking light on my answering machine and felt guilty.

"Sorry, Dad. I should have called you right away. I'm fine, but it has been a terrible day."

"What's going on up there?"

"I wish I knew," I said. "I'm safe, though. You don't need to worry about me." I gazed at the wreckage of my apartment while I uttered this lie. I hoped he couldn't hear the fear in my voice, but I knew he wasn't convinced all was well.

"It looks as though you won't be able to work at your office for a while. Why don't you fly down here and visit for a couple of weeks?"

"I'd love to, Dad, but I can't. This is my busiest time of the year. I'm planning on a collection trip over the fourth, so I'll get out of town for a few days."

That seemed to appease him, and I didn't say anything to alter his assumption that I would be going on this collection trip with a group of people.

I promised him I would keep in touch and then disconnected and checked my answering machine messages. I had two from him and one from a man with a deep voice and a slight accent that I couldn't place.

"Dr. Marcus," the man said. The words were measured and exact. "We are tired of playing games. More people will die until you decide to cooperate. We will give you one more chance. Do not leave your telephone. We will call you later with a time and location." That was the end of message. I pushed the save button. I would have to let Morgan listen to this. Perhaps FBI experts could identify the accent and possibly even the voice if he was a well-known terrorist.

I was certain of two things: I never had heard that voice before, and the caller had not been Jack Justin. Either Jack had associates, or he had been telling me the truth when he said that someone else wanted his father's briefcase. *But what happened to Jack, and why did everyone think I had the confounded briefcase?*

I changed into sweats, and then, beginning in the kitchen, I cleaned my apartment, trying not to think about the evidence I was destroying. I wondered if the intruder had left fingerprints, but I shuddered at the thought of a forensic crew dusting every surface of my home. Since the airplane explosion, my life had been in shambles. It was time I took control again. For the last few days, I had been blindly following the instructions of terrorists and police. Now, I wanted to think for myself and take charge of my own life.

At 6:00, Morgan called. I told him about the message on my answering machine, but omitted the part about my apartment being rifled through.

"You shouldn't be there alone, Jane." His voice sounded weary and strained.

"I'll be fine," I said.

"At least record every call," Morgan said. "If the guy calls back, we'll want to have it on tape."

"Okay," I said.

"I have it arranged so a police car drives past your apartment complex every few minutes, but that's the best I can do. Between the marine center bombing and trying to locate Jack Justin, we're spread a little thin."

"I'm fine." I glanced at my living room floor. I'd put the cushions back on the couch and swept up the broken glass, but papers and debris still covered the floor.

"I'll try to stop by later," Morgan said. He paused a moment. "Your life is in danger, Jane. Don't take this lightly."

"What about my purse?" I said.

"I have it. I'll try to get it over there tonight."

"Thanks," I said. "I'll be careful, I promise."

I resumed cleaning, moving lethargically from room to room. I felt drained, and my stomach growled from hunger, but the thought of food made me sick.

At 8:15, the phone rang again. I hurried to it and pushed the record button on my machine. My heart pounded in my head as I picked up the receiver.

It was a life insurance salesman, and I would have laughed if I hadn't been so irritated that this guy had unwittingly scared me half to death.

"I have life insurance," I said.

"You can never have too much." My hand grew clammy, and I began to wonder if this was one of the terrorists. Then, he launched into a description of the specifics of the policy, and I relaxed.

"I don't want your insurance, and I'm going to hang up now." I dropped the receiver into the cradle. I was doing him a favor. If he had any idea what a bad risk I was, he wouldn't be trying to sell me life insurance.

When my apartment was reassembled, I turned on the television and flipped through the channels. I caught a glimpse of the marine center on CNN and changed channels. I stopped at a sitcom, but I kept hearing noises and having to mute the television to listen more closely. Finally, I shut it off and leaned back against the couch.

I closed my eyes and was almost asleep when the phone rang again. I fumbled with the answering machine and the phone, trying to clear my head and sharpen my senses.

"Hello," I said.

"Jane, are you okay? You sound out of breath."

"Peter." I was surprised to hear my boss' voice. "I'm fine. How about you? Where were you during the blast?"

"I was home eating," he said. "I didn't even know about it until I drove back to work at 1:00."

"Thank goodness you weren't there."

"Poor Gant wasn't so lucky."

"What about the others?" I asked.

"Both Steve and Glenda are in the hospital. I haven't talked to them, but they're listed in stable condition."

"Did Steve regain consciousness?"

"Yes," Peter said, "but I understand the doctors think he may have some hearing loss."

I pulled the bar stool over and sat on it. "What a mess," I said.

"The detectives tell me the blast originated in the area of your office."

My neck stiffened. I should have known this was not just a friendly call to check on my safety and state of mind. I said nothing, but waited for Peter to continue.

"Do you know anything about it?"

"Since the airplane crash, I've been receiving threats, Peter. I told the FBI, but neither they nor I expected anything like this." I wanted to cry. I was too weary to explain this to Peter.

"I don't understand, Jane. What are you involved in?"

"I don't understand either, Peter. I swear to you that I'm innocent, but somehow I got caught in the middle of this."

"The explosion today is related to the plane crash?"

"The FBI thinks so."

"And when did you get involved in this?"

"After the plane crash. Someone thinks I took something from the crash site, but I didn't. I keep trying to tell them that I don't have what they want, but they won't believe me."

"So they blew up the marine center?"

I rubbed my head. "I guess so, Peter. I don't know."

"I see," Peter said, and then I heard several seconds of dead air.

"Are the police going to let us back into the marine center tomorrow?" I asked.

"They said we can go to the basement labs and take out anything we need, but then we have to move out until the structural stability of the building can be tested. I've been on the phone all afternoon and evening lining up an engineer for that and a contractor to rebuild." He sighed. "It will cost a fortune, and I don't know what we'll do in the meantime. Fish and Game has offered us some office space, but they can't give us what we need."

I fought back the urge to apologize. Despite what Peter thought, this was not my fault. I'd been blaming myself for too many things, and I was not going to take the rap for this. I knew my job was in jeopardy, and I had to be careful.

I changed the subject. "I'm still planning my collection trip. I don't think I can afford to wait on that."

"By all means, yes. What about your research?" His voice rose in pitch.

"Don't worry. I have it backed up here."

"Good. I wonder how much data the other researchers lost. I'd better call everyone."

"Okay, Peter. I'll be at the marine center first thing in the morning."

"We'll have a meeting then." He paused a moment. "And please let me know what's happening with this."

The phone went dead, and I slammed it down. I knew from Peter's last comment that he blamed me for the chaos in his life. *Was it already time to polish up my resume? Who would hire someone whose previous boss blamed her for demolishing the workplace and killing one of the researchers?*

I usually could blame myself for my problems, and I had blamed myself for Craig's death, but now I was beginning to feel like a victim, and that made me mad. I wasn't planning to let anyone but me screw up my life.

I walked to the back bedroom and turned on the computer. While I still had a job, I would work. I began thinking up test questions to torture my students with. I didn't know where we would hold class, but somehow, we would finish this term.

It took awhile for my brain to click into gear, but once it did, I was able to push everything else from my mind. At 11:15, the telephone rang, and without even thinking, I picked up the extension near my computer.

As soon as I said hello, I remembered I should be recording the call, and I stood, unsure whether I should run to the kitchen extension or stay where I was. When I heard Nick Morgan's voice, I sagged and sat on the edge of the desk.

The weariness was gone from Morgan's voice. He sounded tense and alert. "Has anyone tried to contact you since I talked to you earlier?"

"No. I've been here all night, but they haven't called back."

"I'm at the boat harbor," Morgan said. "I don't want to go into detail now, but Jack Justin's body just washed up at the boat ramp."

# Chapter Eleven

My throat was too dry to respond.

"Are you there, Jane?"

"How long?" I asked.

"It's hard to tell, but the coroner is certain he's been dead at least twenty-four hours."

Justin hadn't planted the bomb. He'd been telling the truth about the dangerous men who would stop at nothing to get what they wanted.

"It looks like he was tortured before he died," Morgan said. "I suspect he told his attackers that you were the person who had the briefcase, and that's why you've suddenly become so popular."

"What; you're serious."

"Get out of your apartment now, Jane. I'm surprised these people haven't been there already, but you can't take any more chances."

"They have been here."

"What?"

I told him about my apartment being trashed. As far as I could tell, nothing had been taken, but whoever had been in my home had been destructive and violent. I tried to explain to Morgan that I hadn't called him because I didn't want police trooping through my apartment.

"Jane!" he said. "You should be smarter than that."

"I don't have anywhere to go," I said. "If I stay with a friend, I put her life in danger. I can't feel responsible for more deaths."

"Okay, then check into a motel. Stay where I'm staying at the Baranov Inn. The FBI has six rooms reserved, and right now, two are vacant. I'll call the front desk and tell them to give you the key to one of the rooms."

"Okay."

"Hurry, Jane. I sent a police officer to watch your apartment complex. I'll have him follow you to the hotel."

I hung up the phone. My hands were trembling, and my mind was filled with the desire to run. I forced myself to sit and think about what I needed to take with me. I took a small duffel bag from my bedroom closet and filled it with clothes and toiletry items. I took enough for two days, but I would have to come back here to pack for my field trip.

I grabbed my keys, locked the door, and sprinted for my Explorer, expecting to be attacked from behind at any moment. I started the engine, turned on the lights, jammed the gearshift into reverse, and backed out of the space. I took a deep breath and forced myself to relax, easing into forward and driving from the lot at a normal pace.

As soon as I left the lot, a police car pulled away from the curb and followed me. If Jack Justin's murderers were watching, I didn't see them. The streets of Kodiak were nearly deserted. Except for the police car, I saw only two other vehicles, and they were driving toward me, not following me.

I collected the room key from the desk clerk and then hauled my bag up the staircase to the second floor. I locked and bolted the door to my room, changed into an oversized T-shirt, and climbed beneath the covers. I didn't think sleep would be possible, and I planned only to try to relax until Morgan returned to the hotel. I wanted to hear about the investigation, to know if the FBI had uncovered any leads to the identity of Justin's murderer. I also didn't think I would feel safe enough to sleep until Morgan was in the hotel.

I was wrong. I drifted to sleep soon after I closed my eyes, exhaustion forcing my mind to shut down. If Morgan tried to contact me after he returned to the hotel, I didn't hear him. I didn't hear anything until the front desk called me at 7:00 with my wake-up call.

I sat on the edge of the strange bed, groggy and disoriented. Bit by bit, I remembered the nightmare of the previous day and the reason I had slept in a hotel room. I stumbled to the shower and stood under the hot spray. My right thigh was bruised and my shoulder hurt from where I'd hit the ground when the young policeman tackled me. These were small inconveniences when compared with the fate of Barry Gant or Jack Justin.

I searched for the bravado and anger I had tapped into the previous evening, but fear was the emotion of choice this morning. I didn't want to leave the safety of the locked hotel room. *What if Jack's killers were waiting for me?*

I took my time dressing and applying makeup. The hotel room was dark and the building quiet. I considered turning on the television, but I didn't want to see the news. I pulled back the heavy curtain and was delighted by the view of blue sky. The world seemed slightly friendlier.

Knuckles rapped against my door, and I instinctively pushed into the far corner of the room.

"Jane," a familiar voice called.

I exhaled and walked to the door, checking through the peephole before I unlatched the bolt. I pulled the door open. Nick Morgan was freshly showered, shaved, and immaculately dressed in a dark suit, white shirt, and pinstriped tie. However, his grey face revealed that he had slept little, if at all, the previous night. In his right hand, he clutched my purse.

"Come in." I pushed the door open.

He handed me my purse and then crossed the room and sat stiffly on the edge of the bed.

"Are you hurt?" I asked.

"Oh no. Just tired." He rubbed his face with his right hand. "I think I'm getting too old for this job."

"How did you find Jack Justin?"

"We didn't. He washed up on the boat ramp at high tide. A fisherman called the police."

"He'd been tortured?" I leaned against the desk. I wasn't sure I wanted to know the answer to my question.

Morgan braced his hands behind him on the bed and leaned back. "His wrists were tied behind his back, and his ankles were bound together. He had multiple abrasions across his face and chest. He'd been badly beaten."

"Do you know yet who did it?"

Morgan sighed and looked at the ceiling. "I'm sure you know this is confidential, but under the circumstances, I feel you have a right to know."

"I don't plan to talk to reporters," I said.

"Luckily, Kodiak is an island, and as you know, airplanes are the only way to quickly get back and forth to the mainland. Since only two airlines fly between Kodiak and Anchorage, it requires no great detective work to scan the passenger lists."

"But people can use fake I.D.'s and travel under false identities," I said.

"Yes, it's not as easy as it used to be, but it can still be done, and with all the newspeople travelling to Kodiak, it makes our job more difficult, but we can still trace most of the passengers, and we came across a couple who have no business on the island. We haven't located them yet, but I think they are the people we're looking for."

"So you're searching for them?"

"Yes," Morgan said. "And, we should be able to stop them from leaving the island."

I wondered if I still would be alive when they tried to leave the island.

Morgan read my mind. "You will have your own personal guard until they are caught. I know I can't keep you locked in a hotel room, but I insist that you accept protection."

I nodded. He didn't have to twist my arm.

"What are you planning to do today?" he asked.

"I'm getting ready to go to the marine center. We're supposed to get our gear out of the labs and then have a meeting about what to do next. We have to find temporary office space somewhere."

Morgan slowly pushed himself off the bed and stood. "If you're ready to go, I'll walk downstairs with you and introduce your guard."

"Does he have to ride with me?" I wanted protection, but I needed my space.

Morgan smiled. "He'll follow you in an unmarked car. You won't even know he's there."

We walked down the stairs and across the lobby. The young man who had been assigned to watch me the previous day jumped up from the couch and stood as soon as he saw us. He was not wearing his police uniform today, but was dressed in black slacks and a dark green sweater.

We walked up to him, and in a low voice, Morgan made the introduction. "Jane, this is David Wesley."

I held out my hand, and David shook it. "Dr. Marcus," he said.

"I believe we met yesterday." I smiled at the young man, and his face turned beet red.

"I hope I didn't hurt you."

"I'm fine." I glanced up at Morgan. "I'll talk to you later, then."

He nodded and then looked at Wesley. "If anything unusual happens, call me right away."

"Yes sir," Wesley said.

Morgan nodded and then strode toward the stairs. Wesley and I started out the door, but the cold morning air reminded me that I had forgotten my jacket.

"I have to run upstairs for a minute, I'll be right back."

"Yes ma'am," Wesley said, looking back and forth from the street to the stairs.

"You can wait for me in your car; I'll be back in a minute. I just need to grab a jacket."

He thought about this for a moment and then nodded his head. "Okay."

I hurried up the stairs and started down the long corridor toward my room. I saw a couple at the far end of the hall, locked in a passionate embrace. I could see the side of the man's face and recognized him as David Sturman, the man who had eulogized Darren Myers at the memorial service. I couldn't see the woman's face, but I knew who she was from her bright red hair. I took several steps back and watched the couple from a distance as Sturman smoothly unlocked the door and they slid into his room. *Had Darren Myers known that the superintendent of his cannery was having an affair with his estranged wife? If so, the working relationship between the two men must have been strained at the least.* I would have to report this information to Morgan.

I continued to my room and unlocked the door. The phone was ringing when I pushed the door open, and I assumed that Morgan had seen me go one way and my guard the other and was calling me to scold me.

I grabbed my jacket and then snatched up the phone. "Hello.

I sat hard on the bed when I heard the caller's voice. It was the same deep, accented voice I'd heard on my answering machine. "Dr. Marcus," the man said. "We know where you are hiding. You can't escape us. We are not playing a game. We want the briefcase."

My heart pounded like a bass drum in my ears. The room appeared particulate and grainy, my head light. "I don't have your briefcase." I was surprised at how calm my voice sounded. "I'm not a fool, and I don't have a death wish. I never had your briefcase, but if I did, I would have either given it to you or the FBI by now."

I stopped talking, waiting for a reply, and thinking about what to say next. Instead, the phone went dead. I pulled the handset from my ear and stared at it, the plastic shaking in my trembling fingers. I dialed the front desk and asked to be connected to Morgan's room. There was no answer.

I pulled on my jacket, grabbed my overnight bag, and sprinted down the stairs to the lobby, hoping to catch Morgan on his way out of the hotel. When I didn't see him, I ran out the front door and to the driver's window of the unmarked Ford parked on the street in front of the hotel.

Wesley rolled down the window. "You look upset, ma'am, is everything okay?" His eyes were wide.

"Did you see Agent Morgan leave the hotel?"

"Yes ma'am, he left a couple of minutes ago."

"Dang it!"

"He's probably on his way to the police station."

I looked at my watch. I was already late. "Can you call him and tell him I just heard from the man he's looking for? I don't have any information, but I'll be at the marine center, and he can call me on my cell if he wants to talk to me."

"Yes ma'am," Wesley said. "Were you threatened?"

"In a vague way," I said. "I received a phone call in my room, and the caller wanted to let me know that he knew where I was staying."

"He could be watching us, then." Wesley scanned the street in both directions.

"I'm on my way to the marine center."

"I'm right behind you, ma'am."

I didn't see anyone who looked out of place as I drove to the marine center, but then I hadn't seen anyone follow me the previous night. *Maybe my home phone was bugged.* The person or people who trashed my apartment would have had plenty of opportunities to plant a listening device in my telephone. If they were listening to my phone calls, they would have heard Morgan tell me to go to the hotel. *What would they do now? Had I finally convinced them that I didn't have the briefcase?*

The marine center was a depressing site. It had that eerie aura of death that hangs over disasters the morning after the storm. I showed my I.D. to a guard stationed at the entrance to the parking lot, and he waved us into the lot. I parked and walked slowly toward the front doors. Wesley followed several paces behind.

The bomb only had destroyed a small portion of the building. The section that housed the offices was sealed off, but the rest of the building appeared untouched by the blast. I hoped the structural damage was not as bad as Peter feared and that we could move back into part of the building while the rest was repaired.

Peter stood in front of the glass doors addressing a group of my colleagues who formed a semicircle in front of him. I hurried to join the group. Some turned toward me and nodded, dazed expressions on their faces. The rest concentrated on Peter's depressing news. While I'm sure everyone knew that Dr. Gant had been killed and two others injured, most didn't understand until now that they would have to move their laboratory gear out of the building or suspend their research until the building was declared safe to reenter.

"How will we teach our classes?" Diedre Spreate asked.

"I haven't worked out everything yet, Dr. Spreate, but perhaps the community college will loan us some space. They don't have much going on there during the summer session."

Peter looked grey and was dressed in a sweatshirt and blue jeans, instead of his usual well-cut suit. *If this didn't give him wrinkles, nothing would.*

"If possible, though," Peter said, "I will ask you to call your students if you have their phone numbers, or perhaps meet them here outside the building during your assigned class time. They will not be allowed to enter the building, but if they have something in one of the labs that they need, they can tell you or another staff member, and we can get it for them. We have access to the labs until 3:00 this afternoon."

"And then what?" Arnold Nelson, a small, grey-haired man with a pinched face asked. I didn't know him well, but he had a reputation as a whiner.

Peter sighed. "Realistically, I don't think we'll be able to go into any part of the building for a week. If the engineers determine that the lobby and labs are structurally sound, then we should be able to move back into that portion of the building. Of course if they aren't safe," Peter shrugged, "I don't know."

"What about our offices?" Sam Norman asked. "I have papers in my office that I need." Sam was a bright-eyed young researcher. I knew he wouldn't be bothered by a change of office and laboratory space, as long as he could continue with his research. His office was several doors further down the corridor from mine, and I sincerely hoped his work was still there.

"I understand, Sam," Peter said. "I'm working with the police on that. They absolutely refuse to let us go into that section of the building, but I think they might haul things out for us."

Sam groaned. "No, Peter. I don't want someone shoving my files of research into a box. They'll lose half of it, and I'll never be able to make sense of what they've done."

Peter held up his hands. "That may be the best I can do. I think we should get everything out of there before a construction crew begins the repairs."

"At least you have an office to clear out," Jen Wang, a petite Chinese woman whose office had been next to mine, said. "I have nothing left to worry about: no computer, no files, no correspondence, no classroom materials. I have nothing."

"Yes," Peter said. "Next to Dr. Gant's death and the injuries, that's the worst of the news. Dr. Wang's, Dr. Marcus', Dr. Gant's, and Dr. Taylor's offices were destroyed." Wang's and Taylor's offices were on either side of mine, and Gant's was across the hall.

"Luckily," Peter continued, "Wang, Marcus, and Taylor all kept copies of their research elsewhere, so it's not a complete loss." Peter looked around the crowd. "I hope this will convince the rest of you to back up your research and keep copies of it stored at your home or someplace safe. I know I tend to get sloppy about that myself, but I'll be more diligent from now on."

"What about the offices next to those, do you know how much damage was done there?" Arnold Nelson asked. His office was on the other side of Wang's.

"I don't know, Arnold. The police are supposed to tell me the full extent of the damage this morning. I took a walk around the building yesterday, and your office is severely damaged, but I think you'll be able to retrieve most of your files. I doubt you have a computer, though."

"Oh no!" Nelson wailed, and the group turned in unison to glare at him. None of us believed he was foolish enough to store raw data on the hard drive of his computer. Even if he hadn't made several copies, he should at least have one copy on a thumb drive at his office, and the thumb drive was probably okay.

Peter held up his hands. "This won't be pleasant for any of us, Arnold, but we'll have to do our best to get through it."

"Why would anyone want to bomb a marine science center?" Diedre Spreate asked.

Betty, who was standing at the front of the group, turned and glared at me. I felt my face grow hot.

"I have no idea, Dr. Spreate. I hope the FBI and police figure it out soon." Peter paused and looked around the semicircle, but the group was silent, too overwhelmed for more questions. He sighed again. "Get what you need out of the labs today. Fish and Game has offered us space to store our equipment, and I've rounded up a few vans to move things. After that, we'll take off the rest of this week and Monday and Tuesday of next week. By Tuesday, I'll get in touch with each of you and let you know the plan. Until then, if you want to meet with your students at your home or some other place, that's up to you. Otherwise, give them a week off, too."

Peter stopped speaking, but no one moved. "I have a van in the parking lot. We can begin loading gear any time," Peter urged.

Sam Norman was the first to move, and after he entered through the lobby doors, a procession of researchers straggled after him.

I walked up to Betty. "How's Glenda?" I asked.

"She has a broken arm and a concussion." Her tone was sharp, and her assignment of blame crystal-clear.

"Is she still in the hospital?"

She folded her arms across her body and thrust her chin in the air. "You stay away from her!"

"You bitch!" I said. The muscles in my right arm tightened as I fought the desire to slap her.

Peter had been talking to a police officer, but when he heard my raised voice, he pivoted on the balls of his feet.

Betty glared at me and hurried away toward the parking lot. Peter approached, his head tilted, studying me as if he'd never seen me before. "What was that about?"

"Betty has a problem with me," I said. "Her attitude is starting to irritate me."

Peter reached out and rested his hand on my shoulder. He squeezed gently. "This has been a bad week, hasn't it, Jane?"

"I'd say so."

"And I haven't been much help."

"I understand that the marine center is your first concern, Peter."

"I don't blame you for this. You know that, don't you?"

I didn't, and his words made me feel better.

"I don't understand what's going on, but I don't think you do either."

"I wish I knew, Peter. I'd tell you if I did."

"You have a police guard, don't you?" He nodded behind me, and I turned and saw Wesley standing twenty feet behind me. I'd almost forgotten he was there.

"Yes, the FBI thinks someone is trying to kill me. They believe yesterday's bomb was meant for me, but it's not because of something I did. I would never intentionally put anyone at the marine center in danger."

Peter nodded. "I know that," he said. "Listen, your research is important, but I don't expect you to continue under these circumstances. Why don't you take some time off and go away for a while? I'll get someone to take over your class. When the police catch the people responsible for this, you can come back."

"No," I said. "I have a collection trip planned for tomorrow, and I'm going on it." I realized I'd raised my voice, and looked around, alarmed. Several of my coworkers still stood in the courtyard, their eyes fixed on me.

*What was I doing, shouting my plans so everyone could hear? While I was at it, I might as well announce the time of my flight and which plane I was chartering.*

Peter gripped my elbow and walked me toward the building. "Be careful, Jane," he whispered. "Too many people have died already."

I went down to the lab and began packing my gear. Except for the cloying smell of smoke, the basement labs appeared untouched by the blast. At first, I'd thought this would be an easy task. Since I'd already gathered most of my camping gear, I planned to haul it upstairs and throw it into my Explorer. It wasn't until I walked into the lab that I realized I also would have to pack and move my centrifuge and my chromatography and spectography equipment.

I collapsed on the lab stool, propped my elbow on the table, and rubbed my temples. *Maybe Peter was right. Perhaps I should just go away for a few weeks.*

"Hey, Doc, you okay?" Geoff's voice brought an instant smile to my face.

I swiveled on the stool and looked at him. He wore a faded denim sweatshirt and dirty blue jeans. "You're a welcome sight," I said.

"That must mean you need help moving things."

"Now that you mention it..."

He grinned. "All the women want me for my back."

"It must be hell."

"I have a few more things to move from my lab, and then I'm all yours."

"My heart's racing now," I said.

Geoff's cheerful mood and offer of help lifted the storm clouds a little. I would get through this somehow. For now, I could move my equipment to the Fish and Game building, but I would need a lab to test the bivalve samples as soon as I returned from my collection trip. *It will work out*, I told myself. If nothing else, I could work at night in someone else's lab.

It took us three hours to load and move everything to the Fish and Game building. The biologists in the second floor crustacean research lab greeted me with more cordiality than I could have hoped for. They not only allowed me to store all my equipment there, but gave me workspace in the corner of the room. I made a mental note to thank them in my acknowledgments when I published the article on my work.

Geoff was given a small work area in the basement of the Fish and Game building, and I helped him carry his gear down there. I then made one more trip to the marine center to grab my camping gear and load it in the back of the Explorer.

I called Kodiak Flight Services and asked the dispatcher if I could speak with Steve. A moment later his deep voice came on the line.

I told him I had most of my gear with me and asked him if I brought it over to the hangar today if he could assure me that it would be kept in a locked room.

"I'll lock it in my personal storage room," he said. "No one but me has the key to that."

"Great," I said. "There's one more thing I need to ask you."

"Yes, Jane. I will be your pilot tomorrow, and I will check every square inch of the plane."

I laughed. "You don't get paid enough to put up with customers like me, do you?"

"I never get paid enough," Steve said. "Bring your gear over here as soon as you can, and I'll store it for you."

The tent, radio, antenna, battery, shovel, collection bags, buckets, sieve, shotgun, and shells were already in the back of my Explorer, but I would have to stop by my apartment for my sleeping bag and clothes, and I was not looking forward to going back there. I knew Morgan would not approve of me returning, but under Wesley's protection, I would be safe.

Wesley followed me to my apartment, and I walked up to his car to let him know what I was doing. He nodded. "I'll follow you upstairs to your apartment, check it out, and then stand guard outside while you get your things."

His confidence relaxed me. Anyone would be crazy to attack me in the middle of the day while an armed policeman was escorting me. *Of course, someone could have planted a bomb in my apartment, rigged to explode when the front door was pushed open. A platoon of policemen couldn't protect me against that.* I shook the thought from my head as Wesley followed me up the stairs of my complex and waited while I inserted the key into the door lock. Wesley was tall and muscular, and his bulk felt reassuring as he stood behind me.

I closed my eyes, turned the key, and pushed on the door. The door opened easily, and after a few seconds of silence, I opened my eyes.

My apartment was just as I had left it. If anyone had been there since I had, he'd left no visible trace. Wesley pushed past me and quickly checked all the rooms. I walked into the kitchen to wait for him and saw the light blinking on my answering machine. I reflexively pushed the replay button and then wondered if I should have waited to do that until Wesley was there.

I had one message, and it was from Dana Baynes. "My goodness, girl," her husky voice rasped from my machine. "What's going on? If half of the rumors I've heard are true, you're up to your eyebrows in crap. Call me as soon as you get this."

"Ma'am?" Wesley had heard the voice and hurried to my aid.

"Just the answering machine, David. Sorry, I guess I should have waited for you before I played it."

His expression remained wide-eyed and serious. "I can't tell if anyone has been in here, but there's no one here now."

"Thanks, David, I'll hurry."

"I'll be outside if you need me."

It took me less than five minutes to collect my gear and lock the apartment. Wesley carried my sleeping bag, while I hauled my backpack down to the Explorer. I climbed into the driver's seat, told Wesley my next stop would be Kodiak Flight Services, and then waited while he got into his car and started the engine.

I drove on the Chiniak Highway. Even though my flight would leave from Trident Basin, near the marine center, the Kodiak Flight Services office was located at the airport, five miles southwest of town. I would fly on a float-plane, but the bulk of Kodiak Flight Services' business was conducted on three wheel planes that flew passengers and freight between Kodiak and the six small villages on the island, so the main office, hangar, and warehouse were located at the airport.

I parked in the charter service's lot and was opening the back door of the Explorer when Steve Duncan hurried out the front door to help me.

"How are you doing?" he asked.

"I'm a little jumpy, but fine otherwise."

"I know what you mean. I keep expecting someone to come after me, looking for the briefcase. I was at the crash site, too."

"I don't know," I said. "For some reason, Jack Justin got it in his head that I took the briefcase, and before he died, he apparently convinced some very nasty people of that."

"You're sure you still want to go on that camping trip tomorrow?"

"As long as you still want to fly me."

Steve smiled. "I'm not worried. I've been checking my planes over pretty carefully the last few days, and tomorrow I'll triple check the plane I plan to use for your flight."

"I'm actually looking forward to this trip," I said. "I'll feel safer when I'm out of town."

"As long as no one follows you," Steve said.

# Chapter Twelve

S teve and I piled my gear in a small room, and I watched him shut off the
light and lock the door.

"Is that all your gear?" he asked.

"Except for some personal things I'll need tonight."

"What about a heater or cook stove?"

I shook my head. "I've decided to keep it simple. It's warm enough that I
shouldn't need heat, and I'll eat sandwiches."

"Jane," Steve gripped my shoulders. "Fuels did not cause the Beaver
to explode. You can bring propane, kerosene, and Blazo. I'll be careful
where I load them."

"It's not that, Steve." I looked down. "Really, I just don't want to fool
with all that."

I knew Steve didn't believe me. Why should he? I didn't believe it either.

When I got back to my vehicle, I called Dana.

"What's going on?" she asked as soon as the refuge receptionist put my
call through. "Are these rumors true? Was the bomb at the marine center
meant for you?"

"I don't know, Dana." I'd grown up in a small town and knew all about
rumors and gossip, but sometimes the grapevine in Kodiak astounded me.

"You really sound tired." She paused a moment. "Okay, I'm taking over.
You are staying with me tonight. I'll get off work early."

"No," I said. "You don't want me and my problems in your home."

"Yes, I do."

"You don't understand, Dana. The people who planted the bomb at the marine center think I have something they want. I have a police guard following me everywhere."

"Then get rid of him. Tonight you'll stay with me, and no one will find you. Besides, I've got two shotguns if we need them."

"This isn't a joke, Dana."

"I'm not joking. Where do you think you'd be safer, tucked away at some friend's house in the country, or in town with a policeman following you around? You might as well wear fluorescent pink, so the terrorists can fix their rifle scopes on you."

"Thanks, I feel so much better now."

"I'll meet you at my place in an hour."

I got out of the Explorer and walked over to Wesley's car. "A friend who lives in Bell's Flats has asked me to stay with her. I guess I won't need your protection anymore."

Wesley straightened. "No ma'am. I have direct orders to stay with you all day. I can't quit trailing you until those orders are rescinded."

I sighed. "I'll call Morgan."

"Are you okay?" Morgan's voice was strained. "Have you heard from the man with the accent again?"

"No, I'm fine. I'd just like you to tell Wesley he can go home."

There was a brief pause, and then Morgan said, "I won't do that."

"Dana Baynes, a friend, has invited me to stay at her house in Bell's Flats. I'll go there and stay there until my flight tomorrow. I'll be fine."

"I don't think that's a good idea."

"Morgan, you can't force me to have a bodyguard. I can take care of myself."

"It's your call." Icicles hung from his words, and I understood why he was angry. He'd gone out of his way to protect me, and now I was refusing his protection.

"There is something I need to tell you, though," I said. "When I went back into the hotel this morning to get my jacket, I saw Maryann Myers hugging David Sturman, and it was more than a friendly embrace."

Morgan sighed, and I could imagine him rubbing his forehead. "I'll check into it," he said.

I handed the phone to Wesley and watched him as he stood straight, receiver to his ear. I wondered how long he had been out of the military. He still stood at attention while receiving orders.

"Yes sir," he said after a few moments, and then listened again. "Yes sir," he repeated, and handed the phone to me.

"Listen, Nick, I appreciate the guard," I said. "David has been great, and I've felt very safe under his protection. I just don't need him anymore."

Morgan was silent, and I thought for a moment that he'd hung up. "Are you there?" I asked.

"Yes." His voice had thawed a couple degrees. "Do you have room on your charter tomorrow?"

"Yes, why?" I wiped a sweaty palm on my jeans.

"I want to spend some time at the crash site. I may even stay a night or two there."

So, convenience and economy were the only reasons Morgan wanted to share my airplane. I didn't know why I felt disappointed. The arrangement was logical and splitting the charter with Morgan would save my department money.

"You're taking a sideband radio?"

"Yes."

"I'll take one, too, so we can communicate with each other."

"Okay," I said. "That sounds good. Can I ask why you're going out there?"

"I want to take a better look at the debris; make sure we didn't miss anything."

I knew the briefcase was the "debris" he was searching for, but he probably didn't want to mention the briefcase over the phone.

"Are you still planning to camp alone?" he asked.

"Just me."

"I wish you would reconsider."

"I have a shotgun; I'll be safe."

"A bomb specialist will look over the plane before we get on it."

"You'd better talk to Steve Duncan about that," I said.

"I will, but I'm sure he'll be happy for the assistance."

I wondered how happy Steve would be if a television crew filmed a bomb expert crawling around one of his planes before a flight. That sort of publicity would not help reinstate public confidence in the safety of his charter company.

"The flight is at 10:00," I said. "I'll meet you at Trident Basin fifteen minutes before the flight."

"Promise you'll call me, Jane, if anyone contacts you, or if anything unusual happens, and I mean anything."

"I will."

"Call the police if you can't reach me."

"Thanks, Nick," I said. "For everything."

Wesley still stood beside me, his arms folded across his chest.

I smiled at him as I hung up the phone. "I guess you can go home."

"Yes ma'am."

"Thanks for taking care of me." I held out my hand, and he gripped it in a firm shake.

"Just doing my job, ma'am."

I sat in my Explorer and let the engine idle until I saw Wesley exit onto the highway and turn toward town. I pulled out of the lot and turned in the opposite direction. I followed the Chiniak Highway for five miles and stopped at a small grocery/liquor store. I bought bread, bologna, and mayonnaise to make sandwiches for my camping trip, and I also picked up a twelve pack of Diet Pepsi and three bags of chips, one for tonight and two for the trip. I selected a bottle of Merlot and hesitated in front of the frozen pizzas, but I didn't want to second-guess Dana's plans for the evening.

I paid the cashier for my groceries and walked slowly toward the Explorer. I loaded the bags inside and looked at my watch. I was twenty minutes early, but I didn't have anywhere else to go, and I felt vulnerable sitting in the grocery store parking lot.

I meandered down Russian Creek Road and climbed the steep drive to Dana's cabin. A large Golden Retriever greeted me, barking and jumping up and down in front of the Explorer. It seemed as if everyone in Bell's Flats owned at least one dog, and if there was a leash law, no one obeyed it.

I opened my door. "Hey, Sergeant, how you doing? He jumped up on me, smearing muddy paws across my jeans. "Good dog, just what I needed." I tried without success to push him away. Only the sound of an approaching vehicle distracted his attention, and I turned and smiled as I saw Dana's blue Ford pickup bounce up the drive toward me.

"You're early," she said as she swung out of the door of the pickup, a grocery bag in one hand and two rented videos gripped in the other.

"I hope those aren't horror movies," I said.

"Romantic comedies."

Its previous owner, who was a carpenter and cabinet maker, had built Dana's tiny home. There was no wasted space in the cabin that consisted of a small bathroom and one larger room with a loft. The downstairs portion was divided between a living room and a kitchen. I knew my bed for the night would be the living room couch that pulled out into a bed. The cedar walls were loaded with cubbyholes, drawers, and hidden closets that opened to reveal an amazing amount of storage space. Dana's home was perfect for one person, and I always jokingly was trying to convince her to sell it to me.

I looked around as I piled my bag of groceries on the kitchen counter. The house was spotless, as it always was, and it struck me that Dana took better care of her home than she did herself. Her hair never appeared combed, she wore very little makeup, and except on those few occasions when she was forced to wear a refuge uniform, she rarely dressed in anything other than jeans.

"You sure you want me in your home?" I asked.

"Why, do you have some disgusting habit I don't know about?"

I smiled down at my friend. "You know what I mean, Dana."

"Don't be silly. Besides, I want to hear everything about the investigation, and what better way than to trap you in my home?"

I laughed. "I'm sure you know more about it than I do. You must have informants all over this island."

"Agent Morgan isn't bad," Dana said, as she began unloading her bag of groceries onto the kitchen counter. I moved my own bag to the side to give her more room. "I heard you two had dinner the other night."

"What," I said. "Where do you get this stuff?"

"Oh no," Dana said. She thrust her head in the air and put her right hand over her heart. "I never reveal my sources."

I rummaged in my grocery bag and plucked out a sack of chips. I pulled it open, stuffed a chip in my mouth, and pushed the sack toward Dana. "Morgan's okay, but he's married, and I don't need that grief."

Dana's right hand, gripping a potato chip, froze just short of her mouth. "Now that I didn't know. I heard he was single."

"Well, actually, he's separated from his wife."

"Mmmm." Dana shook her head as she chewed the chip. "That's even worse. Stay away from marital trauma."

"Not that a relationship with Morgan is even an option," I said, "but I would never get involved with someone who lived five thousand miles away."

"What do you mean?" Dana began washing a head of romaine lettuce. "Long distance is the only kind of relationship I want. I don't want a man around all the time, messing up my lifestyle. I just want him to pop in occasionally for sex and then leave me alone. If I want to talk to him, I can call him."

I laughed and shook my head. "What are we doing here?" I nodded toward the lettuce. "Can I help?"

"I thought we'd have an early supper," Dana said. "Then, we can watch those movies I picked out. If we can't have romance, we might as well watch it."

"Put me to work," I said.

"No, you sit down. There's only enough room for one in this kitchen. I think I see a bottle of wine peeking out of your shopping bag. Let's uncork that, and you can relax."

While Dana cooked, I went out to the Explorer to get my overnight bag. The aroma of wild roses and cow parsnip filled the air. The evening was perfect, no clouds in the sky, and it was dead calm. I looked around and sighed. *Tomorrow would be a good day, and I would have a good flight.* Unless fog settled in overnight, this weather should hold.

I pulled the key from the right front pocket of my jeans and unlocked the cargo door of the Explorer. I swung the door up and froze, my hand still clutching the handle. I heard a faint rustling of leaves and grass in the woods to my left. I felt helpless, a gazelle on the open savannah surrounded by a pride of lions. Why had I dismissed Wesley?

The rustling grew louder, and I turned to face the danger, backing into the cargo hold of the Explorer. Then, I heard a familiar panting, followed by galloping feet and muddy paws that sent me sprawling across the vehicle's floor.

"Sergeant. You could get shot doing that." I allowed myself to breathe, gasping for air. I tried to push Sergeant off of me, but he had me down and was licking my face.

I began to laugh, which rendered me completely helpless and sent Sergeant into a licking and slobbering frenzy.

"Sergeant!" Dana yelled. "Get down."

Sergeant turned reluctantly, looked at Dana, put his head down, and backed out of the Explorer.

I pushed myself up on my elbows, smelling Sergeant's pungent breath all over me. "Some watchdog," I said. "Is he trained to lick your intruders to death?"

"Hey," Dana propped her hands on her hips. "He had you restrained."

I grabbed my bag and returned to the safety of Dana's house. I headed straight for the bathroom and washed the doggy drool off my face. My jeans were stained, but not too badly. They were the only jeans I had with me, so I hoped Steve and Morgan didn't mind the smell of wet dog. It might be overpowering in the cabin of the small charter plane.

I sipped wine and read the latest copy of *Outdoor Photographer* magazine while Dana prepared our supper. I tried to relax, but I was uncomfortable sitting there while she worked. She divided the salad into two wooden bowls and carried mine to me.

"This is wonderful," I said, after swallowing the first bite of lettuce and chicken. "That's the best Caesar dressing I've ever tasted."

Dana smiled. "I got the recipe from my sister. It's good, isn't it?"

After dinner, Dana popped in the DVD *French Kiss*, and then we watched *As Good as it Gets* with Jack Nicholson and Helen Hunt. I'd seen both movies years ago but enjoyed them again, and Jack Nicholson had Dana and I laughing so hard, we were crying.

It was 10:30 when Dana turned off the television. The evening had evaporated, and I felt better than I had in days.

"Thanks Dana," I said. "That was exactly what I needed."

She beamed. "I'm a good doctor, and now you're going to sleep. I seriously doubt that you've gotten a good night's sleep since the plane crash, and you need to rest if you're going camping. I never sleep well on field trips. There are too many animals in the woods here."

I knew she was right. The mind could conjure an enormous bear from the sound of a deer walking through the woods at night, and on this trip, I would have more than wild animals to haunt my nightmares. I had an active imagination, and I already could see terrorists in night-vision goggles stalking me in my sleep.

Dana gave me sheets and blankets, and I made up the hideaway bed. I pulled on my nightshirt, climbed under the covers, and was asleep before Dana turned out the lights.

My sleep was deep and untroubled until 3:15. Then, I sat straight up in bed, disoriented and panicked. I'd heard something, but I didn't know what. I looked around. *Where was I?*

I threw back the covers and jumped out of bed, alarm bells blaring in my head. A low growl sounded in the entryway, and I remembered Sergeant. I was at Dana's. I tried to calm down. I sat on the edge of the bed, and then I heard the noise again. Something bumped the outside wall of the cabin.

I stood and backed toward the kitchen. Sergeant issued a short, sharp bark.

"Jane?" Dana called, her voice groggy with sleep. "Are you okay?"

"There's someone outside," I said in a low voice, my head pointed toward the loft, hands cupped around my mouth.

"What?"

"Shhh," I warned

Dana came to the loft railing. "What's wrong?"

"I heard something bump the wall of the cabin."

"Jane. Go back to sleep. It was probably just a deer. You'll never survive a camping trip."

Dana returned to bed, but I stood in the kitchen for several minutes, concentrating on the silence. Finally, when I didn't hear another sound, I edged back to the couch and climbed under the covers. I remained awake and alert until Dana's alarm beeped at 7:00.

I let Dana use the bathroom first, and then I soaked in a hot shower, trying to clear my sluggish brain. The dull headache from not enough sleep was back to visit.

When I opened the bathroom door, the aroma of freshly-brewed coffee lured me to the kitchen, where Dana stood with a mug in her outstretched hand. I took the cup from her and sipped.

I leaned against a kitchen cabinet. "You'd make someone a good wife."

Dana's right eyebrow arched. "People have been banned from my house for saying that."

"Just kidding," I smiled. "Honestly, Dana, thanks for taking me in last night."

"Don't sound so pathetic." Dana dumped the last of her coffee down the sink. "You're not indigent."

"I feel like I am."

Dana wiped her hands on her jeans and slipped past me out of the small kitchen. "I hate to rush off, Jane, but I have a conference at 9:00, and I have to get there early to prepare."

"Sure," I said. "I should be going, too."

"No. I think you should stay locked in my house until half an hour before your flight and then drive straight to Trident Basin. Don't make yourself a target."

I sighed. Dana was right, but I wasn't anxious to stay in her small cabin alone. I couldn't shake the unease I'd felt in the wee hours of the morning. If someone was watching Dana's home, the observer would see Dana drive to work and know I was alone in the secluded cabin.

I stood in the doorway and watched Dana drive away. Sergeant hopped up and down on his front paws and barked at me. Maybe he would keep an intruder away.

The next hour and a half crept past. I made eight sandwiches for my trip and packed them and the chips in the plastic grocery bag. I then tried watching television but couldn't stomach the morning programs. Everyone was too cheery. I called Kodiak Flight Services and confirmed that my flight still was scheduled for ten, and then I thumbed through Dana's magazines and paced her tiny living room, glancing at my watch every two minutes. At 9:20, I'd had enough. I gathered my overnight bag, my purse, and the food bag. I locked Dana's door, told Sergeant goodbye as I was pushing him off me, and climbed into my vehicle.

I drove slowly to town, enjoying the perfect view of fishing boats cruising over the calm waters of Chiniak Bay. Only a few days earlier, the bay had churned like a boiling pot, but this morning its smooth surface reflected the unblemished blue of the sky. The morning fog had not materialized, and the weather was perfect for flying. The conditions were just like the day I'd stood on the floatplane dock waiting for Craig to return.

I shuddered and tried to close my mind to the memory of the crash. I needed to be brave today, and I could not accomplish that feat if I dwelled on the events of the last few days.

I eased my foot off the accelerator as I entered the city limits. I scanned the faces of people on the sidewalk and watched the drivers of vehicles I passed. Everyone was a stranger; nothing looked the same to me today. I felt like a slow-moving target in a crowd of snipers, but I already was pushing the speed limit and didn't dare drive any faster.

I exhaled a long, slow breath when I turned onto the Near Island Bridge. Just a few more minutes and I would be there.

I drove past the marine center and was surprised to see a large construction crew already at work. Had Peter gotten the building surveyed already, or were these bomb experts, sifting through the debris? I hope they would find the answer to this mess in the rubble that used to be my office, but I doubted this crisis would be solved so easily.

I turned my attention from the marine center just in time to see a red pickup truck barreling down the center of the road toward me. I veered off the side of the road and jammed on the brakes, my heart thundering.

A cloud of dust surrounded the pickup, but when it was adjacent to me, the driver turned and looked into my eyes, an angry frown on her young face.

I parked my Explorer in the lot above Trident Basin, grabbed my gear, and ran down the road and then down the ramp to the base where the two-oh-six was tied.

Steve and another man, whom I assumed was the bomb expert, were inside the plane on their hands and knees. Morgan stood on the dock, hands on his hips, watching them.

Despite my distress, I smiled when I saw him. He wore new blue jeans that looked stiff and uncomfortable and a bomber-style jacket that sported the logo of the local sporting goods store on the back. I bet they were happy to see him walk into their store. He had probably purchased all his camping gear there on the spur of the moment.

I stopped a few feet from him and caught my breath. I knew he'd heard me run down the metal ramp, but he must not have picked up on the fear in my pace. His attention was riveted on the men in the airplane.

I walked up and stood beside him, and he looked at me and smiled. "Hello, how was your night?"

"Fine. No problems," I said. "But I just passed Toni Hunt on the road near the marine center. She was driving very fast and coming from this direction."

Morgan spun to look at the road. "I didn't see her drive by here."

He walked toward the edge of the dock and called to Steve. "Jane passed Toni Hunt on the road near the marine center. You were here before I was; did you see her?"

Steve backed out of the plane and stood on the float. He wiped the back of his right hand across his sweaty forehead. His voice was low and calm. "No, but I wouldn't worry. She's been coming down here several times a day since Bill died. She just sits in her truck and stares at the water."

I wondered why Steve was so unconcerned by Toni Hunt's actions. A few days earlier, he'd felt she was the prime suspect in the plane bombing. *What had happened to quiet his suspicions?* Maybe if he had seen her tearing down the road in her truck, he wouldn't dismiss her so easily.

Morgan looked at me, shrugged, and clicked his tongue. "I'll tell Saunders," he gestured to the man in the plane, "to have someone watch her." He shook his head. "She might have had something to do with the plane bombing, but I doubt she planted the explosives at the marine center."

"Why?" I turned toward him, hands on my hips, legs spread apart. "Remember the note on my office door? I think Toni Hunt wrote that note."

Morgan stepped closer to me, his voice barely above a whisper. "Maybe," he said. "But, the bomb experts combing through the debris at the marine center told me this morning that the device used in that bombing was a sophisticated plastic explosive with an expensive timer and maybe even a multiswitch detonator. Those aren't items you'd pick up at the local hardware store. They came from somewhere else and were assembled by someone who has made bombs before. The bomb boys are relatively certain that the device that blew apart the Beaver was nothing more than dynamite and a kitchen timer."

I wrapped my arms around me, suddenly noticing how chilly the morning air felt. "You said before that a smart terrorist might build a simple bomb to confuse the authorities."

Morgan nodded. "That's possible, but the marine center bomber is an experienced bomb maker, and these guys are arrogant. It is unlikely he would build one highly complex bomb and another bomb that was nothing more than an inaccurate homemade job. These guys generally learn their trade and then refine their technique over time."

"I can't believe that two bombings on Kodiak Island within a week of each other aren't related." I strained to keep my voice low. "I think that's a bigger coincidence than your experienced bomb maker bundling together some dynamite to throw off the police."

Morgan rubbed his chin. He was freshly shaved and showered, but he looked tired, as if he hadn't slept in days. "I'm not saying the bombings aren't related, I'm saying the bombers were two different people. If I know that, I look at these crimes differently."

"What do you mean?"

Morgan spread his arms and was about to explain when a brown van sped down the road and stopped at the top of the ramp. The logo on the door said, "Bear View Charters."

The four doors of the van opened and people climbed out. The driver walked to the rear of the van, swung open the back doors, and began unloading gear.

One of the passengers from the van walked down the ramp toward us. "Hey, Steve, how's it going?"

Steve crawled out of his plane. "Hi John, where are you headed?"

"Taking a party to Red River. Everything alright there?" He squinted and turned his head to one side, studying the activity in Steve's plane.

"Fine. I'm getting ready for a flight to Uyak."

John nodded his head, frowning. He watched for a few more seconds and then turned toward the blue-and-white two-oh-six tied directly across the dock from Steve's plane.

The van driver and the other two passengers weighed their gear on a scale in the parking lot and then began hauling it down the ramp toward the plane.

I watched the activity for a few minutes and saw a grey-haired man shuffle down the ramp, both hands gripping a large, cardboard box. He nodded to us as he passed and then lowered his load on the dock in front of the blue-and-white plane. His partner, a younger man, followed, hauling two large duffle bags. They returned up the ramp together, discussing whether they had remembered to buy coffee. I watched them walk by a load of bags and equipment piled at the top of the ramp and then blinked my eyes. Some of the stuff in that pile was mine.

I turned to Morgan. "Our gear is up there." I pointed toward the palettes near the scale.

"Yes."

"While a bomb expert looks over our plane with a microscope, our gear sits exposed where anyone can drop something into it."

Morgan shifted his weight from one leg to the other. "I've been watching it. These are the first people to arrive since we've been here."

I didn't point out that he hadn't seen Toni Hunt. Instead, I turned and marched toward the ramp. I smiled again at the older man, who was setting a large, wooden box on the scale as I passed. I grabbed my duffel bag, swung it over one shoulder, and grasped the handle of the wooden radio box that housed the sideband. I began down the ramp, passing Morgan, who was on his way up.

"Jane, we have to weigh this gear."

I let out a long sigh and felt certain steam was coming out of my ears. I turned and smacked into the grey-haired man and his wooden box.

"Sorry," I said.

"We're done weighing things if you need the scale," he said.

I plopped my bag and radio on the scale and felt in my coat pocket for a pen and paper. I recorded the weight, grabbed the gear, and took it down to the dock.

We weighed and hauled all our equipment down the ramp, placing it in a neat pile near Steve's two-oh-six, while Steve and the FBI bomb specialist continued their search. Steve was still in the plane, but the FBI agent was outside, checking the propellers and then the engine.

I sat on my duffel bag, while Morgan stood a few feet away, watching the bomb search. The blue-and-white two-oh-six was gone from its stall, taxiing for takeoff. I watched it break the plane of the water and soar lazily into the sky. I inhaled a deep breath of processed fish and rotting kelp and my brain instantly associated the aroma with the day I had waited for Craig. My mouth went dry and my stomach burned. I put my head between my knees.

"Are you okay?" Morgan moved closer and bent over to look at me.

I swallowed deeply a few times and wiped away the tears running down my cheeks. I didn't look at him when I answered. "I'm sorry," I said. "I don't mean to be such a bitch today. I guess I'm just tense."

Morgan pulled his duffel up beside mine and sat down. He leaned forward, his head near mine. "I understand, Jane, and you haven't been *that* terrible."

I looked into his eyes, only a few inches away. They were iridescent in the sunlight, framed by small wrinkles at the corners. His mouth turned upward into a small grin. I could smell his aftershave.

"Thanks. I'll be better after we get this trip over with."

My attention was diverted by the sound of engines. Morgan and I looked toward the parking lot and saw two large pickup trucks pull up to the top of the ramp. Two men got out of one of the trucks and three out of the other. They began unloading the trucks and hauling gear down to a grey Beaver, the only other plane tied to the float we were on.

A grey van pulled into the parking lot and stopped near the ramp of the adjacent float. Five people climbed from that van, and the noise level of Trident Basin rose.

"We're ready for the gear," Steve called.

I stood and stretched my cramped legs. Morgan walked up to the other FBI agent, and they began talking in hushed tones. I picked up a box and walked to the plane, handing it to Steve, who was standing on the end of the float.

Morgan shook the bomb expert's hand, and the man left. I handed Morgan a box, and he carried it to Steve. I returned for another load, regretting the coffee I'd had to drink that morning.

I handed a duffel bag to Morgan. "Mind if I run up there for a minute?" I pointed toward the portable toilets.

Morgan smiled. "By all means. Steve and I can load this stuff."

I ran up the ramp and stepped into the small, white cubicle. It smelled just as I expected it would, and I held my breath as long as I could. When I exited the toilet, I looked down at the plane; the gear and Morgan were on board.

I began walking quickly toward the ramp. There were five vehicles and several people in the parking lot now, but I paid little attention to any of them as I hurried toward the plane. I had just reached the top of the ramp, when a large hand gripped my arm, jerking me to a stop.

I spun around and tried to yank my arm from his grasp, but he was too strong. My gaze jerked from the oil-encrusted fingernails to the wide, unshaven chin, the greasy, shoulder-length black hair, and the wild, slightly-crooked brown eyes. He breathed chewing tobacco into my face. "So, you're the bitch causing all the trouble."

I tried to pull my face away from his, but when I moved, he applied more pressure to my arm. I didn't know who this man was, but I thought I was dead. He could drag me into a truck and drive away with me, and Morgan never would know what had happened.

"You leave me out of this, you hear?" The wild eyes looked capable of anything, and I didn't doubt he could murder me right then. "I have enough problems, and I ain't done nothin' to you." He put his mouth next to my ear, "But I will if you don't back off."

He shoved me and I fell, whacking my head on the gravel parking lot. I closed my eyes, waiting for the next blow, but when I opened them a few seconds later, he was gone.

I sat and rubbed the back of my head. I'd spent too much time lately on the gravel in this parking lot. I stood and shook my head, trying to clear the dancing black dots from my vision. I walked to the top of the ramp and looked down at the plane. Morgan stood on the float, cupping his hands over his eyes, looking for me. I waved, and he waved back.

I gripped the handrail on the ramp and then turned around to see if I could spot my attacker. I felt as if I were moving in slow motion. *Why hadn't I yelled to Morgan for help?*

People moved in double-time around me, and I gripped the railing tighter as a man brushed past me and sent me reeling.

There he was. My new acquaintance was unloading gear from a black van. I couldn't see his face, but there was no mistaking the hair and physique.

The side of the van faced toward me, and I should have been able to read the large, yellow lettering, but everything was blurred. I blinked my eyes and squinted. "Afognak Logging," I muttered the words as I deciphered them.

I started slowly down the ramp. Morgan was on the dock walking toward me. I had no idea how long I had been standing at the top of the ramp, but apparently it had been long enough to worry Morgan.

"Are you okay? You're not walking straight." Morgan gripped my arm. I leaned against him and he put his arm around me.

"I just met George Wall," I said.

"The guide on probation?" Morgan asked. "He hurt you? Is he still here?"

"Forget it," I said. "He's a bully. Let's just get out of here."

Morgan helped me onto the float and steadied me while I climbed into the right rear passenger seat. He took the front seat next to Steve.

"Your headset is hanging on the back of the seat," Steve yelled to me above the engine noise.

My brain slowly was beginning to clear. I put on the headset, leaned back, and closed my eyes. This day was not starting out well. *How had George Wall known who I was, and how had he known I'd been asking questions about him?*

The blow to the back of my head calmed my fear of flying better than any tranquilizer could. I'd have to remember to thank George Wall. We were half way to Uyak before I began to imagine all the places the bomb could be hidden, and the day was so beautiful that I couldn't manage to work myself into a state of apprehension.

I listened to Morgan and Steve chatter in my headphones. Morgan had a map unfolded on his lap, and Steve pointed out geographical points to him. He told Morgan the story about Port Lions, the Alutiiq village named in honor of Lions Club International, the service group that helped build the village and relocate the survivors of Afognak village after the 1964 tsunami wiped out their homes. Morgan listened with interest and asked Steve several questions about the tsunami and about the history of the Alutiiq people.

The more I was around Morgan, the more the man impressed me. Nothing about the history of the people of Kodiak Island pertained to his case, but he was interested and seemed to want to learn as much as he could about this island while he was here. I wondered if he showed this amount of interest on every assignment or if Kodiak intrigued him. *Perhaps he could be persuaded to relocate here.*

I felt my lips curl. I must have a concussion; I was beginning to hallucinate.

"How are you doing, Jane?" Steve asked.

"Better. Nothing a handful of Excedrin won't cure."

"Jane, do you mind if Steve drops you off first?" Morgan asked.

"Of course not. The fewer landings and takeoffs, the better."

"Can we do that, Steve? I want to get a better look at the area and follow the flight path Bill would have taken that day."

"Sure," Steve said. "I can only guess he made a straight path from Craig's camping site to Uganik Pass."

"Why does it matter?" I asked.

"It probably doesn't," Morgan said, "but it might give me a new perspective."

I didn't understand how it would help to know the flight path, but Morgan was the pro. I would just be happy to get out of the plane and sit on the beach.

I closed my eyes and leaned back when we flew over the crash site. Morgan and Steve were silent, and I knew they must be peering down at the ground.

"This is Spiridon Bay," Steve said a few minutes later.

I sat forward and watched out my window as we flew over one more point of land, and then Steve announced we were now over Uyak Bay. In the shade of the mountains, the water was a deep, murky green, but in the sunlight it was a silvery mirror, reflecting the blue sky.

"It must be hard to land when it's this calm," Morgan said.

"It's no picnic," Steve said. "I'll circle to get a good look at it"

"What's wrong?" I asked. The conditions looked perfect to me. I was finally beginning to relax, but now my stomach tightened again.

"It's okay," Steve said. "Just hard to tell where the water is when it's so calm." Steve turned and smiled at me. "Don't worry, Jane. I've done this a couple of times before."

I smiled at him but didn't release my grip on the seat cushion. I bit my lip and stared out the window until we glided smoothly across the water and Steve turned off the engine.

"Got you here in one piece," he said.

"Sorry, I'm just a little tense."

We glided to the edge of the beach and stopped. Steve and Morgan climbed from the plane, and I saw that at some point, Morgan had pulled on shiny, new hip boots. I looked down at my hiking boots. My hip boots were somewhere in the jumble of gear in the rear of the plane.

Morgan held onto the plane, while Steve climbed back up onto the float. He opened the door and looked in at me.

"My boots," I said.

"That's okay. This is a steep beach," Steve said. "You can jump from the float, and I'll hand your gear to you."

We unloaded my gear in a few minutes.

"You all set?" Steve asked.

"I think so." I suddenly wasn't so sure I wanted to be left alone, but I pushed the thought to the back of my mind.

"Let's have a radio schedule at 6:00 tonight," Morgan said.

I nodded. "I'll have the radio antenna up by then."

Steve leaned his head to one side, studying me. "Call Kodiak Flight Services at any time if you have a problem."

I felt the threat of tears, which made me angry with myself. *Why was I becoming such a marshmallow?*

"Hey, I've got a present for you. I almost forgot." He opened the pilot-side door and reached under the seat. He walked back to the front of the float, carrying a green hat. "One of our new hats. This will keep you from getting sunburned."

I reached for the cap and turned it around in my hands, caressing the corduroy fabric. The white, embroidered logo depicted a floatplane gliding over a mountain, surrounded by the words, "Kodiak Flight Services."

"This is nice," I said. "I like the colors."

Steve's smile faded. "We got those in the mail the day of the accident. I'd just given Bill his before his last flight. After the crash, I didn't want to look at them, but that's stupid. I've got a thousand of them to get rid of."

"Why aren't you wearing one?"

"Nah. I'll stick with my trusty grey one a while longer."

Steve and Morgan turned the plane around, pushed it away from the beach, and then climbed up on the floats and into the cabin. I stood on the beach and watched the plane take off and fly out of sight. Then, I sat on the shale rocks and cried. I'd never felt so alone in my life.

# Chapter Thirteen

I wrestled with the small tent for an hour before I got it secured the way I wanted it. I tied it to three trees and covered it with a waterproof tarp. The weather was beautiful now, but I knew how quickly a raging storm could appear.

I didn't have much gear, and it didn't take long to drag it inside the tent, but I fought with the radio antenna for twenty minutes before I could pick up the voice of the dispatcher at Kodiak Flight Services. Radio signals baffled me. Craig could figure out the proper direction to aim the antenna in a few minutes, but for me, it was trial and error to get it lined up right. I hoped if I could receive Kodiak, I would be able to hear Morgan, but he had a smaller antenna than the stations I was receiving from Kodiak, and radio waves do funny things. I'd have to wait until our schedule at six to know if I needed to make adjustments.

Some researchers carry satellite phones instead of sideband radios into the wilderness, and others take both. I preferred the sideband to the sat phone, because satellite signals are often tough if not impossible to pick up on the heavily wooded mountainous island where I live. Usually, you have to climb up to an open hill or rocky cliff to get a signal. Also, you only can make outgoing calls and not receive incoming messages. With the sideband radio, once the antenna is aligned properly, you have reliable two-way communication any time of the day or night with multiple sources in Kodiak and with other remote camps. I wished now, though, that I'd rented or borrowed a satellite phone as a backup, but things had been so hectic in town that I hadn't thought about it.

I unrolled my rubber mattress and my bedroll on the tarp floor of the tent. The small tent was dome-shaped and was too small for me to stand up straight inside it, so I was left with the two options of kneeling or sitting on my sleeping bag. Neither choice was comfortable, but I didn't plan to spend much time in my tent.

I looked at my watch – 3:00. The tide would be going out for another three hours. Mr. Cycek probably had seen the plane land and wondered why someone was camping here, and I didn't know how much he had heard about the plane crash. It was difficult to believe that anyone on this island could miss that news, but Mr. Cycek kept to himself, and from what I'd heard, he didn't welcome outside news. I hoped my visit wouldn't upset him, but I couldn't very well call ahead. I knew he had a sideband radio, because he'd called for help the night his wife got sick, but he apparently rarely turned it on. Before Craig's collection trip, we tried unsuccessfully several times to contact Cycek by radio. In the end, Craig had to walk down the beach and talk to him, just as I planned to do now.

I pulled on my hip boots and slipped the strap of my camera around my neck. A northerly breeze ruffled the water now, and four puffy, white clouds huddled on the horizon. The sun beat down, but the breeze was cool, and I wrapped my jacket around me.

I wondered if I should have carried my shotgun for bear protection, but lugging the heavy gun only would have put a damper on my stroll. I felt safer in the wilderness than I had the past week in town. I'd take my chances with the bears today.

I played like a child on my way to Cycek's cabin, stopping to inspect tide pool residents and peeking under rocks to see what lived there. I watched a noisy oystercatcher strut along the beach, his long orange bill outstretched. He watched a geyser of water squirt from a buried clam and then stuck his beak into the sand, withdrawing it a moment later with the clam attached. He pried open the clamshell and ate the animal.

I snapped a photo, even though I knew I was too far away for a good shot. I wondered what the PSP level was in the clam the bird had just eaten. Many marine birds have evolved aversions to PSP, either avoiding toxic shellfish or regurgitating the offensive bivalves soon after consumption. I watched the oystercatcher strut and squawk. He seemed to be complaining about something, but I couldn't tell if it was his recent meal. I watched him eat two more clams and then fly away. Perhaps oystercatchers were not susceptible to PSP. I made a mental note to check the literature on this point.

I waded out into the water to edge around a pile of large boulders and surprised a fox that was digging in the beach around the corner. I don't know which one of us was the most frightened. The fox ran into the woods, but I might have too if my reflexes had been faster.

I leaned against one of the rocks and laughed, shaking off the adrenaline rush. I pondered the difference between good and bad fear: the excitement of a roller coaster ride, the thrill of being near wild animals, the terror of having a gun pointed at you, or the dread of being told you have a terminal disease.

I kicked a rock and began walking again. Maybe the last example didn't fit, but I could think of nothing more terrifying than being told I had cancer or some other terminal disease. Once you've seen someone die from a terminal illness, other deaths pale in comparison. The final outcome may be the same, and we'll all die, but I'd just as soon avoid the suffering if I could.

The piercing cry of an eagle brought me back from gloom. I looked up. The bird was perched high in a cottonwood on a cliff above me. I knew his mate and nest must be nearby. They probably had one or two eaglets in the nest by now. I hurried past so I wouldn't disturb him. I thought about snapping a photo, but I resisted the urge to add to my photo collection of small white dots backlit by a bright sky.

I knew I was nearing Mr. Cycek's cabin when I saw the small, wooden dinghy tied to a running line. I walked a few more steps and inhaled a deep breath of fragrant alder smoke. Mr. Cycek must be smoking salmon. I climbed the steep bank and looked down at the white cabin. The small house sat several feet above sea level, but it was blocked from the ocean by a hill. It was not visible from the beach and didn't offer the occupant a view of the ocean, but it was well protected from winter storms, and apparently warmth was more important to Mr. Cycek than an ocean view.

I walked down to a stone path that curved up around the other side of the hill from the beach. I followed the flat stones to the cabin and knocked on the weather-beaten door. There was no answer. I knocked again and waited a few minutes. Then, I followed the smell of the alder smoke around the side of the house to the back. I came to the small smoke shed fifty feet behind the house, but Mr. Cycek was not there. He was behind the smokehouse on his hands and knees, pulling weeds from a garden plot.

"Mr. Cycek?" I hoped I wouldn't give the poor man a heart attack, but he turned slowly and didn't seem surprised to see me standing there.

"Hello." He stood and faced me. "May I help you?"

From my one meeting with Mr. Cycek, I remembered him as a small man with big ears. I realized now that he was not that short. If he could stand straight, he would be at least five-feet-eight-inches tall. Time and a hard life had bent him permanently a few inches shorter. He was thin but not gaunt, more of a wiry leanness that suggested strength. His ears were large and their size was accentuated by the way he wore his tight blue baseball cap.

He squinted at me in the bright sun, adding more and deeper furrows to the wrinkles around his eyes.

I stepped closer. "You probably don't remember me," I said. "My name is Jane Marcus. I met you at the hospital when your wife was sick."

His face brightened into a toothless smile. "Dr. Marcus, I believe it is. I usually don't forget a pretty face, but that wasn't a good night."

"No," I said, "and I'm sorry to trouble you again."

"No bother. I'm ready for a coffee break; won't you join me?"

"Sure," I pointed to the garden. "What are you growing?"

He pulled a handkerchief from the right front pocket of his overalls and wiped his face as he sauntered toward the house. "Lettuce, spinach, bush beans, snap peas, carrots, potatoes, onions, and radishes." He waved his hand in front of his eyes as if swatting at bugs. "More than one old man like me can eat." He shrugged. "But it's a hobby. Keeps me out of trouble."

"The fish smells good," I said.

"Take some home with you. I'll never eat all of it."

He bypassed the back door and walked around the house to the front. He pulled off his muddy boots outside the door, and I followed his example. He opened the door and I trailed him into the house.

I don't know what I expected, but I was surprised by Mr. Cycek's domestic skills. The interior of the cabin was spotless. Everything appeared to be in its place. The floors were swept and scrubbed, the furniture dusted, and even the doilies looked freshly laundered.

My heart ached for this lonely man, trying to resist the change his wife's death had brought. My father had been the same way after my mother died, wanting to freeze time and keep everything the same as if she were still there.

"It will just take me a minute to heat up the coffee. Have a seat." He gestured to a lumpy couch draped with a crocheted slipcover and then turned and walked out of the room.

I took in my surroundings as I lowered myself to the cushion. Everything in the room was handmade, from the cover on the couch, to the needlepoint samplers on the wall, to the painted bookcase stuffed with reading material. I fingered the doily on the willow table in front of me. It was crocheted in beautiful shades of purple, yellow, and rose thread. On top of it sat a framed photograph of a young woman in her twenties. I picked up the photo to examine it. It was black and white and a little blurry. It had been taken a long time ago. The subject wore a light, flowered dress and a wide-brimmed hat. Her dark eyes shined, and her smile was wide. She had a long, graceful neck and shoulder-length black hair.

"Easter 1967," a low voice said.

I looked up. Mr. Cycek was leaning against the door frame between the living room and the kitchen. He had removed his cap and slicked his thin grey hair into place, but he still wore his coveralls.

"She was beautiful," I said, carefully lowering the photo to its place.

"Yes, she was." His voice cracked and he turned abruptly, retreating into the kitchen.

A small wooden table sat near the kitchen door, and when I saw the kerosene lantern on it, I realized that Mr. Cycek must not have a generator. This time of year, that wouldn't be so bad, but I couldn't imagine spending the long winter nights alone here in the dark. *No wonder the books in the bookcase looked so worn.* Over the years, the Cyceks must have reread each one several times.

I stood and walked over to the case. It was six feet long from floor to ceiling and had six shelves. The top three shelves held hardback and large paperback books, neatly arranged side-by-side. On the second shelf down, in front of the books, stood a crude, eight-inch-tall, painted carving of a raven. Warped and stained paperbacks and magazines filled the bottom three shelves, and these had been stacked horizontally and vertically, any way they would fit on the shelf. Great care had been taken to stack the books on the shelves in the neatest way possible.

I now knew who would appreciate my old paperbacks. I hated to part with them, but I was running out of shelf space, too, and my stacking job didn't look as good as Mr. Cycek's. I scanned the titles to see if my taste would interest him. Except for a spy novel, an anthology of Robert Service poems, and two romance books, the hardback books were all nature guides: *Wildflowers of Alaska, Discovering Wild Plants, Edible and Poisonous Plants of Alaska, Gardening in Alaska, Guide to the Birds of Alaska, Eagles, Under Alaskan Seas, The Emerald Sea, Whales of Alaska, The Great Bear Almanac,* and many more. The paperbacks included everything from romance to gothic horror, mysteries, and humor.

"Do you need something to read?"

Mr. Cycek's soft voice startled me. I hoped he didn't think I was snooping.

"You have a better selection of Alaskan wildlife books than the bookstore in town."

He handed me a mug of coffee, and when he smiled, I saw he'd put in his dentures.

"I try to buy a new book every time I go to town, which isn't often." He sipped his coffee and then shook his head. "Books have gotten so expensive. I think they try to discourage people from reading, and everything is digital now."

"Wildlife books filled with glossy photos are especially expensive," I said. I put the cup to my lips, but when I felt the searing steam, I decided to let it cool awhile longer. I settled back on the couch and set the cup on the willow table. "I have several paperbacks at home that I've read. Could I send them out to you?"

"Box 283, Larsen Bay," he said. "I never say no to books."

"You have quite a variety on your shelves. Is there anything you don't read?"

"I don't want any romances. Those were Doris'. I can't stomach those."

I laughed. "No romances, I promise. By the way, I like your raven sculpture. Do you know the artist?"

Mr. Cycek beamed. "That would be me. I dabble in a little carving from time to time."

"It's very nice," I said. "You should do more of it."

Mr. Cycek's cheeks flushed, and he looked down at his coffee cup. I wasn't sure how to approach the subject of the reason for my visit, but Mr. Cycek took care of the problem for me.

He pulled an old wooden armchair from the head of the dining room table across the room and set it on the other side of the willow table from me. He lowered himself into the chair and set his coffee cup on the arm. "Terribly sorry to hear about your associate," he said, looking down at his lap, shaking his head. "Such a nice young man."

*So he did know. Good.* I wouldn't have to tell that story. "I was afraid you hadn't heard," I said, and then a sickening thought occurred to me. "You didn't see or hear it from here, did you?"

"What? The crash? Oh no," he said. "I didn't hear about it until several days later when a fisherman friend of mine stopped by with the salmon I'm smoking." His eyes met mine. "He said the plane blew up. That someone planted a bomb. Is that right?"

I nodded. "I'm afraid so, Mr. Cycek."

"Who would do something like that?"

I sighed. "Everyone from the troopers to the FBI is trying to figure that one out. There were five passengers plus the pilot on the plane. One of the passengers was a U.S. senator. The police think she may have been the target."

He shook his head in long, slow swings. "I know the world is crazy, but I didn't think the insanity would ever reach here; things have gone too far. I never thought I'd live to see something like this." He balanced his coffee cup on the arm of the chair with his left hand while he reached into the front pocket of his coveralls with his right hand, extracting the dirty, white handkerchief. He wiped his eyes and nose and then dropped the handkerchief onto his lap.

I blinked back my own tears and gulped a mouthful of blistering coffee. My first instinct was to spit it out, but I tilted my head back and swallowed. At least the physical pain took my mind off Craig for a moment.

We sat in silence for several minutes. I watched Mr. Cycek's far-off gaze and wondered what he was thinking about. He looked old and fragile as he sat slumped against the wooden frame. *How sad it must be to live alone all the time.* I thought I lived alone, but living by myself in the midst of a community was completely different than Mr. Cycek's existence in the wilderness. If he was sick or having chest pains, there was no one nearby to call for help. There was no one to share in his happiness, and no one to comfort his grief.

"Why are you out here?" His question penetrated my thoughts.

"To take more samples. I don't want you to think we've forgotten about your wife."

He leaned forward. "It's not too late?"

"No. The PSP levels may not be as high as they were when your wife ate the clams, but we will still get very high readings and should be able to confirm the cause of her death."

He sat back. "It doesn't matter, you know. It won't bring her back."

I sipped coffee. It had cooled, but it was still hot enough to sting my blistered mouth. "I know this won't help you," I said. "But maybe some good can come from her death. I'm sure her death has stopped most people on this side of the island from digging and eating clams, at least for a while, and by testing the clams, I hope to develop an easier, quicker method to monitor PSP in the clams and mussels on the beaches around the island."

Mr. Cycek nodded. "I know. I just wish Doris hadn't had to die for all of this."

I sighed and stared at the woven willow table. *This was depressing.*

"I still don't understand why no one checked her stomach contents. They should have measured the PSP from the clams she'd eaten. Maybe she died from natural causes. There might not have been anything wrong with the clams."

Why her stomach contents had not been tested was a subject I didn't want to talk about. It involved negligence and incompetence in two separate laboratories, and I didn't understand how it had happened, either. I needed to be diplomatic, though, so I thought about my answer.

"I believe Doris died from PSP, and the lab should have tested your wife's stomach contents," I said. "There was a mix-up, but I'd still be here taking samples even if we had tested the digested clams from Doris' stomach. The level of saxitoxin in digested clams is not the same as it was before they were eaten, and I need to test the level in live tissue. Does that make sense?"

I was not certain Mr. Cycek understood or believed much of what I said. In truth, a contaminated sample of Doris Cycek's stomach contents had been tested, and the PSP levels were as high as any ever recorded. The problem was that even though an autopsy had been performed on Mrs. Cycek's body, her stomach contents had not been sealed properly in a sterile container. While this was an unfortunate oversight, I didn't consider it significant. The unsterile sample could affect the quantitative but not the qualitative results. In other words, if the lab in Palmer tested a high level of saxitoxin in her stomach contents, we could be certain Mrs. Cycek died from PSP.

Unfortunately, the comedy of errors continued when the sample reached the Palmer lab, where a new technician working on the weekend did something wrong. What he did, I never would know, but it must have been a serious error, because the Alaska Department of Environmental Conservation admitted the problem and fired the technician. I was told the toxicity of the sample tested extremely high, but that the sample had been contaminated, and the lab did not consider the result official. This meant the mouse died from something, but the lab would not say it was PSP. No one would sign off on the official cause of Mrs. Cycek's death, but if I found toxic levels of PSP in the clams on the beach from where Mrs. Cycek's last meal came, then everyone concerned would agree that was how she died.

I thought it was easier to let Mr. Cycek think Doris' stomach contents never had been tested. He did not know that I had good reason to believe she had died from a concentration of saxitoxin two hundred times the lethal limit. She was dead, and that was all that mattered to him.

"I see," Mr. Cycek said. "You're welcome to stay with me while you dig your samples." A grin spread across his face. "I don't suppose though that a pretty young woman like you would want to stay in a cabin with an ugly old man."

I laughed. "Thank you, Mr. Cycek. I haven't been called pretty or young in a very long time, and while I appreciate your offer, I've already set up my camp about a mile down the beach."

"Tomorrow's the Fourth of July," Mr. Cycek said, and from the tone of his voice, I couldn't tell whether it was a statement or a question.

"Independence Day," I nodded my head.

"You shouldn't spend it alone. Would you be my guest for dinner?"

"I'd be honored," and I was. I doubted Mr. Cycek invited many people to dinner, and I knew by the following evening I would be bored with my own company and sick of lunch meat sandwiches.

Mr. Cycek beamed when I accepted his invitation. "How does 5:00 sound?"

"Perfect." I made a mental note to tell Morgan I would not make radio schedule the following evening.

I swallowed the rest of my coffee and stood. Mr. Cycek also stood and took the cup from my hand. "Do you need help digging the clams in the morning?" he asked.

"No," I said, "but I would like you to confirm, as near as you can remember, where Mrs. Cycek dug the clams."

Mr. Cycek's gaze dropped to the floor. "I dug the clams for her," he said. "She had arthritis in her back and couldn't do things like that anymore, so she asked me to do it."

I patted Mr. Cycek's arm. The poor man must feel as if he murdered his wife.

"Let me put the cups in the kitchen," he said, "and then I'll walk outside with you."

Mr. Cycek pulled his cap on his head, and I followed him out the front door and down the path to the beach. We discussed the recent storm and the perfect weather of the last few days. A cold breeze blew off the ocean, and I pulled my jacket around me.

"Do you ever get tired of living out here?" I asked.

"Never!" Mr. Cycek shouted his reply. "I've lived in this cabin thirty-three years, and I'll stay here until I die."

"It's beautiful out here, but I think I'd get lonely."

"Young folks these days aren't used to solitude," Mr. Cycek said. "You don't know how to be alone with your own thoughts."

I considered arguing this point with him, but perhaps he was right, or maybe I just liked being called a young person.

We walked around the rocky point north of the Cycek cabin. The tide was a foot lower than it had been when I'd walked to the cabin. Earlier I'd had to wade around this point, but now there was a stretch of beach between the rocks and the water.

As soon as we rounded the point, Mr. Cycek pointed to a flat, muddy, intertidal area in front of us. "We always get our clams right here," he said.

"Okay," I said. "Do you remember how low the tide was when you dug the clams?"

"Let's see." He rubbed his forehead. "It was a minus four something, and I started digging about a half-hour before low tide."

"Did you dig near the water's edge?"

"Mostly, yes." He shrugged. "As well as I can remember."

I smiled. "Thanks Mr. Cycek, and thanks for the coffee."

Mr. Cycek smiled. "Don't forget, 5:00 tomorrow."

"I won't." I waved and watched him walk around the point, and then I squatted on the beach and studied the area where I'd be digging my samples.

The next morning's low tide would be a minus five point one at 7:10. I would need to get down here by 6:00, set up a quick transect, and collect samples from the low tide mark up the beach to the top of the clam population. Since tomorrow's tide was lower than the next morning's tide, I would concentrate my efforts on the lower portion of the beach tomorrow and work on the upper beach the next day.

I wondered if this was how Craig had done it. I had trusted his scientific approach so completely that I had left the methodology up to him, telling him only to keep exact records. During our last radio conversation, the night before his death, he had assured me that his notes were a thing of beauty. Unfortunately, the notes, like the samples and Craig, had been blown to bits. I could collect new samples and write a lifetime of notes, but I never could replace Craig. He was bright, self-motivated, charismatic, and honest. He had been too good for this world, where people murder each other for greed, jealousy, and revenge.

I walked slowly back to my campsite, my head bent against the chilly wind. I pushed depressing and frightening thoughts from my mind and concentrated on work. I planned my morning, reviewing each piece of equipment I would need to haul down the beach with me. Since my collection time was limited by the tide, I would collect, bag, and label the clams, and then, when the tide was too high to dig, I'd shuck each clam and pack the samples on dry ice.

I decided to shuck the clams at my campsite, even though that would mean lugging the clamshells a mile down the beach. The clams still would be alive until I shucked them, and I wanted to put the live tissue on ice as quickly as possible.

I planned to organize my gear and put it in my pack as soon as I reached the tent, but when I climbed over the berm at the top of the beach and out of the wind, the warm sun anesthetized me. I spread out my coat and lay down on the rocks, turning my face toward the sun's rays. I stayed like that for twenty minutes, drifting in and out of sleep, feeling at peace for the first time in several days.

A fly landed on my nose, and when I brushed it away, I felt the heat rising from my skin. I didn't want to move, because the sun felt so good. I tried putting my hands over my face, but that position was uncomfortable and suffocating. I pushed myself into a sitting position and then remembered the cap Steve had given me. I got stiffly to my feet and walked to the tent. The cap was just inside, propped on my pack.

I picked it up and turned it around. I didn't often wear this type of hat, but this was a good-looking cap. As I held it in the sunlight, I saw that it was more teal than green, and the embroidery thread was cream-colored. I shivered and popped the cap on my head so I wouldn't have to look at it. I wished Steve hadn't told me that these caps had arrived on the day of the crash and that Bill had worn one on his final flight. I felt as Steve did. This cap would end up in the back of my closet, because I wouldn't be able to bear the memories it evoked each time I looked at it.

I edged past a large cow parsnip plant, or pushki as it was called locally; the sap of that plant could make my life miserable for weeks. I learned my first summer on the island that I was extremely allergic to it, and simply grabbing the stalk would burn my hands and leave my fingers covered with pus-filled blisters that would take weeks to heal. I'd seen Dana once with a blistered cheek, and she'd told me she had sliced a pushki plant while using her weed eater, and the sap had squirted her in the face. The plant had my respect.

I sat on my jacket and looked around me at the plants and wildflowers. I knew so little about the plants of this island. Pushki had caught my attention, and I knew wild geraniums, chocolate lilies, bluebells, and the beautiful, poisonous monkshood. I could also point out a rose bush as long as there were roses on it. Without the flowers, though, I could not distinguish a rose bush from a salmonberry bush. I should have borrowed one of Mr. Cycek's wild-plant books. Instead of sleeping, I could have spent the afternoon learning about my environment.

I stretched out and pulled the bill of the cap over my face. The lapping ocean lulled me to sleep, and forty minutes later, the harsh call of a raven woke me like an alarm clock.

I sat up, startled, and then remembered where I was. My head and shoulders were in the shade now, and I felt chilled. I slid into my jacket and leaned my head onto my bent knees. I felt drugged by too much sunlight and fresh air. I pulled the cap from my head and ran my fingers through my hair. When I finally sat up and opened my eyes, I was staring at the cap.

I jumped to my feet and dropped the hat as if it were on fire. *What was wrong with me? Why had it taken me so long to realize the significance of the cap?* Had Morgan pieced it together?

I looked at my watch – 5:30. I had radio schedule with Morgan in half an hour.

The tranquility of the afternoon was shattered. My stomach vibrated, and my mind and feet paced. I'd wanted to get away from everything, but now I felt helpless. I pulled a sandwich from my pack and tried to eat it, but it tasted like rubber and warm mayonnaise. After two bites, I wrapped it up and stuffed it back into the pack.

At 5:45, I turned on the sideband radio to let it warm up. I faintly heard someone on a boat trying to call one of the charter plane services in town. They must have answered him, because I picked out bits and pieces of his end of the conversation, but I couldn't hear Kodiak. I remembered that hot, sunny days did not provide ideal radio conditions.

I left the tent and walked down to the beach. *What would I do if I couldn't talk to Morgan? I'd never make it through the night if I couldn't share my thoughts with him.* I ordered myself to calm down and then climbed back up the beach into the tent and sat on my sleeping bag next to the radio. I heard nothing but static for the next several minutes, and was about to try Morgan when I heard his voice, a bit muffled but loud.

"KVT04 this is WXT890. How do you read?"

"WXT890. I've got you fine. How 'bout me?"

"Loud and clear. How's it going?" Morgan asked.

"I have my tent up, and I'm ready to start my collections in the morning."

"Sounds good. I didn't find much today, but I'll try again tomorrow.

"Are you planning to spend tomorrow night there, too?" For some reason, I felt safer knowing that Morgan was camped a few miles away, even if he only could reach me by airplane.

"I have a tentative schedule to be picked up at 4:00 tomorrow afternoon. Unless I find some reason to stay here longer, I'll fly back then."

"I thought of something that might be important," I said. I didn't have a powerful antenna, and the radio reception was poor right now, but I had to assume that anyone on the island with a sideband radio could hear me. I'd been thinking for the last several minutes about how to word my explanation.

"Maryann thought Bill looked good in his teal cap." I paused, giving Morgan a moment to pick up on my meaning. "Bill didn't have the cap until right before the flight."

My radio hissed static but nothing else. I thought I'd lost Morgan. "WXT890, are you there?" I shouted into the microphone.

"Sorry, Jane. I was thinking," Morgan said. "You're right. Good catch. I'll check into that when I get back to town tomorrow."

I wanted him to question Maryann Myers immediately, but Morgan was right, he could do nothing until he got to town.

"Do you want to set up a radio schedule for tomorrow?" I asked.

"Yes. How about 3:00? By then I'll know whether or not I plan to spend another night."

"I have a dinner date with Mr. Cycek, but I'll be here at 3:00."

"I'm glad you can work it into your schedule." I could picture Morgan's smile. "You're the only person I know who needs a social calendar when you go camping."

"Don't invite any bears into your tent," I said. "KVT04 clear."

"WXT890."

I listened to the hiss of the radio for a few minutes and then turned it off, suddenly feeling very alone. The peaceful serenity I'd enjoyed a few hours earlier now felt like isolation. I'd become a prisoner instead of an escapee.

I forced myself to go to work and get my gear ready for the following day. I first took everything out of my pack, and then stuffed the folded army shovel, collection bags, garbage bags, a pocket knife, stakes, rope, my notebook, a pencil, a sandwich, and a can of pop into the pack. My project was as simple as field work ever got, but I didn't want to hike a mile down the beach just to find I'd forgotten something essential. The tide wouldn't wait for me to run back to my tent to grab the missing piece of equipment.

Once my pack was ready, I set my watch alarm for 5:30. It would be light enough to see by then, and I could begin hiking to my collection spot.

I walked down to the beach and strolled in the opposite direction from Mr. Cycek's cabin. The tide was low now and soon would be coming in. I had to be careful not to walk too far, or I would get stranded by the rising tide and be forced to climb the bank and hike back through the thick jungle-like growth of the woods. I had no desire to hike by myself through head-high weeds in bear country.

I wasn't looking forward to the night. Darkness only lasted a few hours this time of year, but I knew I'd have trouble sleeping during those hours. It took a few nights to get used to wilderness sounds, to realize that every thump was not a bear five feet from your tent, and that you probably would survive the night.

I crouched on the beach and watched a seiner on the horizon. The wind had calmed to a light breeze, and mosquitos buzzed around my face.

"Mosquito repellent," I said. "That's what I forgot." I stood and walked back to my tent.

The night was as bad as I expected. I tried to read, but I soon felt groggy. I put down the book and fell asleep for two hours. When I woke, the light had faded, and the dusk was muffled further by the fabric of the tent. I fumbled beside my sleeping bag until my hand closed around the cool plastic grip of my flashlight. I clicked on the beam and directed it at my watch. It was 10:30.

I'd placed the shotgun near the tent flap. I got it now and put it under the edge of the sleeping bag. I crawled back into the bag, closed my eyes, and hoped for slumber, but the noises outside the tent increased in proportion to the dimming light.

I knew not to let my imagination roam, but my logic couldn't rein it in. Usually when I camped, I imagined bears ripping apart my tent and then me, but tonight, marauding terrorists, not wild animals, topped my creature list.

*What if someone had followed me from town, hired a plane, and had the pilot drop him a few miles from my campsite?* "And why would anyone do that?" I asked myself out loud, but I couldn't guess what had precipitated any of the violent acts that recently had touched my life. I knew I was safer sleeping here than in my apartment.

I thought about Jack Justin. He had been so terrified the last time I'd seen him, and rightfully so, as it turned out. *Had he been involved in the death of his own parents? Why not?* He wouldn't be the first offspring to do away with his mother and father, and the guy was cold and manipulative. He didn't seem to mourn the loss of his parents. He'd only been concerned about the briefcase. No, concerned was too light a word. He'd been obsessed with the briefcase; crazed to the point of believing that I had taken it. Then, when his life was in danger, he apparently had given my name to his killers. I chuckled to myself. My evening out with Jack Justin had not been one of my better dates

I heard a twig crack and pushed the sleeping bag away from my face. How could I joke about Jack Justin? The guy had been brutally murdered. *Too little sleep.* I was beginning to feel giddy.

If Jack had told me any part of the truth, he only wanted the briefcase to give to the terrorists who had bombed the airplane. I hadn't believed him, but now I didn't know. Someone very bad had killed him, and someone with a great deal of knowledge about bombs had blown up the marine center. Had this same person or group of people planted the bomb on the Beaver? I couldn't work out another answer, and I wished I had been able to talk to Morgan more about his two-separate-bomber hypothesis.

When I cleared my mind, I could hear the faint lapping of waves against the shore. I concentrated on the ocean and tried to sleep, but before I knew it, my brain was flashing facts about the Beaver bombing.

If I discounted everything that happened after the plane exploded, I still found the terrorist theory weak. The bomb was a simple, homemade job, probably several sticks of dynamite wired to an alarm clock trigger. Such a device would be the more likely weapon of an individual with limited knowledge and access to explosives. A group of terrorists would use a more finely-honed instrument that was both reliable and could avoid detection. *Wouldn't they*? Maybe I'd seen too many James Bond movies.

The second obstacle I had, even though it didn't seem to bother Morgan, was that terrorists from somewhere other than Kodiak would not be familiar with the way Kodiak Flight Services operated. Granted, the small charter company was not a top-secret organization, but certainly a stranger would have to ask at least one question to know which plane would be used for a particular flight. None of the employees of Kodiak Flight Services remembered a stranger asking any questions about which plane would be used for the Justins' flight. Even if the terrorists were invisible and could avoid detection, how would they know where to plant their explosive bundle?

Problem three I had with the terrorist theory was that if the briefcase was so important, why in blazes would they blow it up? Did they not know the Justins had it with them on the plane? Did they hope to kill the Justins and then steal the briefcase from their hotel room? I propped my hands under my head and wondered if I ever would know the answers to all my questions.

I didn't believe that the man with the accent who had called me was still in Kodiak, because if he was still on the island and wanted to find me, he would have succeeded. I hoped I finally had convinced him I did not have what he was after. I wanted the man and his associates caught and punished for their crimes, but I wanted even more never to meet him face-to-face. I'd choose a keen sense of survival over bravery any day.

I stretched and turned over on my stomach. My thoughts began to wander, and I was fading into sleep, when I heard small, scampering feet. I twisted around in my bag and groped for the flashlight. The rapid ticking continued as I fumbled for the button and switched on the beam. I spotlighted the tiny noise-maker, and once I steadied my breathing, I laughed as the small vole fought for traction on the slippery, plastic tarp floor of the tent. Caught in the spotlight, the bucktoothed little creature looked like a cartoon tap dancer. His poor little heart must have been fluttering as he tried to figure out what he'd stumbled into. I clicked off the flashlight and let him continue to safety. I sank back into my bag, but the more I thought about the vole, the harder I laughed. The release of tension felt great.

I wiped the tears of laughter from my eyes and once again turned my attention to sleep. I could make a case for Toni Hunt, George Wall, or Maryann Myers as the mad plane bomber. Maryann Myers seemed the most stable and least prone to violence of the three, but she had lied to us about knowing which plane would be used for her husband's flight. *If she was innocent, why lie? Toni Hunt was psychotic, but would she kill her boyfriend?* I didn't know her well enough to answer that question.

I'd only met Mr. Wall once, but that one meeting had impressed me. I believed he was capable of killing five people, and he knew how to make a crude bomb. He admittedly hated Dick Simms and had access to the dock. *How did he know Simms would be on that plane?* The problem always came back to that question. Toni Hunt knew her boyfriend would be flying that plane, and Maryann Myers knew her husband would be a passenger on that plane. Either of them could have handed Bill the fatal package, and he wouldn't have been suspicious. Toni Hunt's black room was the last image in my mind when I finally fell asleep.

# Chapter Fourteen

I awoke slowly from a deep sleep and fumbled to turn off the alarm on my watch. I unzipped the sleeping bag and shivered as I reached for my jacket and pulled it around me. I clicked on the flashlight and stood, hunched over in the small tent. I shuffled toward the tent flap and untied it. It was lighter out than I expected. The sky again was cloudless and the air still.

I wandered a few feet from the tent and relieved my bladder. The lack of a bathroom was one thing I hated about camping, although, I missed a shower more than a toilet, and on this trip, I hadn't even brought a stove to heat water. That meant no shower and no coffee. I'd survive, but it wouldn't be pleasant.

I glanced at my watch. It was 5:10. I had just enough time for a sandwich and a Diet Pepsi. I forced down the mushy bread and meat, shouldered my backpack, and hiked down to the edge of the cliff above the beach. If I ignored the small bugs buzzing around my face, the morning was perfect. The sweet fragrance of wild roses mingled with the salt air, and chirping birds and the far-off rumble of a boat engine were the only sounds I heard. A bald eagle swooped down and plucked his breakfast, a four-pound salmon, from the ocean. He landed on the beach and began tearing the fish apart. I didn't want to disturb him, so I walked several feet along the cliff before descending to the beach.

Wildlife is abundant when you don't have a camera or the time to photograph it. Two does and four fawns walked to within thirty feet of me before they detected possible danger and angled up the bank. I slowed my pace as they approached, expecting them to see me and bolt at any moment, and I finally stopped and watched them strut toward me. I cursed myself for not having my camera accessible. I had it with me, packed in the zippered pouch on my pack, but I knew I would spook the deer by the time I removed the pack and unzipped the pocket.

The fawns were tiny, with big white spots covering their golden bodies, and their large brown eyes trained on their mothers' hooves. When the two does began climbing the bank, the fawns looked bewildered, heads turning in every direction to locate the source of their mothers' concern. They didn't seem to see me, but after only a moment's hesitation, they followed the does at a leisurely pace.

I also saw six foxes on my walk, but they were all a long ways off. The tide would be forty-five minutes later tomorrow, so I could afford a more leisurely pace and stop to snap a few photos.

I reached my destination and set up my crude rope grid. If I'd been about to perform a population-density study, my grid would not have been adequate. My only goal, though, was to gather a random sampling of clams, and with the grid, I wouldn't have to depend on my memory and holes in the sand to know where I had dug. My memory was faulty, and holes disappeared when the tide rose. I'd drawn a replica of the grid in my notebook, numbering the squares, and planned to mark each square with an X when I gathered my samples from that plot. I would drop each bivalve I collected into a collection bag and write the home plot number on the bag. I got my gear ready, assembled the shovel, and went to work.

I began digging at 6:30, and by 8:30, my lower back muscles screeched at me to stop. I looked at my pile of sample bags and checked the grid in my notebook. I was well over half done. I could finish the rest the following morning. I carefully layered the samples in my pack and groaned when I lifted it onto my back. I slid my notebook and extra sample bags into the pack, but carried the shovel so I wouldn't smash the delicate bivalves.

I'd collected three species of clams, as well as cockles and mussels. Mr. Cycek reported that his wife had eaten steamers and butter clams, so those two species were my primary interest. However, I knew that certain species of bivalves concentrated the deadly saxitoxin much quicker and to a greater degree than other species, and I hoped someday to study this phenomenon. For now, I just collected the data.

I spurted breath in short, shallow gasps when I climbed the bank to my tent. I nearly dropped my pack to the ground, but then remembered the fragile contents. I eased it off my shoulders and lowered it like a case of eggs. Then, I plopped beside it and squeezed my back muscles. My shirt was soaked through with sweat. I unzipped my coat and tossed it into the tent. I remembered why I hired strong, young college students for this work.

I closed my eyes and nearly succumbed to the heavy swirl of fatigue. Sleep would have been so easy, but I had work to do first. I sat and shook my head. I pulled each collection bag from my pack, removed the clam from the bag, carefully sliced the adductor muscles holding the shells shut, removed the tissue from the shells, re-bagged and labeled the tissue, and placed the bag on top of the dry ice in the Styrofoam cooler. After all the clams had been shucked, I set the cooler inside the tent and stretched out on my sleeping bag. I awoke shivering a half-hour later and crawled into the bag.

I began to drift to sleep again when the low rumble of an airplane engine passed overhead. I knew the plane was headed for Larsen Bay, but the sound made me edgy, and I shed the cloak of fatigue, blinking rapidly to clear my head and sharpen my senses. I crawled out of the bag and tried to eat another sandwich, but one bite was all I could stand. I got my camera and walked to the edge of the bank.

The tide was coming in now, and by 1:00, the water would be nearly to the top of the bank. A beach walk was out of the question, and I decided instead to take a short hike through the woods. I could practice with the macro adjustment on my camera lens and shoot a few photos of wildflowers and bumblebees.

I dug work gloves out of a side pocket of my pack, not wishing accidentally to brush my bare skin against a pushki plant. I walked along the bank, where the vegetation was sparse. My goal was to avoid pushki and bears, especially the latter.

I knelt by a wild geranium, zooming in my camera lens on the pale violet flower. I snapped three photos of it and walked a few paces further. I photographed wild roses, forget-me-nots, lupine and a small, delicate white flower whose name I did not know. I spent several minutes photographing a large monkshood plant, examining its narrow stem and five, navy blue, helmet-shaped flowers. It was beautiful, but deadly. I'd learned from the Alutiiq Cultural Center in town that hundreds of years ago, the natives of Kodiak distilled the sap of monkshood plants and rubbed the poison on their spear tips before a whale hunt. The poison was so potent, it could bring down a large whale. The plant contains the alkaloid aconitine, and as few as three grains of the root can kill a large man.

I backed away from the plant and wondered why I found nature's toxins so intriguing. Monkshood was not the only deadly plant on the island. Baneberry and water hemlock also grew here. Baneberry I could identify from the bright red or white berries on the plant, but water hemlock closely resembled wild celery, and I would not trust myself to differentiate between the two.

I climbed a steep hill, staying near the edge on a game trail. I walked out onto a grassy knoll at the top and emitted a squeak of pleasure as I devoured the view. I was a hundred feet above the ocean, and below me, the ground fell away in a sheer cliff with small, choppy waves lapping at its base. I faced the mouth of Uyak Bay and could see the end of the earth, beyond Shelikof Straight to the snow-capped mountains on the Alaska Peninsula. Not a cloud blotted my view, and the air was clear, free of the volcanic ash that often blows across from the mainland with a westerly wind.

I found a sunny spot and sat, trying to remember the last time I felt this good. The danger and grief of the past week diminished. The apprehension I'd felt upon awakening in my tent less than an hour earlier was gone. I was able to put everything except Craig's death aside for a while.

I smiled, but tears trickled down my cheeks. No one would have appreciated this moment, this piece of paradise, more than Craig, because nothing passed by him unnoticed. While I concentrated on work, he pointed out trees, flowers, and colorful starfish. He would have known the name of the small, white flower I'd photographed.

*I really missed him. Why did someone as special as Craig have to die?* I braced my head between my knees and sobbed. Then, I lay back in the grass and slept for two hours.

My eyes opened, but I didn't move. Panic coursed through me. Brush crashed inches away from my head. *What had I been thinking?* I hadn't even brought my rifle with me. There were three woofing noises, a popping sound, and then more crashing brush. I willed myself to lie still, but I couldn't do it. I sat and looked behind me. A big, brown, furry butt was disappearing into the woods. The fur jostled from side to side as the big animal ran from something that had smelled like danger. I'm grateful he hadn't figured out how helpless I was and hadn't decided to see how well I bounced down a cliff.

I pulled my knees to my chest and allowed myself to breathe. Adrenaline surged through me, and every instinct screamed, *flee!* The bear, however, had galloped down the game trail I'd followed to the top of the cliff, and I knew it would be wise to give him some lead time. I hoped I'd smelled so repulsive that he'd run for several miles before he stopped.

I laughed, but when I released my knees, I saw that my hands were trembling. I closed my eyes, leaned my head back, and sucked in air, but then a terrible thought hit me: *What if the bear stopped at my tent? He could tear everything to shreds with just a few swipes of his paw.*

I stood, grabbed my camera, and rushed down the trail, listening for cracking brush, but focusing my eyes on the uneven ground and gnarled vegetation. Fear pulsed through me, but I gritted my teeth to hold it at bay. Sweat ran down my back and stomach. I tripped over a fallen branch once, but caught myself before I fell. I didn't hear the bear, and I didn't look for him. I was so convinced that my campsite would be destroyed that when I burst through a clump of alders and stood a few feet in front of the small blue tent, I sagged to the ground, panting hard. The bear had not been here, or if he had, my things hadn't interested him.

All I wanted to do was climb in my sleeping bag and stay there until morning, but Mr. Cycek was counting on me for dinner. I thought about trying to raise him on the radio, but dismissed the idea. I really didn't want to sit alone in my tent from now until dark, and I planned to walk on the beach to Cycek's so as not to surprise any bears. I knew I'd frightened the bear as badly as he had frightened me, so I doubted he would return to this area soon. *Get a grip*, I told myself. *There are thirty-five-hundred bears on this island. You're bound to see one once in a while.*

I checked my watch – 2:00. One hour until my schedule with Morgan. I went into the tent and sat on my sleeping bag, too wired to sleep or read, and I doubted I would sleep again until I returned to town. Then, I remembered the man's voice on the telephone, and wondered if I ever would be able to sleep again. *Maybe I should accept Peter's offer and take a long vacation.*

I replayed the bear encounter in my mind and told myself that the episode should make me feel more and not less secure in the wilderness. I'd been asleep and quiet, but when the bear sensed my presence, he fled. Bears weren't going to bother me here. I was safe. So why were my fingers quaking, and why did my stomach feel queasy?

I knew I needed to hire another assistant; camping alone in the wilderness was not for me. I considered field work the least attractive side of my profession. Most fish and wildlife biologists choose this field of study because they love the outdoors; lab work and publications were the necessary evils. I was an anomaly, and I thought this gave me an advantage. I sought out lab jobs, while other fish biologists only wanted field positions.

I knew how to operate an outboard, shoot a shotgun, and set up a tent, but I never felt secure on the ocean or in the woods. If the outboard quit running, I could change the spark plugs, but there my expertise ended. If I had to shoot the shotgun to protect myself, would I, and would my shot be accurate? I didn't know, and I hoped I never would find out. Craig had been good at all things outdoor. He knew outboards and guns and was confident with both. I hated the thought of searching for a new assistant.

My mind drifted from Craig to the explosion, and then to the device that caused the explosion. *What had happened that day?* Morgan believed the bomb had been nothing more than several sticks of dynamite hooked to a timer. I couldn't remember ever seeing a stick of dynamite, but I had seen Westerns where the bad guys blew the bank vault with a bundle of the long red sticks. *How many of those sticks would it take to explode an airplane?* Surely several to inflict the carnage I had seen at the crash site.

*So, how could a bundle of dynamite have been slipped onto the plane without the pilot's knowledge? It couldn't.* Bill must have believed the dynamite was something else, a legitimate parcel to load on his plane. *Did that mean he knew the person who had planted the bomb?* I reclined onto the sleeping bag while I pondered the question. *Not necessarily.* If a stranger walked down the dock, handed Bill a box, and told him the package was for someone at Uyak Cannery, Bill probably wouldn't have doubted him or inspected the box. As long as he had room on the plane, he would have flown the box to the cannery.

I rubbed my forehead. This line of reasoning brought me back to the same two questions: How would a stranger know Bill was flying to Uyak Cannery, and how would a stranger know who Bill's other passengers would be?

If Toni Hunt wanted to kill her boyfriend, though, the scenario played easier. All she would have had to do was wrap up the dynamite, put a bow on it, and tell Bill not to open the gift until later.

Maryann Myers had been at the dock that day and knew that in two or three hours her estranged husband would be a passenger on that plane. "Take this box to the cannery," she could have said, and Bill would have stuffed it in the back of the plane.

The gap in my logic smacked me in the face. Any parcel sent to Uyak Cannery would have been offloaded at the cannery. The bomb hadn't exploded until Bill and his passengers were flying back to town. Maybe Bill had forgotten to unload the offensive package and it was meant to explode somewhere else. I didn't think this likely though, so that left two choices: Either the dynamite had been hidden from Bill's view, or Toni Hunt was the bomber. The only freight going back to town should have been Bill's personal gear and the luggage of the passengers.

"Oh my …!" I said aloud and sat up. *What if the bomb was put on the plane somewhere other than Kodiak? Perhaps someone at Uyak Cannery sent a surprise package with Darren Myers. Had Morgan examined this possibility?* The more I thought about it, I warmed to the idea. Darren Myers ran Uyak Cannery, and a boss is bound to foster some resentment in his employees.

I glanced at my watch. It was 2:50. I considered how I would word my thoughts when I talked to Morgan on the radio. Discretion was imperative.

I turned on the sideband to let it warm up. At 2:59, Morgan's voice crackled through the speaker. "KVT04, this is WXT890."

"WXT890, KVT04. You're weak, but I can read you," I said.

"Happy Fourth of July. How did your collecting go?"

"Fine," I said. "How did you do?"

"No luck. I've made plans to fly back to town this evening. I'm needed there."

My throat tightened. Whether Morgan was twenty or a hundred miles away made little difference in the wilderness, but I felt safer knowing he was nearby and I could contact him by radio. He must have read my mind.

"Have you talked to Kodiak? Is your radio signal strong enough?" he asked.

"I should be able to."

"Are you still planning to go to Mr. Cycek's for supper?"

"Roger. I'll head that way in a few minutes."

"Let's set up a schedule for 10:00 tonight. Will you be back to your tent by then?"

"Roger." I hoped to return to my campsite hours before then. Mr. Cycek was a nice old man, but a couple of hours of melancholy stories about his late wife were all I could handle.

"I'll use Kodiak Flight Services' radio. Stand by from 10:00 to 10:30."

"Roger," I said again. "If the reception is down, though, you may not be able to hear me."

"I understand."

"Nick." I squeezed the mike and spoke loudly into it. I didn't want to repeat myself, and I hoped Morgan would understand what I was saying. "Have you considered that the package could have been put on the plane at one of the stops instead of in Kodiak?"

"Roger." There was a pause. "Which stop do you think the most likely?"

"The cannery," I said. I thought it was the only possibility, and I wondered what Morgan was thinking.

"We're looking into it," he said.

"That's all I have then. I'll stand by tonight and see you tomorrow."

"Okay. Have a good evening. This is WXT890, clear."

"KVT04."

I switched off the radio and sat for a minute, still clutching the mike in my hand. I felt empty and alone. I wished more than anything that Morgan was here, that we could discuss the case, that I could feel safe in the presence of a strong man.

"What," I said, and dropped the mike by the radio. *Since when was I such a wimp? Since when did I need a man to take care of me? Men were like drugs; they made you weak and dependent.* Better to leave them alone and depend on yourself.

I changed into a clean shirt and wiped my face and hands with moist towelettes. I combed my hair and pulled it away from my face in a ponytail. I didn't think Mr. Cycek would notice my lack of makeup. As long as my hands were clean, and I didn't smell too bad, I should pass general muster.

I pulled on my boots and hoisted the twelve gauge on my shoulder. This time, I would be ready for any surprises. I knew I had three shells in the magazine, and I dropped three more into my pocket.

I walked to the cliff and looked down at the beach. The tide was at its mid-point, but there was plenty of walking room on the beach. I would have to wade around a few of the rock outcroppings, but I thought I could make it to Cycek's without having to find a trail through the woods. As I stood staring at the beach, I heard a loud squawk above me. I swiveled my gaze upward to the large, sleek, black bird sitting in the cottonwood.

"You stay out of my tent," I said. I hoped I had tied the flap tightly enough to keep this guy out.

"Auuk," he replied, and we stared at each other for a moment. Was this the raven Craig had told me about in his last radio broadcast? Was this the guy who had been giving him trouble?

"Did you meet my friend Craig?"

The black feet tapped back and forth on the branch limb, and it occurred to me that this bird was possibly one of the last living creatures to see Craig alive. *If only he could talk.*

I tried to shed my gloom on the walk to Cycek's. A slight breeze ruffled the water, not enough wind to chill me, but enough to keep the bugs out of my face. I inhaled a fruity, salty breath, a mix of ocean, wildflowers, alders, and cottonwoods, and marveled that my sinuses hadn't objected to all the pollen.

The shotgun felt heavy on my shoulder, but I welcomed the weight and the secure feeling it offered. I didn't like guns. I wasn't good with them, and I didn't feel comfortable around them. On my first field trip, two weeks after I started my job at the marine center, I told Peter I wasn't taking a shotgun with me. He'd replied that only a fool camped on Kodiak Island without a firearm. He was right, and many hours of target practice later, here I was with a gun I knew how to load, shoot, and clean. The question was, would I shoot it if I had to? Craig had assured me when I confessed my doubts to him that I would shoot the gun without hesitation to protect my life.

"You won't even think about it," he'd said. "If you know your weapon, you will instinctively use it when you need to."

I wanted to believe him, but I had doubts, not only about my marksmanship, but about my ability to judge when killing an animal or a man was the only option left to me.

I waded around a large pile of rocks and was surprised to see smoke curling in the air on the cliff above me. I'd been so engrossed in my thoughts that I hadn't realized I was nearing Mr. Cycek's cabin.

I walked up the steep path and knocked on the door. A few moments later, the door swung open and I was embraced by the warm fragrance of a busy kitchen. I picked out garlic, basil, and dill from the spicy mix, but that didn't begin to describe the complex aromas wafting from the small kitchen.

Mr. Cycek, who bowed slightly when he opened the door, was a sight to behold. He wore Carhartt pants, a red-and-blue flannel shirt and a narrow blue tie. His false teeth were in place, and his grey hair was slicked neatly back from his forehead. Apparently, I had underdressed.

I smiled. "Happy Fourth of July."

"And to you, my dear." He bowed again.

"It smells great in here," I said. "What are you cooking?"

He shook his finger in front of his face. "A chef never gives away his secrets." He gestured toward the couch. "Please, sit down. You can leave the gun by the door and hang your coat on the hook."

I followed his instructions and perched on the edge of the couch. The room was as spotless as it had been on my last visit, and for our dinner, Mr. Cycek had draped the small table with a white sheet, placed a canning jar of wildflowers in the center, and laid two place settings. The only other decorative change I noted was that the photo of his wife that had adorned the alder coffee table had been moved to the bookshelf, and in its place stood the raven carving I had admired. I smiled. My praises must have inspired Mr. Cycek to display his artwork front and center.

"Would you like a glass of salmonberry wine?" Mr. Cycek walked from the kitchen clutching a juice glass of dark red liquid.

"Yes, thank you." I reached for the glass and stared down into it. I braced myself, expecting a syrupy sweet concoction. Mr. Cycek was watching me carefully, and I didn't want to grimace when I sipped his brew.

I rolled the liquid around in my mouth, acquainting it with my taste buds, and then carefully swallowed. The taste surprised me, and I glanced up at my host. "This is very good," I said. "Did you make it yourself?"

He nodded, smiled, and returned to the kitchen.

I swallowed more of the crimson liquid. I had tasted homemade berry wines before, and they had been sickeningly sweet. This wine was fruity but dry. It resembled a Merlot in both color and taste. *Maybe Mr. Cycek would share his winemaking tips with me.* I took one more sip and then set the glass on the table. I reminded myself that the alcohol content of this homemade wine could be quite high, and I didn't want to end the evening staggering down the beach in search of my campsite.

Mr. Cycek glided from the kitchen, one hand holding a plate of crackers, the other a bowl of pink spread with a knife sticking out of it.

"Try some of my smoked salmon spread." He placed the dishes in front of me. "Don't eat too much, though. I want you to be hungry for supper."

I dabbed some of the spread onto a cracker and took a small bite. A moan escaped my lips as the smooth salmon flavor slid down my throat.

"This is wonderful," I called to Mr. Cycek, who had returned to the kitchen. He stuck his head around the corner of the door, smiled, and nodded.

I sipped more wine and then heaped a pile of the spread on the next cracker. I ate four laden crackers before I stopped myself. I could have made this my meal, but from the smells drifting from the kitchen, Mr. Cycek was preparing a feast, and he would expect me to eat healthy portions. I was glad I would have a long walk back to my tent to burn off some of the calories I was about to consume.

I leaned back on the couch and sipped more wine. The warm house, food aromas, and potent wine were making me sleepy. I leaned my head back and closed my eyes.

"You're tired."

My eyes flew open, and I sat forward. I hadn't heard him walk across the room, but now Mr. Cycek stood over me, wine bottle in hand. He bent and filled the glass I still held.

"I haven't been sleeping well," I said. "Today I fell asleep in the woods and was awakened by a bear."

Mr. Cycek stepped back and smiled. "You must be careful."

"At least I know my heart is strong." I laughed.

"How did your clam digging go?"

"Fine. One more morning, and I'll be done." I paused. "I would like to ask you a few more questions about the onset and development of your wife's symptoms. I know Craig asked you those questions," I shrugged, "but I don't have his notes."

Mr. Cycek nodded his head but said nothing. He turned and disappeared into the kitchen. I sipped more wine and stared at the raven sculpture. Up

194

close, I saw the work was crude, the features choppy. This only added to its charm, though, and as I ran my finger over the bird's head and down its back, I wondered if Mr. Cycek would sell this to me. *He must need money, and I could put the carving in my office to remind me of Craig.*

A few minutes later, Mr. Cycek walked from the kitchen, his arms laden with serving bowls and platters.

I stood. "Can I help you?"

"No, no," he said. "Please, sit at the table, and I will serve you." He plopped a full salad bowl down in front of me. "I dished up our salads in the kitchen."

I was charmed and amused. This was the best date I'd had in years. I wondered if Mr. Cycek was looking for another woman to fill the void left by Doris. *I could do worse.*

Mr. Cycek loaded the small table with food and then sat in the chair across the table from me.

"This all looks wonderful," I said, "but I hope you don't expect me to eat everything."

He flashed a broad smile, showing off his even white dentures. "I won't let you leave the table until everything is gone." He snapped his fingers. "I forgot the wine." He stood and scurried to the kitchen.

"Maybe I should slow down with that," I said when he returned with the bottle.

"Nonsense. This is a holiday." He refilled my glass and set the bottle on the table. His glass was full, and I wondered how much of the ruby brew he'd already had to drink.

"Please help yourself. Taste the salad first." Mr. Cycek gestured to the full bowl he had placed in front of me. "I will explain what you're eating."

It was a green salad, but unlike anything I ever had seen before. There was no lettuce in the mix, just shades of green leaves and lavender and pink petals.

"It's okay," Mr. Cycek said. "I like to eat natural food. Most humans, even people who have grown up in the wilderness, think they have to buy their food from the grocery store, while much more nutritious and better-tasting food grows in their yards."

"What's in the salad?" I asked.

Cycek shrugged. "Let's see. Fiddleheads, young birch leaves, salmonberry flowers, watermelon berry shoots..." he stared at the bowl and made a face of concentration. "Rose petals, geranium flowers, fireweed leaves, and let's see, I sprinkled in a few wild chives and some spring beauty. I don't believe I have any sorrel or dock in this one, but the salty flavor comes from the sea lettuce seasoning and the beach greens. I also put dandelion greens and chickweed in it. Those, of course, grow in my garden, no matter how much I try to discourage them." He shrugged again and then nodded his head. "Oh yes, wild mustard leaves and goose tongue."

"Wow," I said.

"It doesn't need much of a dressing; it's flavorful by itself. Just put a little of this oil and vinegar on it." He handed me a bottle and I shook several drops over my wild salad.

"Try it," he said. "Tell me truthfully what you think."

He studied me while I lifted a forkful of salad to my mouth. I pushed the greens into my mouth and instantly regretted taking such a big bite. My cheeks involuntarily drew together in a pucker, and I had to fight the urge to spit the vile-tasting leaves onto the floor. I chewed slowly and forced myself to swallow. I felt tears run down my cheeks.

"Well?" Cycek asked.

"Good." My mouth had not yet recovered its normal shape, and the word sounded strange. "It has quite a kick."

"Oh yes." This was the compliment Mr. Cycek apparently wanted. "So much better than the bland stuff you buy in the store."

"It's definitely not bland." I swallowed wine and then looked around the table. "What else do we have?"

He handed me a bowl of dark green leaves that looked like spinach. "Try the nettles. I steamed them with morels."

"Nettles?" You mean the leaves that sting you when you touch them?"

Mr. Cycek laughed. "Don't worry. They lose their sting when they're cooked. You'll be pleasantly surprised."

I spooned a small mound of the mushy plants onto my plate, and this time took only a small bite under Mr. Cycek's watchful eye.

I glanced up. "This is good. It tastes like spinach, and these brown things are mushrooms?"

"Yes, morels."

"Isn't it difficult to know which mushrooms are safe to eat?"

Cycek shook his head. "I only pick the morels. Nothing else except false morels looks like them, and I know the difference, so I know they're safe."

He handed me the bread basket. "This is my work of art," he said.

I lifted a piece of heavy, dark bread with green specks from the basket and waited for Mr. Cycek's explanation before I bit into it.

He smiled. "I made that from a mixture of cattail and wheat flour. The green specks are dried nettles and chickweed."

"You made flour from cattails?"

"Yes, from the rhizomes. It's a lengthy process, but quite rewarding."

I held the bread to my mouth and prepared myself for something bitter, but the bread tasted bland, and bland was good.

"Mmm," I said. "You are some chef, Mr. Cycek. Tell me how you make flour out of cattail rhizomes."

Mr. Cycek smiled. "I scrub and peel away the tough outer rind of the rhizome while it's still wet. Then, I pound it into mush with a mallet, place it in a jar, and cover it with water. The flour settles to the bottom, and I pour off the water and stringy fibers. I then dry and store the flour until I need it. Of course, it takes a lot of cattails to make enough flour for bread, so I usually have to mix it with wheat flour. I like the flavor of the cattail flour, though."

"It's delicious," I said, and bit off another small piece.

Mr. Cycek helped himself to the nettles and bread and then handed me a bowl of cooked, white grain that I thought was rice.

"These are steamed chocolate lily bulbs," he said, as I dumped a large spoonful on my plate.

I looked from the grain to Cycek's face. "The flowers that smell like a baby's diaper?"

Cycek smiled. "That's right. Try it, though. I think you'll be surprised."

My adventurous spirit was flagging. I longed for Minute Rice, iceberg lettuce, and Wonder Bread. I nibbled a bite of white grain.

"It tastes like garlic."

"I seasoned it with garlic butter. The lily roots are bland by themselves, so they need to be livened up."

I was surprised but thankful Mr. Cycek had chosen a conventional spice to season the lily roots. "It's very good," I said, and this time, I was telling the truth.

"And this I'm sure you've had before." Mr. Cycek handed me a platter loaded with chunks of white fish.

"Oh yes. I love halibut. How did you cook it?"

"I basted it with lemon butter and baked it."

Thank heavens. Something I could identify and liked. I took two pieces, but that didn't make a dent in the large platter of fish.

"We'll never eat all of this," I said.

Mr. Cycek shrugged. "I guess I got carried away. It has been a long time since I've had company."

"And you outdid yourself." I gestured to the food. "This is all wonderful. Thank you for inviting me."

We ate in silence for a few minutes. I alternated bites of delicious, flaky halibut with the bland and bitter side dishes. After each bite of salad, I gulped wine, and before I knew it, Mr. Cycek again had refilled my glass. I felt flushed and light headed and knew I should ask for water, but instead, I sipped more wine.

"If you don't mind me asking," I said. My mouth tingled and the words sounded strange. I shook my head, trying to clear it. "Why didn't you eat clams with Doris the night she got sick?"

Mr. Cycek chewed slowly while I waited for his answer. "I don't like clams," he said. "I only ate a salad that night, but clams were Doris' favorite meal." He ate another bite of fish. "I did all the cooking, you see. Oh, Doris cooked when we were first married, but she was never any good at it, and I like to cook. Doris usually dug the clams and I cooked them, but when her arthritis got worse, she wasn't able to dig."

"How did you cook them that night?"

"Steamed them. That was her favorite."

"And did she drink wine with her meal?" This was an important question, since liquor magnifies the effects of PSP, and I could testify that the liquor content of this wine was high.

"Yes. Doris always had a couple of glasses of wine with supper."

"Do you remember how long it was from the time Doris began eating clams until she began feeling ill?"

Mr. Cycek lathered butter on a slice of bread and took a bite, chewing slowly. He picked up his wine glass and stared into it a moment before sipping.

"A few minutes after we began eating, I noticed Doris kept scratching her mouth, and then she slurred her words. I thought it was the wine." Mr. Cycek's eyes gleamed and a smile spread across his face. He chuckled and took another bite of salad.

I felt as if I were a guest at the Mad Hatter's tea party. The interior of the Cycek cabin lost its sharpness, and I seemed only able to focus on one object at a time. Everything else was fuzzy, and when I moved my head too quickly, the room blurred into a swirl of colors. Sound also was distorted, and Cycek's laugh sounded louder than it should have. *And why was he laughing?* His reaction was out of place; it didn't seem to make sense. *Had I missed the joke?* He was telling me about his wife's death. Laughter had no part in that story.

I closed my eyes, shook my head, and then scratched my tingling mouth. I was beginning to imagine I had Doris' symptoms. "I've had too much of your wine," I said.

"After supper I'll brew coffee. Don't worry, I won't send you back to your camp drunk."

I tried another bite of salad, hoping the bitter taste might clear my head. Instead, my eyes began to water, and I pushed the bowl away from me. I ate two large bites of halibut and reached for my wine glass. I brought the glass to my lips, inhaled the potent brew, and set it down.

"Then what happened to Doris?" I asked.

Mr. Cycek slid his fork into his pile of chocolate lily grain. He tilted his head to one side, recalling the last night of his wife's life.

"She dropped her fork three times and said she was dizzy." He lifted his fork to his mouth, and I watched him chew.

"How do you like your food? You're not eating very fast." He nodded to my plate.

"It's delicious," I said and stuffed a forkful of nettles into my mouth. "Excellent," I said after I swallowed, slurring the word so that instead of sounding like an "s," the "c" sounded like "sh." I licked my lips, which felt thick and numb, and I wondered if I was having a reaction to the nettles.

"What was Doris' next symptom?" I asked.

Mr. Cycek waved his hand in front of his face and frowned. "I don't know. Is this important?"

"I'm afraid so," I said. "But if you'd rather wait and talk about it later, I understand."

"No, no. We might as well get it over with." He ate a bite of fish and then wiped his mouth with his napkin. He looked at me, and I focused on his small, black eyes. The rest of his face was blurred.

"Her words were so slurred I couldn't understand what she was saying, and I told her that, but she wouldn't shut up. She just kept babbling. The woman couldn't stop talking." His voice was low, his eyes hard.

I felt as if I were floating in space. *Had I heard him correctly, or was I hallucinating?* My stomach churned, and suddenly, the room seemed unbearably hot. I tugged at the neck of my sweatshirt.

"Bitch, bitch, bitch. That's all the woman did. I never fixed the leaky roof. I didn't help enough in the garden. She was tired of living like a hermit." He paused and then chuckled. I heard his laugh, but my eyes were still locked on his, and they remained cold and hard. "She was particularly upset that day, because I forgot to bring her groceries from Larsen Bay. She didn't stop to think that maybe I didn't go to Larsen Bay."

Without thinking, I pulled my salad bowl toward me and took another bite. I choked on the acrid leaves and swallowed the rest of the wine in my glass. Mr. Cycek didn't refill it. He was lost in thought now, his eyes gazing past me as he remembered. I felt something wet run down my chin and wiped away a drop of saliva. *Was I drooling?*

"I helped Doris to the couch," Cycek continued. "She could barely walk at that point, but she was still yammering. Finally, about ten minutes later, she began gasping for air. She clutched her throat and rolled off the couch onto the floor. Then, except for the wheezing and choking, she was quiet, and I called the Coast Guard."

I watched Mr. Cycek quietly resume eating his meal. I knew I could not eat another bite. My head spun, my stomach churned, and sweat poured down my face. My heart thumped so rapidly that I imagined Mr. Cycek could hear it beating. I swallowed and looked around the room, trying to force myself to sober up, willing my vision to clear. My gaze fell on the bookcase, and I blinked, trying to read the blurred, jumbled letters on the spines of the books. *Birds of Alaska,* I deciphered after much effort. *Edible and Poisonous Plants of the Pacific Northwest. The Alaska Cookbook. If only the Cyceks had heeded the PSP warnings in that book, Doris would be alive today. The Poor Man's James Bond,* I read. The words went in and out of focus, but this exercise seemed to be sharpening my acuity. *Under Alaskan Seas,* I read on the next book spine, the letters were slightly blurred but easy to make out.

I stopped, the sweat turning cold on my face as my eyes slowly returned to the James Bond book. The author of the book was not Ian Fleming, but Kurt Saxon. This was the homemade-bomb-making book Morgan had told me about.

I swiveled my gaze back to the table. Mr. Cycek's head was bent, his attention focused on his food. My heart beat wildly, and for the first time, I examined the bouquet of flowers in the vase in the center of the table. Pink, white, yellow, and violet flowers filled the vase, but all I saw were the two stems of purple monkshood.

The bouquet blurred, splintering into fragments of color. I tucked my hands between my knees to control their shaking. My sweatshirt clung to my sweaty back, and I felt as if all the air had been sucked out of the room. I lifted my head toward the ceiling and took a deep breath.

Cycek looked up from his plate. "Are you okay? Your face is flushed."

I'm not sure I answered him. My brain was scrambling to recall symptoms of aconite poisoning, a poison so toxic that the original inhabitants of this island spread it on their spears to kill bears and whales. Only a grain of monkshood root would kill a human being. I looked at the grains of chocolate lily in my plate, but no, Cycek also had eaten the lily root. *What had I eaten that he hadn't? He hadn't eaten any of the salmon dip, or he could have dropped some-thing into my wine, because he'd brought the first glass to me from the kitchen.*

I took another deep breath and looked around the table. Cycek's attention again was focused on his plate as he continued to shovel food in his mouth. *The salad.* He'd dished up the salad in the kitchen, and the bitter greens would camouflage any disagreeable taste the toxin might have. Also, monkshood leaves look similar to wild geranium leaves, and I would have to be an expert to spot them in the shredded salad.

I tried to calm down. I hadn't eaten much of my salad, and if the old man had chopped up monkshood leaves in the salad, at least the leaves were less toxic than the roots.

*What were the symptoms of monkshood poisoning?* I'd consumed a great deal of wine. *Was I feeling intoxicated or the symptoms of aconite?*

I wiped drool away from the corners of my mouth. *Yes, that was one of the symptoms of aconite poisoning. Salivation, weakness, chest pain, and in a few hours, death from cardiac arrest.*

# Chapter Fifteen

I sobbed, and Cycek slowly lifted his head to meet my gaze. "You poisoned me."

He nodded. "I'm sorry. You seem like a nice woman, but you shouldn't have meddled in my affairs."

"But why? What have I done?" I didn't know if my racing heart was a symptom of poisoning or terror. I should have bolted for the door, but I couldn't move. I didn't understand why this was happening; although, I now knew that for some reason, Mr. Cycek had placed the explosives on the plane. He had killed Craig, the pilot, and the other passengers.

"I had to get rid of the evidence," Cycek said. "No one could know." He buttered another piece of bread and took a bite.

I pressed the first two fingers of my right hand into my forehead above the bridge of my nose, trying to relieve my pounding head and clear my vision. My eyes fell on the raven sculpture sitting on the coffee table. *How could I have been so stupid?* Cycek was the raven that had bothered Craig. Craig must have known or at least suspected the man had murdered his wife. *Was I ever dumb.*

Cycek was talking again. "I dug clams for Doris' last meal. I told her I got up early and dug them on the beach where you took your samples. She knew those clams were safe, because she'd had some from there just a week earlier. If she'd been thinking, she'd have known the tide wasn't low that day until 11:00, but Doris never bothered to think." He sipped his wine. "Then, I told her I had to go to Larsen Bay, but instead I went to Uganik and dug clams near where the man died from PSP a few weeks ago. I didn't know if the clams would kill Doris, but there was no harm in trying."

"That's why you didn't have her groceries." I scratched my right arm and then my right leg. I felt as if I had spiders crawling on me.

"I never went to Larsen Bay, so how could I get her groceries?" He puckered his lips and shrugged. "I knew if everything went as I hoped it would, Doris wouldn't need those groceries."

My pulse danced and skipped. *If I had eaten a lethal dose of monkshood leaves, I would not survive. I was too far from medical help.*

"Did you put monkshood in my salad?" I ran the sleeve of my sweatshirt across my clammy forehead.

Cycek smiled. "If you and your assistant had just left me alone. I can't let you test the clams from here, because they're clean, and that would give me away."

"And if I die? Don't you think you'll be the prime suspect?" I ran my fingers across my tingling throat.

"An unfortunate accident on the way back to your tent. The bear you saw in the woods today." He leaned toward me. "You didn't even see him coming."

I cradled my head in my hands, fighting nausea. Pain stabbed my stomach, and I wondered how much time I had left. *After I died, Cycek planned to mutilate my body so that I looked as if I'd been mauled by a bear.* My mind screamed for me to run, but I wasn't even sure I could stand. I had to do something, though. I couldn't just sit there and die.

I stood, but my legs buckled, and I grabbed the edge of the table, knocking over my chair in the process. I held onto the side of the table and bent toward Cycek. "If I've eaten monkshood, what can I do? How can I counteract it?"

He leaned back in his chair and smiled. "There's nothing you can do, my dear. You're dead."

My legs dissolved, and I fell to the floor. My sobs sounded foreign to me. The entire evening had been surreal. I looked up, and the room swirled. *If only I would wake up from this nightmare. Was there any way to counteract aconite poisoning?* I couldn't remember.

I pulled my knees to my chest and hugged them. I looked up at Cycek, still sitting in his chair at the table. "Tell me about the bomb."

I licked my lips. My mouth felt swollen and numb, as if a dentist had just deadened my mouth to fill a tooth. I knew that aconite was an alkaloid, and it acted on and eventually paralyzed the central nervous system of its victim. Just as with PSP, the first symptoms of aconite poisoning were tingling and numbness around the mouth and salivation. I didn't know the etiology of the poison, or how rapidly the symptoms progressed, but if I survived the night, I'd be an expert on it.

"I have a shed full of dynamite that I got from that barge found drifting in Shelikof a couple years ago. I bundled up a few sticks, attached the fuse to a kitchen timer, and set the timer for twenty minutes. I had to set the timer on the beach, mind you, just a few hundred yards from where the plane landed to pick up Craig." Cycek grinned. "I wrapped it in cotton to muffle the ticking sound. Those timers are loud. I taped the box, scribbled an address on it, and hurried down the beach and handed it to Craig just as he was climbing on the plane. He agreed to mail it for me and even said he'd pay the postage. I wouldn't have asked him to do that, though. I knew the package would never get to the post office."

"And the marine center bombing? Did you do that too?"

Cycek's eyebrows folded into a solid line, and he slowly shook his head. His cheeks were rosy from the wine, his mouth partly open, dentures shining. *He was insane.* I knew that now. He'd gotten rid of his wife, the torment of his life, and now he wasn't going to let anyone get in the way of his solitude. He planned to spend the rest of his life in peace and quiet here in Uyak Bay, and if I didn't cooperate by dying soon, he would murder me in some other way. *He was planning to mutilate my body anyway, so why not take an axe to my skull?*

I sized him up. If I hadn't been poisoned, I easily could outrun him, but I wasn't sure now. I had to move fast and take him by surprise. I counted to three and rolled onto my knees and pushed myself to my feet. I stumbled sideways and fell.

"Whoa there, dear," Cycek said, and slowly rose from his chair.

Adrenaline surged through me. It was now or never. I got my feet underneath me, bent over, staying near the floor in case I fell again, and loped toward the door. I grasped the door handle, stood upright, and steadied myself while waves of dizziness coursed through me.

Cycek watched me, an amused look on his face. I could see that he didn't believe I would make it far. I hoped he was underestimating me.

My shotgun stood by the door. I grabbed it with my left hand, while I opened the door with my right. I held onto the door and stepped into my boots. I used the shotgun as a walking stick and stumbled down the path. I was grateful it was June and the sun was still high in the sky at 7:00 in the evening. The light made me more visible to Cycek, but without it, I never could have navigated the rocky, uneven path.

"Come back, Jane!" Cycek called from his doorway. "I'll take care of you. You don't want to die alone in the woods."

I didn't look back.

I followed the path to the beach, and when I reached the beach, I bent over, panting hard. I wiped perspiration from my eyes. My body was drenched. I didn't hear Cycek behind me, and couldn't afford to think about him. I didn't believe I had the strength to make it back to my campsite, so I set my sights on something nearer. Hands on thighs, I looked up and focused on the rocky point nearest the Cycek cabin. I could get that far, and once I'd reached that goal, I would reassess my situation. I began moving, and the thing that frustrated me the most was that I couldn't tell how fast I was traveling. Was I walking or running? I seemed to be exerting a great deal of effort, but the landscape moved past me very slowly. My feet were so numb that I couldn't feel them make contact with the beach. I swung my arms back and forth, but the act felt unnatural and didn't seem to make me move faster.

A glob of saliva dripped on my shirt, and I wiped my mouth, alarmed at the amount of drool that had formed there. If only I could think. *What should I do?*

The tide was low enough so that I could walk around the large boulders at the point. I knew this was one piece of luck for me. If the tide had been any higher, I never would have been able to scale the rocks.

I made it around the point and looked back. As soon as the beach in front of Cycek's cabin was out of view, I collapsed and bent forward on the beach on my knees and elbows, wheezing and choking into the wet rockweed. Black dots swirled in front of my eyes, and I concentrated on a clamshell until the ridges came into focus. My stomach contracted. Pain jabbed, followed by nausea too powerful to ignore.

I bent my head and heaved. I made the mistake of closing my eyes and nearly fell over on the beach. I found the clamshell again, locked my eyes on it, and concentrated while sweat and tears rolled down my face. Violent spasms rocked my stomach for several minutes, and I feared they wouldn't stop. Once my stomach was empty, bile and saliva dripped from my mouth. I rolled onto the beach, away from the vomit, and my heaves slowly subsided into sobs.

*Was I going to die like this? Would this be my last night, and would I die without being able to tell my father and my friends goodbye?* After watching my mother's lingering death from cancer, one of my firmest wishes was a speedy death, but not yet, not like this.

"Jane!"

I squatted on my feet. I was beginning to hope that Cycek wasn't following, that he had decided to just let me die and let nature take its course. If I died on the beach, I would be swept out to sea with the tide, my remains consumed in a few days by fish, crab, and sand fleas. Mr. Cycek could claim that I had never shown up for dinner, and he thought I'd changed my mind. Who could argue with him? *Why was he following me? Was he worried I hadn't consumed enough of the poison to kill me, or did he simply want to watch the outcome of his handiwork?*

His reasons weren't important. He was following me, and I had to get away from him. I looked above me for a trail leading from the beach into the woods, but the cliff was too steep, and I knew I didn't have the strength to pull myself up the bank.

"Move!" I said, and even though I couldn't feel them, my legs obeyed the command. I alternated my gaze between the rocky beach and my legs to make certain they still were moving. Other than a loud buzzing noise, all I heard were the snaps and crunches my feet made as they slapped shale and smashed clam and mussel shells. I don't think I could have heard Cycek if he was right behind me, and my scope of focus was so narrow that I had little trouble dismissing him. I only thought about one step at a time.

I felt as if I had been walking for hours, and when I turned around to check my progress, I stumbled over a large rock. I fell hard, smashing my face into a shale slab. The world went black for what I thought was just a moment, but I wasn't certain, and terror coursed through me as my muddled senses returned.

I sat on the beach and ran my right hand over my face. Blood ran from a deep gash above the bridge of my nose, and the pain was so intense when I lightly touched my nose that I feared it was broken.

I remembered Cycek and looked behind me. He was following, his gait steady but slow. He was several hundred yards behind me, but I knew his eyes were locked on me.

I grabbed the shotgun and leaned on it to pull myself to my feet, and then I cradled the gun in my arms and ran. I watched my legs as they moved back and forth, amazed at their speed. I stumbled again and stopped watching my legs and concentrated on the beach, picking my way through the smaller stones.

My body vibrated from the exertion. My heart was slamming against my ribs, and my lungs were pumping to keep pace. I choked, fighting for oxygen. Sweat poured down my face and torso, and I wondered how much fluid I'd lost in the last hour. *Did adrenaline speed the effects of aconite poisoning, or was I sweating some of the toxin out of my body?*

Suddenly, my energy reserves gave out. I fell onto the rocks on my hands and knees, dropping the shotgun. Barnacles sliced the palm of my left hand, my lungs burned with fire, and my heart fluttered. I expected cardiac arrest at any moment, and I reflexively gasped air, but the more air I swallowed, the more my lungs screamed with pain.

I thought about giving up, collapsing, and letting Cycek find me. *Death wouldn't be so bad. I could just go to sleep and not wake up. Who besides my father would miss me? A few tears might be shed, but my death wouldn't alter anyone's life. Another scientist could take over my research and probably do a better job with it.* These thoughts were not so much self-pity as excuses to give up. Going on would require every ounce of strength I had, and I doubted even then I would make it.

I looked up. I was in the middle of a small cove, and I couldn't see Cycek. For all I knew, he could be a hundred feet behind me, or he could have turned around and gone home. I doubted the latter. I held my breath for a moment and lifted my head, listening for the crunching sound of boots on the beach. I heard nothing but the cry of gulls. I turned my head and listened again. Either Cycek was quite a ways back, or he had stopped so I wouldn't hear him.

*How far did I still have to go?* I wasn't certain, because one stretch of beach looked like the next to me. I wouldn't make much of a tracker or guide.

I stuck the butt of the gun into the beach and pulled myself to my feet. Large black dots flashed in front of my eyes, and I felt myself wobbling. I thought I was going to faint, but slowly the beach, the ocean, and the woods came back into focus.

I saw that the beach sloped up to the woods. There was no cliff or steep bank here. If I was going to get off the beach and hike over land, this was the place to do it.

I weighed my options. I could move faster on the beach. In the woods, my progress would be slowed by uneven ground and thick brush. I was having enough trouble navigating level beach, and thick brush, uneven ground, hills, and valleys not only would require more energy, but would increase my chances of serious injury. On the other hand, Cycek would have trouble spotting me in the thick brush. On the beach, he could watch and follow me from a distance.

He couldn't see me climb up into the brush here, and it would slow him down trying to find and follow me. If I became too ill or tired to make it to my tent, my chances of survival were better in the woods, where I could hide and wait for the effects of the poison to subside. If I'd swallowed enough of the poison to kill me, then it didn't matter which path I took. That very real possibility didn't merit consideration.

I looked behind me again but still didn't see Cycek. I walked to the top of the beach, but this time my pace was slow. My knees kept buckling, and I leaned on the gun. I crawled up the small slope and into the thicket of trees. My hands jumped and shook in violent spasms when I leaned on them. The sweat was beginning to dry on my face and back, and the evening breeze chilled me. I crawled into a thick grove of alders and sat. I wiped my hand across my forehead and was shocked to see it covered with blood instead of sweat. I'd forgotten about the cut above my nose. My head throbbed with pain, and I couldn't separate one ache from another.

I knew I couldn't sit there long. Every second I wasted, the poison spread through my body, shutting down my central nervous system. Soon, I wouldn't be able to walk. I had to reach the radio in my tent and call for assistance. Even if no one could help me, I had to let someone know about Cycek. If I couldn't contact Morgan, perhaps I could reach Kodiak Flight Services.

Cycek was a madman, and he had to be stopped. I had to die knowing he would be charged with the deaths of his wife and the pilot and passengers of the Beaver, including Craig. That evil little man deserved to spend his last years locked in a prison cell. To a man who would kill for a life alone in the wilderness, confinement behind bars would be the ultimate punishment.

A spasm contracted my stomach, and I bent my head, trying to throw up. I gagged, but nothing came out, and the effort exhausted me. I squeezed my head between my knees and hugged my legs. Panic invaded my mind. To survive, I needed to perform at my mental and physical best, but my head ached, my thoughts were muddled, and my body refused to obey me. I was alone and being chased by a maniac. I wouldn't survive.

I lifted my head and breathed. *No.* I might not live through the night, but I wouldn't die huddled in fright. As long as I could still move my arms and legs, I had a chance. I gripped the shotgun. One crazy old man was no match for me.

I crawled out of the alder thicket and fought my way through the dense brush until I found a game trail. I followed the meandering trail, hoping I was going in the right direction and that I would be able to find my tent when I got close to it.

Walking on the game trail was easier than fighting my way through the thick brush, but the trail was uneven, and trampled weeds camouflaged rocks and holes. I used the shotgun as a walking stick, but I fell several times, once jamming my right foot so tightly into a deep, narrow hole, that I was afraid I had sprained it. I used both hands to pull my foot out of the hole and massaged the numb appendage, wondering if I had injured it. *Would I feel pain if I had sprained it, or was sensation so lacking that I only would know I'd hurt it when it began to swell?* I stood and leaned slowly on the foot, and when it didn't buckle under my weight, I continued my awkward gait down the trail.

Under the best conditions, I had a bad sense of direction, so how would I find my camp in this maze of trees and brush? Bugs buzzed around my head. I felt a mosquito sucking on my neck, but couldn't muster the strength to slap it. I watched the trail while I walked and stopped every few minutes to look around. I knew this trail might pass several hundred yards from my tent, and the brush was too thick to see the ocean. I had no way to determine my bearings. I decided that when I thought I'd walked far enough, I would hike through the brush until I could see the beach, and from that vantage, I should be able to tell if I had gone too far or not far enough.

I didn't think Cycek was following me on the game trail, or if he was, he was a long ways behind me. He knew the woods better than I did, but his body was stiff, his legs unsteady. He would trip and fall as often as I had on this trail, and if he was behind me, I would have heard him. *Had he continued on the beach?* I didn't know if he knew where my campsite was, but if he did, he could be waiting for me when I arrived. He had been behind me, but he could move faster down the beach than I could through the woods. I would have to approach my campsite with caution.

I was concentrating on lifting my feet when I nearly bumped into a large cottonwood tree. I looked up at the tree and then took several steps back to get a better perspective. I laughed. No two trees had a large, heart-shaped knot like that. I knew where I was. I'd walked approximately one hundred and fifty yards past my tent, but now I knew which way to go. My strength had ebbed, and my hands and feet felt like clubs, but I would make it to my tent. I would not die lost in the woods.

I approached my tent from the rear and stood outside for a moment, listening. When I didn't hear anything, I walked around the tent and peeked through the tied flap. *No Cycek.* I fumbled with the ties, alarmed by how little I could move my fingers. Finally, I gripped the end of the top tie in my teeth and pulled. I repeated this procedure with the other two ties and stepped into the tent.

I sat on my sleeping bag. I wanted to stretch out and sleep, but I knew I couldn't do that yet. With the heel of my right hand, I turned on the radio and then clumsily gripped the mike in both hands and squeezed the transmit button.

"WXT890 – KVT04." I let up on the button and sobbed. My tongue was swollen, and the letters and numbers had sounded like gibberish, as if I had a wad of cotton in my mouth.

I took several deep breaths and tried again, slowly enunciating each letter and number as clearly as I could. I waited, but there was no reply.

I checked my watch. It was only 8:30. Morgan wouldn't be standing by for another thirty minutes. I tried Kodiak Flight Services. I couldn't remember their call sign, so I just said the name and repeated it three times, hoping someone would understand me. I knew I must sound drunk, and I worried that even if the dispatcher heard me, she would ignore my call.

I waited, and when there was no replay, I began to cry. I would try one last thing before I gave up.

I depressed the button. "Mayday, Mayday, Mayday!" I called. "This is Jane Marcus in Uyak Bay. I'm dying. Help me!" I dropped the transmitter. *What was the use?* The mumbled mishmash that had rolled over my swollen tongue didn't make sense even to me. *How could I announce that Cycek was the bomber? I couldn't begin to get my mouth around the name Cycek, and I couldn't even leave Morgan a note, because my fingers were too paralyzed to hold a pen.*

I rolled onto my sleeping bag. There was nothing else to do, and I was so tired. My chest throbbed. What I before thought was a symptom of exertion, I now believed was a symptom of aconite from the monkshood. My heart raced and then slowed, beat wildly as if I'd just run a race, and then relaxed to a normal rhythm for a few beats. I concentrated on taking slow, even breaths, but my heart continued its dance. My hands tingled, and I began massaging my right hand with my left. They weren't as numb as they had been a few minutes earlier, and when I concentrated, I could move my fingers.

I struggled to stay awake, but I finally lost the battle, and I didn't know how much time had passed when I heard a man's voice calling my name.

"Jane, where are you?"

Hope followed confusion. *Had someone heard me on the radio?*

"Jane?"

*Cycek, and his voice was loud. He couldn't be far away.*

I moved with a speed and agility I didn't think possible. I rolled off the sleeping bag, stood, looked around in a panic for the shotgun, and then slid through the tent flaps. The shotgun was outside, lying on the ground where I'd dropped it while I struggled to untie the tent flaps.

I gripped the gun with both hands and looked up. Cycek was watching me. The corners of his mouth twitched into a smile. "You're a strong woman. I expected to find you passed out somewhere."

"You put something in my first glass of wine. A sedative." I knew the wine had hit me too hard, and not all the symptoms I had been feeling could be attributed to aconite.

He nodded. "To relax you."

Cycek didn't have a weapon that I could see. *What did he plan to do?*

"Get out of here," I said. I have a gun."

He advanced two steps. "You don't want to shoot me, my dear. I'm the only one who can help you."

My hands shook as I fumbled with the gun, trying to chamber a round.

"How can you help me? There is no antidote for aconite."

"Brandy blended with flies that have supped on monkshood."

*The man was insane. Why hadn't I noticed earlier, the first time I'd visited him?* He must have displayed some signs of mental illness then, but I'd dismissed them as quaint or chalked them up to him being a lonely old man who recently had lost his wife.

"Leave," I said. "I will shoot you." I pushed down on the shotgun, trying to pump a shell into the chamber, but something was stuck. I held the gun up, shook it, and tried again.

Cycek stepped closer to me and reached his arm out. *Did he expect me to hand him the gun, or was he offering to help me pump a shell into the camber?*

I stepped back, still fumbling with the gun. He walked closer, and I kept backing away. My heart continued its erratic beating, and my vision faded from clear to blurry, bright to dim. I knew I was close to fainting, and I shook my head. I rested the barrel of the gun on my boot and pushed down with all my strength. It gave. *Click*, a shell slid into the chamber.

I continued backing up, and I lifted the gun to my shoulder.

Cycek stopped. "You don't want to do that, Dr. Marcus."

I stumbled over the root of a tree and would have fallen if my back hadn't slammed into the trunk of a large cottonwood.

Cycek scampered toward me, hoping to disarm me before I regained my composure.

I braced the gun against my shoulder and aimed in the general direction of his blurred figure. Everything was beginning to fade again. I heard a loud blast, felt a sharp pain in my right shoulder, and then I felt nothing else.

# Chapter Sixteen

I heard the buzzing of a single-engine airplane, but that was the only thing that made sense. I was freezing and had the worst headache of my life. I opened my eyes and made out the dim outline of trees in the fading light. I was outside and it was evening. No, it must be night. It was almost dark, and in June, twilight didn't settle in until nearly midnight. I closed my eyes and drifted away. I would worry about the time and where I was later.

"Jane!" The voice sounded familiar.

"What?" The reply was just a whisper, but that was all I had. Whoever was looking for me would have to wait until later, after my nap.

"Jane!" He was closer now, and his tone sounded urgent.

"Jane, where are you?" Another familiar voice.

"Oh no. Up here, Steve!"

"Is she okay?"

"I don't think so. Wait, she has a pulse, but she looks terrible."

A cool, firm hand gripped my wrist. I opened my eyes and saw the shadowy face of Agent Nick Morgan hovering a few inches above me.

He took off his coat and draped it over me. Then, he picked me up in his arms.

I heard panting. "Thank goodness, she's alive," the second man said.

"She's in bad shape. We need to get her to town right away."

"What in heavens happened here?"

"He's dead. I guess she shot him."

"This is Old Man Cycek. Why would she shoot him?"

"Because he's the person who blew up your airplane."

"What?"

"Not now, Steve. We have to get her to town."

"We'd better go. We're almost out of daylight."

I drifted in and out of consciousness, aware of Steve helping Morgan carry me down the bank, being pulled and pushed into the two-oh-six, the sound of the engine starting, my head resting in Morgan's lap, and his hand stroking my hair. Then, I slept.

The next time I opened my eyes, I squinted into a bright light. I closed them and tried to figure out where I was and why I felt this bad. I reached my left hand to my forehead and lightly fingered the gauze bandage that covered my nose. The back of my left hand burned, and when I peered at it, I saw that an I.V. tube ran from my hand to a bag over the head of the bed. My right hand was wrapped in gauze, and something was stuck to my chest. I looked down to see what it was, but I couldn't figure it out.

"Hello, sleepyhead. How do you feel?"

I looked into the smiling face of a young, blonde-haired man in scrubs.

"I'm Dave, your nurse," he said. "Those are electrodes on your chest. You're hooked to a heart monitor. You gave us a scare last night, but your rhythm is better today. How do you feel?"

"horrible."

Dave laughed. "I hear you. You have a visitor waiting to see you. Shall I show him in?"

I nodded, and Dave left the room. He returned a minute later with Morgan behind him.

"Don't wear her out. I'll call the doctor to let him know she's awake, and he'll want to see her as soon as he gets here."

Morgan nodded and thanked Dave. Then he walked to the side of my bed and smiled down at me. "That was a close call," he said.

"What happened?" My throat burned, and my voice was just a whisper.

Morgan pulled a chair up to my bed and sat. He touched my right arm. "I don't know much. A dispatcher at one of the air charter companies heard your radio broadcast. At first, she thought you were drunk, but then she could tell something was wrong. She tracked down Steve, who had gone home for supper after flying me to town, and told him that someone in Uyak Bay was calling Kodiak Flight Services and announcing a Mayday. Steve found me, and we flew to your campsite. We found Cycek dead and you passed out. Your heartbeat was all over the place by the time we got you to the hospital. The doctor wanted to medevac you to Anchorage, but you weren't stable enough, so he waited and watched, and finally, your heart slowed to a normal rhythm."

"I was poisoned with monkshood," I said.

"Monkshood." Morgan nodded. "We knew you'd been poisoned, but we didn't know what the agent was."

"Cycek planted the bomb on the Beaver."

"I know. By the time I got back to town, the explosives experts had determined that the trigger was a one-hour timer. I knew the bomb had been placed on the plane at one of the last two stops, and most probably the last stop." He shook his head. "If they'd given me that information over the radio, I could have gotten you out of there before this happened."

"He poisoned his wife with clams from Uganik Bay," I said, my memory of the previous evening returning in a flood. "He didn't want us to test the clams from his beach, because then we would know his wife's last meal hadn't come from there."

Morgan rubbed his eyes, and I saw that they were red and swollen. He had been awake all night. "He murdered six people to destroy some clams? Didn't he know you'd take another sample?"

I shook my head. "He thought it would be too late to do a PSP analysis by the next series of low tides. He didn't know that clams hold the toxin for several months."

Morgan's hand still rested on my right arm, and he gave it a squeeze. "What can I do for you?"

"My gear?" I said.

Morgan nodded. "Steve flew two troopers out this morning to recover Cycek's body, and they packed up your gear and brought it back here with them."

"This morning?"

Morgan smiled. It's 3:30 in the afternoon."

*I'd been asleep all day? Had Morgan been here with me the entire time?*

"Could you send the clam samples to the DEC lab in Palmer? I'll give you the information. I'm sure they are toxin-free, but they need to be tested. I don't want to have to go back out there and get another sample." Tears crept from my eyes, and I turned my head away, hoping Morgan wouldn't see.

He gently squeezed my arm again. "This is not your fault, Jane. You can't blame yourself because some crazy old man decided to kill his wife."

I lifted my left hand to my face and wiped away the tears. Then, I turned back to Morgan. "He was tired of listening to her complain, so he got rid of her." I looked into Morgan's strong face. His eyes were full of compassion, but weary from seeing too much of the dark side of human nature. I doubted much surprised him. "Cycek didn't have anything to do with the marine center bomb," I said.

"In a way, he did." Morgan withdrew his hand from my arm and sat back. "By blowing up the airplane, he set off a chain of events that culminated in the explosion at the marine center and the death of Jack Justin."

"So now what?"

Morgan shrugged. "I didn't find the briefcase. I think the people who were looking for it either found it or gave up, but I don't know that. You could still be in danger."

"I'll be careful," I said, "but I think they're gone."

Morgan sighed. "We'll continue the investigation," he said. "I promise I'll let you know if we learn anything."

"What about Maryann Myers?"

"I called her this morning, and she admitted she hadn't told us everything. She said she didn't want Sturman involved, and that's why she didn't tell us about her relationship with him. She didn't mention taking her package to the dock and talking to Bill that day, because she didn't want to be at the top of our suspect list."

"I hope you gave her what for about withholding information."

"I made her cry. How's that?"

I smiled. "Tough guy."

"I'm flying back to Washington tonight." He leaned close to me. "Will you be okay?"

I felt my heart race, and hoped the nurse watching the cardiac monitor wouldn't think I'd relapsed. "I'll be fine. Will I see you again?" *I usually wasn't so forward, but what the heck?*

He put his hand on my arm. "I hope so," he said.

The door to my room burst open and in strode a heavyset, middle-aged man in a white coat. "Hello, I'm Doctor Hagen, and I would like to examine Ms. Marcus now."

Morgan stood. "Goodbye," he said, his voice soft, and then he turned and walked out of my life.

# Chapter Seventeen

I settled back in my desk chair and propped my legs on the desk. The new computer had been delivered that morning, and I finally felt as if my life was getting back to normal. The summer and fall had been hectic, borrowing lab space here and office space there, always in debt to someone and feeling like an interloper. I'd moved back into my lab two months ago, but the office wing hadn't been reopened until last week.

I circled the date, November sixth, on the calendar. "Today, my life starts again," I said.

"Who are you talking to?"

I spun around and saw Geoff's lanky frame leaning against my door frame.

"You're too quiet. You need to wear taps on your shoes or a bell around your neck," I said.

"The new digs look good." He nodded his head as he glanced around the office.

"It's nice to have my own space again."

"Just came to check it out and congratulate you on your funding."

I laced my fingers behind my head. "Five-hundred-thousand dollars out of the blue. I'm not complaining, but I'll never understand government funding."

"Don't ask," Geoff said. "Think of it as the one good thing to come out of this disaster."

I shook my head. "No. No amount of money can make up for Craig's death or for the loss of Barry Gant. I keep expecting to see him walk down the hall."

Geoff stepped into my office. "I heard on the radio a little while ago that Alfred Eaton won the New York senate race by a landslide."

I shook my head. "The world goes on. Steve Duncan told me the other day that Toni Hunt is attending the University of Alaska in Fairbanks this fall."

"Good for her," Geoff said. "And I suppose you heard that Maryann Myers is engaged to David Sturman."

I laughed. "How do you hear all this gossip?"

Geoff nodded. He was getting warmed up. "What does your friend, Dana, think of her new boss?"

"She was less than thrilled when Marty Shires was named the new refuge manager."

"He'll be as bad as Simms," Geoff said.

"At least Betty still loves me," I said. "It's comforting to know some things remain constant."

Two weeks later, I just had returned to my office after teaching a class when my cell phone buzzed. I dropped the stack of papers I was carrying on my desk and grabbed the phone. "Marcus."

"Jane, how are you?"

Heat rushed through me, and I dropped into the chair. "Agent Morgan." I tried to keep my voice level, as if this were just another in a long line of calls I'd answered that morning. I did not want Nick Morgan to know how often I thought about him, how many times I'd wanted to pick up the phone and call him. I hadn't heard from him since late August, when he called to see if I'd had any more threatening phone calls and to tell me that the FBI hadn't made much progress in determining the identity of the marine center bomber.

We'd talked for fifteen minutes before he told me in a quiet voice that he and his wife were back together, going to give it one more try. I'd congratulated him and wished him well, and then I'd said I was late for a meeting.

Now I said, "I'm fine, Nick. How are you?"

"I have some information. It's highly confidential, and I probably shouldn't tell you, but after all you went through, I think you have a right to know."

I leaned back in my chair and waited for him to continue.

"Six days ago, a deer hunter found a briefcase about a mile from the crash site of the Beaver. The exterior of the case was discolored, but it was still intact and locked. Thank goodness the guy was honest. He gave the case to the police in Kodiak, and they contacted us." He paused a moment and then continued, "Our lab got the case a few days ago, and there is no question that it's George Justin's briefcase."

I sat forward and leaned my elbows on the desk. "What was in it?"

"Documents and photos positively linking Alfred Eaton with a Mexican drug cartel."

"So the briefcase belonged to Margaret, not George Justin. She was the one making the allegations about Alfred Eaton," I said.

"No. From what we can decipher from two letters that were in the briefcase, George was blackmailing Eaton for money and political favors. If Eaton didn't come through, George threatened to give the incriminating documents to his wife."

"In other words," I said. "If Eaton paid up, George would keep his mouth shut and help Eaton win the election."

"It looks that way," Morgan said. "The Justins were a close-knit family, weren't they?"

"What will happen now?"

"The federal prosecutor is in the process of securing an indictment to charge Alfred Eaton with trafficking illegal drugs and with murder."

"Do you think he'll be found guilty of those charges?"

"I don't think the murder charge will stick. It's more of a bargaining tool to convince him to plead to the drug charges. In any event, this will end his political career."

I sighed. "At least now we know why Jack Justin was murdered. I wonder if he was in on the blackmail scheme with his father."

"If he didn't know about it before his parents died, Eaton's friends made him aware of it soon after."

"No wonder he was terrified and frantic to find that briefcase."

Several seconds of silence followed while I waited for Morgan to say something. "Thanks for calling," I said. "I'll be able to sleep easier now."

"Jane," Morgan said. His voice was low and husky.

"Have a nice Thanksgiving, Nick," I said. "Goodbye."

# Afterword

Kodiak Island lies 250 miles southwest of Anchorage, Alaska. The island is 3,588 square miles in area, making it the second largest island in the United States. The city of Kodiak is located at the northeastern tip of the island, and most of the roughly 13,500 inhabitants of the island live in or near the city. Much of the rest of the island is part of the Kodiak National Wildlife Refuge, and since there are no roads on the refuge, the only way to access it is by floatplane or boat. Kodiak is breathtakingly beautiful and rugged, but it also can be inhospitable and dangerous.

I have attempted to portray Kodiak as honestly as possible, and some of the locations I have used in this book are real, while others are fictional. The Kodiak Braxton Marine Biology and Fisheries Research Center where Jane works is entirely fictional. It is located near and is somewhat similar in appearance to the University of Alaska Fairbanks Kodiak Seafood and Marine Science Center, but that is where the similarities end. The staff and students at the marine center where Jane works are figments of my imagination and are in no way based on the staff and students at the UAF Seafood and Marine Science Center. This is also true for the Kodiak National Wildlife Refuge employees. My characters are not based on actual refuge employees, who are much nicer and more efficient than some of my characters.

Kodiak has several fine air-charter services, but Kodiak Flight Services does not exist. Many air charter services now put tracking devices on their airplanes, so the dispatcher always knows where the planes are at any moment. In my novel, Kodiak Air Services did not have that system. Again, none of the pilots in this book are based on actual Kodiak pilots.

The Baranov Inn does not exist in Kodiak, but Henry's Great Alaskan Restaurant does, and it has great food. Check it out if you get to Kodiak. The *Kodiak Daily Mirror* is our newspaper, and the publishers, editors, and writers there do an amazing job publishing five newspapers a week to keep us informed of what is happening on our island.

All characters in this book are imaginary and not based on anyone I know, and any mistakes in this manuscript are mine.

I want to thank Alison at First Editing for her guidance and suggestions on preparing my manuscript, and I want to thank Evan Swensen and everyone at Publication Consultants for their fantastic cover design and hard work preparing this manuscript for publication. Finally, I want to thank my husband, Mike, for the support and encouragement he offered while I was writing this novel. Writing is a lonely endeavor, and it helps a great deal to have someone in your corner cheering for you.